Pieces of Fate

A Collection of Short Stories
by
David P Elliot

[signature] David P Ell 1 | 6 | 2013

RED CAP
Publishing

RED CAP PUBLISHING

Published & Distributed
in Great Britain in 2011
by

RED CAP PUBLISHING
100 Marlborough Gardens, Faringdon, Oxfordshire, SN7 7DN
+44 (0) 7775 858322
Email: info@redcappublishing.com

A CIP catalogue record for this book is available
from the British Library.

ISBN   978-0-9564369-7-9

CONTENTS

For Thomas, Erin & Joshua

INTRODUCTION

'Pieces of Fate' is a collection of six short stories by David P Elliot, which may be described as of the 'Tales of the Unexpected' genre.

Only *'Caroline'* has been published before having been originally written as an entry for the BBC Short Story competition for 2010; it did not win, but was subsequently released as an e-book.

'Medusa' is a story that has its genesis in the author's previous career in the IT industry. From an original idea the author had in the 1980s, before the modern computer games industry became the massive global business it currently is.

'The Cottage' is the first of two tales in this anthology, which explores an investigation into a modern day, alleged haunting incident. Although the name of the house has been changed, the cottage of the story is based on a local Oxfordshire property where the author once lived, and was purported to be haunted.

The title of the fourth tale, *'Shark'*, is derived from the occupation of the main protagonist, a loan shark called Gary Bowler who preys on the weak and vulnerable.

'The Thief in the Waiting Room' was the response to a challenge thrown out to the author to come up with a story which included 'a thief', 'a waiting room' and 'a flat tyre' in ten minutes. This was the result. Whilst the idea was established in the 10 minute time scale, the actual writing took a further 60 minutes to actually put down on paper.

The final story, *'Long Alley'* is also local to the author and uses real locations and an actual historical event as the backdrop for another modern day haunting. Readers may wish to read *'The Cottage'* first, as a prologue to this story.

CAROLINE

ONE

Detective Chief Inspector Matthew Richards stood looking through the one way mirror into the interview room, observing the man sat at the table fixed in place against the far wall.

The man had hardly moved, as far as Richards could tell, since he had been led into the interview room by the desk sergeant George Brown, who had placed him in the seat.

The room was sparsely furnished. Apart from a small shelf fixed to the wall alongside the table, upon which sat a tape machine for recording interviews, a printed plastic notice pinned to the wall, explaining prisoners' rights and the unoccupied chair directly opposite the man, it was empty.

Empty that is, save for the rather bored looking, uniformed police constable leaning with arms folded across his chest against the door to the room, ostensibly guarding the - 'What was he?' Richards thought, 'Prisoner? Witness?'

Without turning his gaze away from the man in the room, Richards spoke to Sergeant Brown who was now standing alongside him. 'Tell me again what he said, George.'

'He came in alone, 30 minutes ago, walked up to the desk and just said, 'He's dead. I killed him. He's dead. I asked him who was dead, but he didn't answer, he just kept repeating over and over, 'He's dead, I killed him.''

Richards studied the man again as he sat motionless, both hands flat on the table before him, with his head bowed, staring at a spot between his hands on the table. For some reason, Richards thought he looked like a medieval aristocrat awaiting the fall of the axe that would decapitate him.

'And he has said nothing else?'

'Nope. I asked, had he knocked someone down in his car, stabbed him, shot him, what did he mean he'd killed him. But he hasn't said anything else.'

Richards nodded, 'Does he have a car outside, have we

checked?'

'Yes, we've checked, and no - no car that we can find. I sent someone out to look in case it was damaged, I thought he may have knocked someone down and was so traumatised by it, he hadn't stopped. It happens. Sometimes people can't face up to what they've done. Thought there might be some damage, some forensics, but we can't find a car. Looks like he just walked in here.'

'Well, at least we know who he is; that's a start,' Richards said. He recognized the man in the room as Jeremy Carlton, just about the town's most prominent citizen. A solicitor by trade, he was rich, powerful and very influential.

If there was a committee somewhere, he chaired it; a charity that needed help, he supported it. In fact, if you wanted anything done - a license granted, planning permission approved, even a new swing in the local playground. If he supported it, it happened, if he opposed it, it didn't.

Richards knew him reasonably well. As a senior police officer, he could hardly avoid regular encounters with the most prominent legal and political person in the town. He had never warmed to him. Perhaps it was just some kind of inverted snobbery. Richards hated privilege, earned or otherwise and Carlton was certainly privileged. It was for others to decide whether he had earned it or not.

'He's on the Police Committee, isn't he?' Sergeant Brown suddenly sounded a little concerned. 'Should I have cautioned him? Don't want to make any mistakes with this guy.' He turned to Richards, looking for reassurance.

'Caution him for what?' Richards finally turned his gaze away from Carlton. 'We have no evidence he has committed a crime or even that one has occurred. He says he has killed someone but we don't know who, whether it's true, whether it was by accident or design, or even if someone is actually dead. We just do our job, Sergeant, makes no difference who it is; we treat them all the same.'

Even as he finished the statement, Richards knew how

naïve it would sound to the cynical desk sergeant. The truth is, Richards wanted things to be that way, and he often fell foul of his own senior officers by his reluctance to compromise or to play the political games he so despised in his own bosses.

'I'd better talk to him,' he said at last.

TWO

Carlton didn't look up as Richards entered the room and took the seat opposite him at the table. He remained resolutely staring at a spot between his hands as if fixed in that position.

Carlton was wearing a very expensive suit but it occurred to Richards that this was the first time he had seen Carlton without a tie or unshaven. Clearly, there wasn't more than a few hours beard growth on him, but it was enough to give a slightly dishevelled appearance to a man who was usually immaculate.

Some people can never look smart, regardless of how they dressed; Richards was one of those people, it seemed no matter how well his suit was pressed or shoes were polished, within minutes of dressing he always looked as though he had slept in his clothes.

His dark brown hair usually needed cutting and, as a consequence, tended to curl up and was impossible to keep under control. His only striking feature was his steely blue eyes which he knew people often found discomforting. He seemed to have an ability to see through lies, which, although not entirely accurate, he was certainly able to use to advantage in interviews.

Carlton, on the other hand, was one of those irritating people, as far as Richards was concerned, who always looked like he'd been dressed by a valet, shaved at least twice a day and never had a hair or a crease anywhere where there should not have been one.

But not today it seemed.

'You remember me, Mr Carlton? Detective Chief Inspector Richards? We last met a week ago at the 'Local Policing' event you arranged as chair of the police committee?' Richards had been obliged to attend the event at the insistence of the Chief Constable who was also there, amongst a host of other prominent local dignitaries.

There was no response to Richards' questions, and he

10

showed no signs even that he had heard him, let alone ever met him before.

'Look, Mr Carlton, I need to know why you are here. You told the desk sergeant you killed someone. Who did you kill? When? Where? What is this all about?'

'He's dead, I killed him.' came the quiet reply, which seemed to be directed at the table or to himself, rather than as a direct response to Richards' question.

'Who? Who did you kill?' Richards repeated. Again, there was no response.

This one-sided interview continued for the best part of two hours, interspersed briefly with short breaks that were more for Richards' benefit than Carlton's.

Despite the fact that suspects were regularly advised to 'say nothing' by their defence solicitors, Richards was well aware that, if you talked long enough to a suspect, whilst he may not directly incriminate himself or admit to whatever transgression he was accused of, mostly they would say something, eventually. It was, he knew, actually very difficult to sit for hours and not say anything.

Usually, totally unconnected to the crime, the suspect would open up some form of dialogue, and once they were talking, the flood gates would eventually open.

Any seemingly unrelated conversation would lead to a slow and painstaking teasing-out of information. Soon, inexorably and despite a determined effort to 'say nothing,' the suspect was singing like a bird!

But not this bird and not this time.

Eventually, frustrated, Richards gave up. 'I need you to sit here and think about what you're doing, Mr Carlton. You don't need me to tell you that at the very least you're wasting police time, and I can't afford to sit here any longer to indulge...,' he paused as if searching for the right word, 'your problem - any longer. If you decide you want to tell me anything then speak to the officer, but I have better things to do with my time.'

He had decided Carlton had had some kind of breakdown.

He would get a psychiatrist to talk to him, maybe he could find out what was going through this obviously disturbed man's mind.

He started to leave, and as he opened the door, his back to Carlton, he heard a quiet voice, so quiet he was not quite sure he had heard anything at all.

'Terry Belling.'

Richards turned to face Carlton who, for the first time since he had entered the room, had raised his head and turned to look at him; his haunted eyes, heavy, tired and lifeless sent a chill down Richards' neck.

'Terry Belling.' Carlton repeated quietly. 'I killed Terry Belling. He is at The Blue Boar.'

Carlton slowly turned away, returning to his previous position, head hanging, hands palm down in front of him, staring at the table.

Despite Richards returning to his chair and continuing to question Carlton for a further hour, not a single additional word passed Carlton's lips.

THREE

'The Blue Boar has been derelict for 7 years,' George Brown said to Richards as he returned to the canteen table with a mug of tea and a rather unappetising looking sandwich. He peeled back the top slice of the thin bread, staring suspiciously at the content which was allegedly bacon.

'There was a fire there,' he continued, 'started in the kitchen, apparently. It was just about the last straw for the place. It was already losing money. The landlord had had enough, I guess, moved on. It never re-opened. Been boarded up ever since.'

Richards sipped his coffee. 'Get a car out there, tell them to look around. Get Detective Sergeant Willis to go with them, see what they can find – and tell them to be careful. If it is a crime scene I don't want the evidence destroyed, especially when the suspect is a bloody solicitor. And find out who owns the place now. I assume it's one of the breweries, but we'd better check.'

'Aren't you going out there?' Brown said as he stood up to leave.

'I'll go if they find something. I'm going to his house, see his wife. I met her at the 'do' last week; she seemed like a nice enough lady. A lot younger than Carlton. Maybe she can throw some light on what the hell is going on. What about this Terry Belling - what have we got on him?'

Brown shrugged, 'Bit of a tearaway, it seems; couple of minor convictions for possession of cannabis, personal use, nothing heavy, and one for criminal damage following a fight. Apparently, more of a drunken punch-up really, broken window in the pub, that sort of thing. Oh! And one for handling stolen goods, bought an 'iffy' iPod, apparently, that had 'fallen off the back of a lorry' – not exactly a master villain. Most of this was a few years back. Doesn't seem to have been in any bother, recently.'

'Do we have an address for him?' Richards asked.

'Last known address was from his last conviction over

seven years ago. Local Panda has been round there; it's all small bedsits, mostly students and the like. The residents change every 5 minutes. There's nobody there now who remembers him, and no luck so far with a current address. One interesting thing, though - his last conviction, one of the possessions of cannabis. His occupation was down as an office clerk. Guess where he worked?'

'I don't guess, Sergeant.' Richards was irritated by anything he considered flippant or unprofessional where a potentially serious crime was concerned.

Brown cleared his throat, slightly embarrassed by the implied criticism before continuing. 'He worked at 'Carlton & Messenger', our local solicitors. Messenger died 30 years ago; the practice is owned by our guest downstairs.'

It was four hours after Jeremy Carlton had walked into the police station that Richards climbed into his car and drove off in the direction of Manor Lane.

Presumably named after the Manor House owned by Carlton, it was one of a small number of very expensive properties in an extremely expensive part of town, but before Richardson had got out of the centre where the police station was situated and into the suburbs, the radio crackled into life and he heard the familiar voice of Detective Sergeant Willis.

'Gov, we're at the Blue Boar,' Willis said, 'the place was pretty securely boarded up, but we've managed to find a way in. We're in the cellar. We've found a body. I've called Scenes of Crime and the pathologist. I think you'd better get over here.'

'Do we know who it is?' Richards asked.

'Sorry Gov, no way of telling without forensics. But it's not natural causes, that's for sure, his face is completely crushed, no way it could be accidental or a fall.' And as if to reinforce the point, he added, 'Somebody smashed his face in.'

14

FOUR

It was 3.00pm by the time Richards and Willis left what Richards had now designated a murder scene, in the cellar of the Blue Boar, and it had begun to rain as they climbed into the front of the car.

Richards turned on the ignition without starting the engine, putting the windscreen wipers on intermittent and watching the build-up of the increasingly heavy rain on the glass before it was wiped away by the sweep of the wiper blade.

He sat, running through the facts they had accumulated so far before he eventually spoke.

'Hand me the file on Belling,' he said, holding out a hand towards Willis.

Willis reached over into the back of the car to retrieve the file and handed the buff folder to Richards who paged through the assortment of loose pages before speaking again.

'Okay. We wait for the forensic report and the PM, but I think it is a fair assumption that the body is Belling. The face is too badly damaged for any identification and that has probably put paid to dental records as well. According to his file we have no DNA sample, but we do have fingerprints, so hopefully we can identify him from that. He seems to be the right height, weight and age and, unless we've missed another body, we also have Carlton telling us it's Belling. So, subject to confirmation of identity and cause of death, it looks like we have a murder, a victim and a probable culprit.'

'Nobody could have survived that amount of facial trauma,' Willis offered, 'But I guess we need the PM to confirm that it was the cause of death. I suppose it's just possible that a frenzied attack like that could have been post mortem.'

'Base to DCI Richards, over'. The two detectives' conversation was interrupted as the radio crackled into life and Richards picked up the handset, 'DCI Richards here; go ahead, over.'

'Yes sir, message from Sergeant Brown, apparently you wanted to know who the owners of the Blue Boar are. We got the name of the agents from the board outside. It seems the building is owned by a commercial property group, Minster Investments plc. They've been pretty active over the last few years, buying up failing pubs. They don't seem to be interested in the pub business, more like long-term property investment. The whole site recently got planning permission for conversion to new homes. Apparently, they are planning to put up 65 apartments and houses on the land. Sergeant Brown says you will be interested to know that the majority shareholder of Minster Investments and the Chairman is one Jeremy Carlton.'

'Okay. Thank Sergeant Brown for me. How is the psychiatrist getting on with Carlton, do we know?'

'Apparently, he's getting less out of him than you did,' the radio operator responded, 'he says he's suffering some deep psychological trauma that could take months to untangle, if ever. It's unlikely we are going to get anything useful from him in the near future.'

'Okay, thanks.' Richards replaced the microphone and turned to Willis. 'Okay, it's unlikely any confession from Carlton is going to be taken seriously, given his mental state. But the fact that he owns the property the body was found at and that he told us it was there is pretty conclusive. But we also need a motive here. We know Belling worked for Carlton years ago. Let's get to his offices and interview the staff. Someone will remember him, and I wouldn't mind betting if there is any whiff of a scandal someone will be only too pleased to tell us.'

'What about Mrs Carlton?' Willis asked. 'You were on your way to see her. Should we get over there?'

Richards thought for a moment and then responded. 'No. Send a panda over there. Tell her we have her husband at the station and that I will be over to talk to her as soon as I can. In the meantime tell her the doctor is with him, and once we have the all clear we will be talking to him again, but in the meantime she

16

should wait to hear from me.'

'What if she insists on going down to the station to see him?'

'We can't stop her, I guess, but tell her she will be wasting her time. She won't be able to see him, as after the medical examination he will be helping us with our enquiries. We'll let her know if and when she can see him.'

'Seems a bit harsh.' Willis said.

'Why do most people kill each other, Willis?' Richards said, and without waiting for a reply continued, 'Sex or money. Sometimes both. If Carlton killed Belling I want a motive before I question his wife. Let's get to his office and see if we can find one.'

FIVE

The offices of Carlton & Messenger were comfortable and quiet, with a subtle air of both efficiency and money. There were around 30 staff in total, but only two, apart from Carlton himself presumably, had any direct recollection of Terry Belling.

Paul Brice and Hilda Burning had been with Jeremy Carlton for 25 and 23 years, respectively.

Hilda Burning was a formidable lady of indeterminate age, with an air of superiority and a permanent look on her face that suggested to Richards that she spent most of her time sucking lemons. She was the Office Manager and appeared to revel in her authority, with a clear attitude of disdain to the many younger staff that she seemed keen to correct even before they had given her cause.

Paul Brice didn't seem to fit at all. 6 feet tall and stocky, he wore a suit like an army sergeant major, and a severe crew-cut and broken nose suggested he had been a boxer in his youth. Richards thought he would have fitted better standing on the door of a nightclub as a bouncer rather than working in a provincial solicitor's office.

His job description seemed unusual, as well. Apparently, he was Carlton's 'Personal Assistant and driver'.

Hilda Burning organised an office for them to conduct their interviews; she seemed insistent on talking to him rather than to Willis. Richards suspected she considered him of too low a rank for someone of her importance.

He organised things so that he and Willis would interview Brice and Burning, who he felt were most likely to have useful information. 'Get the uniformed officers to get statements from all the other staff. Particularly, did they know Terry Belling but more importantly have they heard anything about him. Tell the uniform boys we're not talking evidence here, I don't care if it's rumour, hearsay, gossip or any sort of tittle-tattle. If they have heard anything that might be useful I want it put down in writing. We'll worry about its evidential value later.'

Richards sat himself at the desk and nodded to Willis, 'We'll have Hilda Burning in first. While we talk to her, get someone back at the nick to check up on Paul Brice's background. If that guy's a 'personal assistant', I'm a bloody prima ballerina.'

Caroline's Story

Caroline hated these events and wished wholeheartedly that Jeremy would not be so insistent that she should attend. Not naturally gregarious, attending any event was stressful, but these office Christmas parties were her ultimate nightmare.

She was absolutely certain that Jeremy's staff would enjoy themselves a lot more if Jeremy and she weren't there. It seemed to her that the event amounted to a terribly boring cocktail party, with champagne that nobody really liked and canapés that were not a reasonable substitute for the real food these people would be eating from choice.

It was not until her and her husband left, usually about 9.00pm, that the staff seemed to get on with enjoying themselves when, by all accounts, the 'office party' degenerated into a kind of bacchanalian orgy with the staff drinking beer & Bacardi Breezers and lunging lasciviously at colleagues who, in normal circumstances, they wouldn't pass the time of day with, let alone a night of passion.

For her, it was an ordeal. Jeremy could talk about work, be magnanimous about how well they'd all done this year, knowing nobody would jeopardise their job by saying anything controversial or vaguely interesting. She, on the other hand, had to smile kindly and nod thankfully when members of staff congratulated her on what a wonderful boss Jeremy was, before sidling off to gossip about her, interspersed with sly glances in her direction, as they assessed her clothes and jewellery, makeup and figure.

Caroline knew they thought she was a gold-digger living a privileged life with a rich man twice her age. They were, she thought, not altogether wrong. She enjoyed Jeremy's money, she knew she could never live without the lifestyle he indulged her with, and although he was not strictly 'twice her age', the age gap was as much psychological as anything else. Jeremy was, in outlook, clearly closer to her father's generation than hers.

She had everything – except sexual passion, and that was so deeply buried that mostly she didn't even realise she was missing it.

That was until Terry Belling. Belling was in his twenties and was exactly the kind of young lout who, Caroline imagined, spent his weekends at football matches, followed by binge drinking sessions and fighting outside town centre pubs that she would not be seen dead in.

He was loud, uncouth, uncultured and, from what she could see, not even a terribly useful employee. But when he 'hit on her', as she understood the expression to be, rather than the anticipated revulsion, something seemed to click inside her like a switch that had been turned off for a long time.

She felt breathless and an excitement not experienced since her first clumsy fumblings at the age of 16. Somehow, he had awoken feelings and fantasies in her that she had almost forgotten; feelings that frankly she had never felt with the rather perfunctory, dutiful and very infrequent sex with her husband.

On this first encounter at the office Christmas party, her sense of excitement seemed accentuated by the proximity of her husband, and she had not resisted when Belling had pulled her unceremoniously into a stationery cupboard no doubt often employed for Belling's encounters. With no pretence at foreplay, they had violent sex; she sat on the photocopier, skirt around her waist and her legs around his.

Far from any sense of guilt, disgust or shame afterwards, she found herself yearning for more and it was the beginning of a short but torrid affair that lasted for around 3 weeks, in which time she met with Belling more and more frequently.

There was no pretence at anything involved in this relationship, other than a driving need to indulge themselves sexually. Conversation beforehand was non-existent; no drinks, meals, overnight stays in hotels. Their encounters took place in cars, fields, public toilets, even lifts; their need seemed insatiable and immediate; a fire that needed to be quenched as quickly and as violently as possible, and no sooner had they sated themselves than they separated. No small talk, conversation, even arrangements for the next liaison; a moment or two to adjust hastily removed clothing, and they both returned to their own, quite different lives.

When Caroline was not with Belling, she was fantasising about him, imagining what would happen the next time they met.

Then, no sooner had the affair started, it was over.

The danger of these encounters, which seemed to be an integral part of the excitement for her, inevitably lead to what, had she not been totally blinded by this fantasy, she would have seen coming.

Jeremy discovered the affair.

At first, she was terrified that her indiscretion would lead to her losing everything. She knew enough about Jeremy to suggest that, where money was concerned, he would be clever enough to minimise anything she might claim from the marriage, should he divorce her.

Jeremy was not an overtly mean man, but it was obvious to Caroline that he never spent money which did not somehow reflect well on him. Philanthropy and charitable giving and support were a means to an end for Jeremy. They all reinforced his personal status or were good for business. He did not spend money unless it furthered those aims. Even the beautiful clothes and fine jewellery he bought for Caroline were really to enhance his reputation and standing in the community. She was, she knew, a trophy wife who needed to be on display and beautiful for Jeremy's sake rather than her own.

The minute she ceased to be an asset to him then she also ceased to be a worthwhile business expense, and like any unnecessary business expense she would be ruthlessly cut.

Jeremy's reaction, however, came as a complete surprise and what actually happened was, in many respects it seemed to Caroline, even worse. He said nothing. Well, almost nothing.

He did not get angry, threaten her, or call her any of the many names she no doubt would have used to describe any of her friends who had behaved in a similar fashion. He simply came home from work one evening and told her that he had sacked

Belling and he had left immediately with three months pay, on the understanding he left the area and never came back.

His response was a directive rather than a discussion. She would not embarrass him any further by trying to make any further contact with him. The affair was over, and he never wanted to discuss the matter again.

That had been seven years ago and from that moment on Jeremy never, ever mentioned it again. But somehow, it sat resolutely in the back of Caroline's mind, a niggling thought that sneaked into her consciousness and then retreated as she was constantly aware that something here had never quite been resolved.

At first, she was grateful Belling had not contacted her or even sent her a note to say goodbye. But she did not fool herself into believing that she meant anything more to Belling than a sad, middle-aged and bored woman who he could use for his own purposes.

He would have known that he was lucky to get money out of Jeremy, and there were always other women. But now, lately, she had begun to find that in almost every waking as well as dreaming moment she found herself fantasising about him.

At first, there was anger at him leaving without even a hint that she meant slightly more to him than a quick sexual thrill. Then, as more and more of her time was taken up with images and memories of their times together, she found herself fantasising not only about all the things that they had done, but all that they might have done had the affair continued.

At night she would awaken, body drenched in sweat, reaching out to her imaginary lover. There were hours spent half dozing in the bath, as she allowed her thoughts to drift to him. Sometimes, it seemed she could feel his breath on her neck or the touch of him. She wanted him. More than anything else she wanted him. Her head told her she was obsessing, infatuated, but her body hungered for his touch.

Then, without warning, seven years after the affair had ended, on this quiet Wednesday morning, he returned.

23

She had been sitting in her favourite place, the conservatory at the rear of Manor House. The warm sun through the glass soothed her as she lay nestled in the high-backed wicker chair, enjoying the warmth and soft breeze from the open window that caressed her face deliciously. She felt a familiar feeling in the pit of her stomach as her mind drifted once again to her lost lover, when suddenly she was shaken from her reverie by the sound of the front doorbell ringing.

Stopping to adjust her hair and clothing in the mirror in the hallway, as if her innermost thoughts would somehow be reflected in her outward demeanour, she coughed nervously before composing herself and opening the front door.

She felt her head swirl and her legs almost collapsed beneath her, as there, standing on her doorstep, was Terry Belling.

Caroline stood, open-mouthed, as she stared at the lover she had not seen or even heard from for seven years, and now here he was, standing before her.

He had changed very little, although he looked pale and was unshaven, perhaps a little thinner, with dark rings below his eyes. He looked dishevelled, and his clothes were crumpled and dirty, as if he had been sleeping rough. He smiled. 'Hello Caroline,' he said as without being asked. He stepped into the hallway and stood before her.

As if the preceding seven years had not existed and without any conversation, they came together hungrily, kissing passionately and tearing at each other's clothes. Caroline frantic, afraid she might be dreaming and that at any moment she would awaken and unable to control the passion of their coupling; they collapsed, half on the floor, half on the stairs as they hungrily fed their respective desires.

Finally, lying half naked and panting, Caroline looked across at Belling, as if checking it was not her imagination and that he was really there. 'Why are you here, Terry?' she asked eventually.

'I came back for you,' he answered, 'I want to be with you.'

Perhaps now, her desire having been fed, Caroline began to

realise what a dangerous game she was playing. What if Jeremy caught them? He surely would not forgive her again. She would lose everything, and as if her sanity was returning after weeks of obsessive longing, she began to panic.

'This is stupid, Terry. You must go, you can't be here. You can't just come back into my life after seven years without a word. You must go before you are seen. If Jeremy finds out you are back I will lose everything. You must go.'

Belling looked at her longingly. 'I have nowhere to go. I have no money, no clothes, nowhere to live.'

'I can't help you Terry. Look, you can stay long enough to take a shower and clean yourself up a bit. I'll see if I can find some clean clothes you can have. I don't have much money, but what I have I will give you. But you must go.'

Belling looked helpless, but Caroline's fear of Jeremy, or more accurately, the fear of losing everything she had, was now uppermost in her mind. It seemed the weeks of obsession and fantasy had been somehow exorcised, and the reality of her situation had become more important than her desires.

She forced herself to be strong. She did not want to give Belling any small hope that further begging would weaken her resolve. 'If you want to clean up, Terry, do it quickly, otherwise leave now. I must have been mad to let you in. Please go, and go quickly.'

He opened his mouth as if to argue, but seeing the sudden coldness in her eyes, he seemed to accept that it would be useless. 'I'll take that shower,' he said as he rose stiffly to his feet and climbed the stairs to follow Caroline to the en-suite bathroom off the master bedroom.

Whilst Belling showered, Caroline hunted through the endless rack of expensive suits in her husband's wardrobe. Finally, she settled on a dark-grey suit, covered by a see-through plastic dry cleaning cover that she had collected the week before. There had been a small tear above the left elbow of the jacket where Jeremy had caught it on a nail during a visit to one of his building sites.

Unable to cope with even the slightest defect in his dress,

Jeremy had returned home immediately to change, throwing the expensive hand-made suit into the rubbish bin in the bathroom from where she had rescued it. Her frugal upbringing had come into play and rather than throwing it out, she had taken it to the dry cleaners who had 'invisibly mended' the small tear before dry cleaning it.

As Belling came out of the bathroom wrapped in a towel, she handed him the suit. 'Take this, I don't know why I bothered getting it mended, you can hardly see the tear on the sleeve, but Jeremy will never wear it again, he can't stand anything that is not perfect, even if he is the only person who can see it.'

As Belling dressed himself in the suit, Caroline searched her handbag. 'If he notices the suit is gone, which I doubt, I'll tell Jeremy I took it to the charity shop. He clearly has no intention of wearing it again, and I haven't got much money but you can have what I've got.'

She handed Belling £300 in new £20 notes. 'That is all I have. Now you must leave.' She led Belling back down the stairs and hurried him to the front door, opening it. Belling turned, leaning forward to kiss Caroline who turned away from his advance. 'Just go, please hurry,' she said

Belling stepped outside, turned towards Caroline and started to speak. Without waiting to hear what he had to say and without a word, she closed the door in his face. She leaned her back on the closed door, standing in that position for a few seconds, eyes closed. Finally, she took a deep breath and held her hand out in front of her. It was shaking uncontrollably.

It was five hours later, just as she was finally beginning to recover fully from Belling's visit, that the doorbell rang again and she panicked again as she approached the window to look outside, terrified that Belling had returned.

Surprisingly, at the door stood a uniformed police officer, a panda car parked in the drive behind him. The officer looked at her as she stared out of the window at him, and she realised her initial instinct not to answer would seem odd, so trying to suppress her feelings of panic, she opened the door.

She felt the tremor return to her hand as the officer explained that Jeremy was at the police station. He was being interviewed by a doctor and would then be helping the police with their enquiries. Apparently, a Detective Chief Inspector Richards would explain in due course. In the meantime she should wait.

SIX

It was not until the next day, Thursday afternoon, when the panda car called for Caroline.

The evening before, after the unexpected visit from the police and when she realised Jeremy was apparently not coming home that night; she had telephoned the police station for news, only to have the same story repeated. He was 'helping the police with their enquiries' and would not be released. Unable to sleep, she had tossed and turned most of the night, wondering why her husband had apparently been arrested and fearing it might have something to do with the unexpected visit of Terry Belling.

The policeman, however, had explained that, apparently, the Detective Chief Inspector was ready to talk to her about her husband; he was there to give her a lift to the police station.

At the police station, she was shown into an interview room by a female police officer who offered her tea which she declined, and the officer then took up position by the door. Ten minutes or so later the door opened, two men entered and took seats across the table from her.

Richards introduced himself and DS Willis, as he placed a folder on the table in front of him, opened it and then read for a few seconds, before speaking.

'There is no gentle way of doing this, Mrs Carlton, so forgive me if I seem abrupt. We have charged your husband with the murder of Terry Belling. Mr Carlton will go before the Magistrates tomorrow morning and will be remanded for trial. Given the serious nature of the crime, we will be opposing bail and, given his mental state as well, I suspect the Magistrates will remand him in custody.'

Caroline stared, uncomprehending as she tried to make sense of what she was hearing. 'I'm not sure I understand.'

'I realise this is a shock, Mrs Carlton, but there is no doubt here. I need to clarify a few points with you, but I have rarely come across a case where the evidence is so clear cut and this, coupled with your husband's confession...'

'Confession?' Caroline said, 'I'm not sure I understand what you are telling me - what confession?'

Richards could see that she still did not fully comprehend what he was saying to her. 'I'm sorry, Mrs Carlton, this must be confusing. Let me clarify things a little. I realise this is difficult to get your head around. Maybe I can make it a little easier. Your husband walked into this police station yesterday, Wednesday. He was obviously in a very disturbed state. He kept repeating that he had killed somebody. Eventually he told us he had killed Terry Belling, and he also told us where we could find the body. You know Terry Belling, I believe.'

Caroline sat stunned, and Richards' voice seemed to be coming from a long way away.

Richards continued, 'He said we could find Belling's body at The Blue Boar, a derelict pub in the town, owned by your husband's company, Minster Investments. The body was in the cellar; it was not a pretty sight. Belling's face was smashed beyond recognition.'

Caroline latched on to the doubt, this had to be some terrible mistake 'So how are you sure it was Terry?' she asked.

'We're sure,' Richards said with emphasis. 'Belling had a criminal record. We have his fingerprints on file. They match. That has been reinforced by dental records. I thought originally, the severe damage to his face would exclude dental records, but apparently his rear teeth were relatively undamaged. We found the last dentist in town to treat Belling and the x-rays match. Look, Mrs Carlton, I realise this is difficult, and under normal circumstances I would not be giving you all this information. But frankly, the evidence is water tight and your husband's defence will have access to all the evidence, anyway. We are not looking for anyone else in this case; the matter is quite clear. We have the murder weapon, a mallet used for tapping barrels in the pub cellar. And the pathologist has confirmed the cause of death as a massive trauma caused by a frenzied attack. In excess of 30 individual blows were identified. The mallet has been forensically confirmed as the murder weapon and it has your husband's fingerprints on it.'

Richards paused to check that what he had said so far had sunk in. He didn't want Mrs Carlton to be in any doubt as to the strength of the evidence. The more convinced she was that the facts were unavoidable, the more cooperative he expected her to be. As if to reinforce the fact he continued, 'As I said, I have rarely been involved in a serious case with so much evidence. We just have a couple of issues I need to clarify with you, primarily concerning your husband's motive for this attack. It is true you had an affair with Belling, isn't it?'

The statement was made with such conviction and authority that it brooked no contradiction. Richard's eyes bore deeply into Caroline's as he sat silently, waiting for a response.

Uncomfortable with the eye contact, Caroline lowered her gaze to the surface of the table. 'Yes,' she replied quietly.

'This started when?' he continued.

Still avoiding Richards' eyes, Caroline continued, her head bowed, 'Seven years ago. It started at my husband's office party, Christmas, seven years ago.' Then, as if to justify herself to Richards, she continued, 'I don't know why it happened, perhaps I was a little drunk, I don't know, it lasted just a few weeks and then it ended.'

Richards nodded in confirmation. 'Your reasons are not important in this, Mrs Carlton. As far as I am aware, adultery may be frowned upon in some circles, but the last time I looked it wasn't a matter for the police. But murder is. I'm interested in motive, not morals. It stopped why?'

'I regretted it. It was not something that I am proud of. I wanted it to stop before it ruined my marriage.'

Richards frowned, it was clear to him this was not the entire truth. 'Look, I realise this is an ordeal, Mrs Carlton, and as far as I am aware, up to now you have committed no offence that is of interest to the police. However, if you lie, and that lie interferes with my investigation of this murder, then that could change very quickly. If I feel you are attempting to pervert the cause of justice, for whatever reason, I will charge you.' He let the threat sink in before adding, 'The whole truth please,' he said, emphasising each word.

'It stopped because Jeremy found out about it,' Caroline said quietly.

'Very well, thank you,' Richards responded. 'What was your husband's reaction to finding out?'

Caroline felt a burning sensation behind her eyes, and she rifled in her handbag for a tissue, dabbing below her eyes to staunch the combination of tears and mascara that threatened to cascade down her cheeks.

'Jeremy was Jeremy. He told me he had sacked Belling. Paid him off. He said I was not to try and contact him again. That was it really. He said he never wanted to talk about it again.'

'How did he pay him off, do you know?'

'I don't know. He said he'd given him three months pay, I think. That's all I know.'

'Okay, thank you Mrs Carlton, I realise this is difficult for you, now, did he mention Paul Brice's involvement in any of this?'

'Paul?' Caroline said, 'I don't understand, what has Paul got to do with this?'

'That's what I'm asking you, Mrs Carlton. You know Paul Brice well?'

'Of course,' Caroline answered. 'Paul has been with Jeremy for longer than I have known him. He is a good friend, not just an employee. Why would Paul have anything to do with this?'

'That is exactly what I am trying to establish, Mrs Carlton. Look, we interviewed all of your husband's staff, yesterday. Everyone in the office seems to have known about your affair with Belling. In fact, it seems Belling boasted about it to other staff members, including Paul Brice. Brice says it was him who broke the unpleasant news to your husband.'

'I thought he was a friend,' Caroline said.

'Don't be naïve, Mrs Carlton. Brice was always going to put his and your husband's interests first. Did you know Brice also had a criminal record? It seems he had a bit of a reputation for

31

violence when he came out of the army. Apparently, he did a little more for your husband than what you would expect of your everyday 'Personal Assistant.' Look, let me explain.' Richards leaned forward onto the table. 'One of the major things I need you to help me with is to establish exactly the extent of Brice's involvement in this.'

Richards continued, 'According to Brice, it was him who 'paid off' Belling. This was not a case of three months pay in lieu of notice, you know. Brice went to see Belling and paid him off in a far more literal way. He went to see Belling on your husband's behalf, gave him a choice. He could take £6,000 and leave forever or get sacked and leave with two broken legs. Not surprisingly, Belling took the first option.'

Richards was beginning to realise that Caroline Carlton had absolutely no idea of the nature of the relationship between Paul Brice and her husband. 'Brice says he took Belling to the train station, bought him a first class ticket to London, one way, handed him an envelope with £6,000 and made it clear what he could expect if Brice ever saw his face again.'

Richards played with a large brown envelope and then said 'It seems he didn't stay away, though. Rather, it seems, after having time to think about it, Belling thought that £6,000 was not sufficient payment for keeping your husband's reputation and dignity intact. He obviously felt it was worth more. So he came back to town and arranged to meet your husband at the Blue Boar, a safe and quiet place to meet; it was unlikely anyone would see them there. It is likely Belling knew your husband owned the property from his time with Carlton & Messenger, and it seems he demanded more money. No one knows exactly what Belling said to your husband. But according to Brice, he pushed pretty hard. Threatened to expose everything to the papers, his affair with you, lots of details, just the sort of thing the tabloids love, you know: a rich and bored wife, prominent businessman. Seems he gave chapter and verse on what the pair of you got up to. It would certainly sell a lot of papers and ruin your husband's reputation at the same time.'

32

Caroline sat stunned as Richards continued, 'It seems your husband snapped. The mallet was to hand. He picked it up and hit Belling in the face. The injuries suggest he lost it completely and just kept hitting him, over and over. According to the pathologist, he was probably dead after the third blow, the rest were just, well, frenzy I suppose is as good a word as any.'

Caroline's face was ashen and she swayed slightly as if close to fainting. Richards turned to Willis. 'Get Mrs Carlton some water.' And he paused as Willis left the room, returning quickly with a plastic cup full of water. He handed it to Caroline who sipped it. Slowly, a little colour returned to her cheeks.

'I'm sorry, Mrs Carlton. A dreadful business, but murder is never neat and tidy.' Richards paused and then tipped the large brown envelope he was holding upside down.

Three clear plastic bags spilled out onto the table, and Richards arranged them neatly in a row before her. 'Do you recognise this?' he said as he held up one of the plastic bags. It contained a single sheet of A4 paper. 'This seems to be a receipt for the dry cleaning of a suit and an invisible mend to a tear on the jacket. It's dated last week.'

Caroline knew exactly what it was. 'Yes,' she replied, 'It is the receipt for a repair and clean on one of Jeremy's suits.'

He then held up another envelope inside which was a small yellow cardboard label with a safety pin through it. 'This was on the trousers of the same suit. Looks like the kind of label a dry cleaner would put on both items to tie them together, in case they got separated.'

The final envelope contained a small pile of mint condition 20 pound notes. 'There is 300 pounds in there. Found in the inside pocket of the jacket. All these things were in the suit taken from Belling's body.'

The sight of these mundane objects was just too much for Caroline and she could maintain her composure no longer. As she sobbed uncontrollably she recalled Belling, dressed in Jeremy's suit and the perfunctory way she had sent him away the previous day. Why had Terry not told her he intended meeting Jeremy? He must have planned it before he had come to see her. She would have perhaps been able to dissuade him. She knew, Jeremy would never submit to blackmail, she could have convinced him not to try. Maybe promised to send some money on to him later. If she had known, perhaps she could have prevented this tragedy. Terry would still be alive and her husband would not be facing a murder charge.

Richards' voice shook her from her thoughts, 'I think that is about it, Mrs Carlton,' he said as he placed the plastic bags, one at a time, back into the envelope. 'Thank you for coming in, I will get a car to drive you home. I am happy you had no part in this. I'm also sorry to be the bearer of such bad news.'

Both he and Willis stood, and as they turned to leave, Caroline spoke, 'I'm sorry, I don't understand. What happens now?'

Richards turned back to face her. 'As I said, we have already charged your husband with murder. It seems we have nothing more on Brice than assisting your husband in concealing a body, concealing evidence, possibly conspiracy to pervert the course of justice, but no way of connecting him to the actual murder. That seems to be a clear crime of passion on the part of your husband. We'll take advice from the CPS on what exactly to charge Brice with, but it looks like he told us the truth.'

He paused, before continuing, 'Your husband called him after he had killed Belling. Seems Brice drove straight over and helped your husband conceal the body under debris from the pub. He brought your husband a change of clothes and took away his blood-stained ones with the murder weapon. For some reason he kept them. Maybe he thought they might be useful if he was ever linked to the crime at a later date. Or possibly, he might have thought to blackmail your husband with them at a later date. Anyway, we have them now. They've been examined. The blood and other body matter on your husband's clothes and the mallet is definitely Belling's. That seems to be pretty much it. There are only two major questions we can't get an answer to. Probably never will, unless your husband recovers from whatever trauma he is currently suffering from. I have no doubt the psychiatrists will tell the judge what they think. Personally, I'm pretty sure he will be declared insane.'

Caroline interrupted 'Why insane? What questions? I have no idea what you are talking about.'

Richards continued, a little puzzled by Caroline's apparent continuing confusion, 'Well, the first question is: Why did he walk into the police station and confess yesterday? Why then? Possibly it was all part of the beginning of a breakdown that had been developing for years and was only now coming to a head. Brice told us he received a phone call from your husband, yesterday. Apparently, he told Brice he was on his way home and he saw Belling leaving your house. Obviously, that was impossible, and clearly it shook him up. Seems he drove straight to the Blue Boar and uncovered Belling's body and dressed it in one of his suits. Does that seem like the behaviour of a sane man to you? Anyway,' Richards continued, 'Apparently he then walked to the police station and gave himself up, finally cracked I suppose.' Caroline's mind was racing, unable to make any sense of what Richards was saying to her.

'I don't understand,' Caroline said, 'You say Jeremy killed Terry after he had been to our house yesterday; Jeremy must have seen him, gone after him and...'

'Mrs Carlton,' Richards interrupted abruptly. 'Let's just put this down to over-tiredness, shall we? I think you have been through enough, don't you? Belling was killed seven years ago, by your husband, when he returned from the train station to try and blackmail some extra money from him. His body, with Brice's help, was buried in that cellar and has been there ever since. There is no doubt here. A few more weeks and Belling's body would have disappeared forever under 65 new apartments. It has obviously been preying on his mind every day for the last seven years, and it seems his mind or conscience couldn't take it anymore. Obviously, the hallucination yesterday, when he imagined seeing Belling leaving your house, tipped him over the edge.'

Caroline sat open-mouthed as Richards continued, 'So, second question: Unless a seven-year-old corpse dressed itself, the only other possible explanation is that your husband dressed him in it, probably yesterday, but clearly, anyway, from the evidence of the dry cleaning receipt, sometime in the last week.'

Richards and Willis left the interview room as the full horror began to crystallise in Caroline's mind, and a terrified scream began to build in her throat.

MEDUSA

ONE

Karl Hudsucker hated this shit.

The countryside was for wild animals, not for humans. In fact, he saw no point in it, whatsoever - wild animals or the countryside for that matter.

There was nothing he wanted out here that he couldn't have in his apartment in Manhattan or in any decent five star hotel anywhere in the World.

Nothing, that is, except Seamus Underling.

Underling lived in, what Hudsucker considered a shack in the middle of woods in New Hampshire.

It had taken him hours to drive here, and as he stepped out of the car, feeling his expensive Italian shoes sinking into vile, clinging mud, he looked at the dark, semi-derelict wooden cabin, surrounded on all sides by trees and darkness.

The cabin was a silhouette against a sky lit by a full moon, its light made milky by the thin, scudding clouds that passed across its face, riding on some slight breeze not present at ground level.

A pale, flickering orange/yellow light emanated from the windows and was so weak that, rather than being a welcoming sign of warmth inside, it gave the impression that they were the last flickering embers in a fire that was slowly dying in the wood.

A thin, wispy plume of smoke trailed from the chimney, suggesting the remnants of an open fire inside would provide very little in the way of comfort in this scene of rural decay that Underling chose to inhabit.

Hudsucker pushed open the door and strode in without knocking. 'That generator cost me a fortune to install all the way out here; if you choose to live in the middle of nowhere, you might at least use it and put some lights on.'

The sight that greeted him was bizarre in the extreme. The cabin which consisted of one large room was filthy. Piles of unwashed clothing, books and magazines were spread across the floor and buckets, pots and pans, presumably strategically positioned to catch leaks that seeped through the roof when it rained, were still half-filled with stagnant water.

A stone sink in one corner was filled with dirty pans, cutlery and dishes and a single, rusting tap dripped relentlessly onto the pile of unwashed detritus.

A large wooden table was covered with opened tins still with vicious looking lids half removed; unidentifiable remnants of moulding food festered in the bottom, and Hudsucker shuddered at the thought of the animal droppings, cockroaches and rats that no doubt infested this filth.

A huge stone open fire smouldered against one wall, the flames seeming weak on the pile of ashes that clearly had not been removed for years as they had, over time, been raked forward, spilling off the hearth onto the floor, so it was now impossible to tell where the hearth ended and the floor began.

The room was lit, ineffectively, by a mixture of assorted church candles and ancient paraffin lamps, despite the fact that the cabin obviously had electricity, for there, sat behind an incongruously modern desk was Seamus Underling, before him an array of computer screens, some connected to the Internet via microwave satellite connections installed by Hudsucker at the same time as the generator.

Some streamed lines of compiling computer code and piles of tangled electrical cables stretched haphazardly across the desk and around small unused spotlights and furniture legs, disappearing into patch-panels connected to solid looking boxes of electronics, power supplies and transformers.

The cold, electric flashings of the displays highlighted the filthy, unshaven and lined face of Seamus Underling.

Looking for all the World like a tramp who had wandered in from the cold, looking for shelter and a handout, he sat staring at the meaningless streams of data.

Hudsucker shook his head despairingly as he stared into the face of the universally acknowledged World's expert on Artificial Intelligence Programming.

'Okay,' Hudsucker said as he stepped forward to the front of the desk. 'I'm here – so what is so important I had to come here personally? Not that it's not nice to come visit y'all,' he leered in an exaggerated and effected accent, he imagined, reflected the hillbilly slum he found himself in.

'I needed to give you this.' Underling's voice was a hoarse whisper, and his bony hand shook uncontrollably as he lifted one of two identical, yellow parchment envelopes and handed it to Hudsucker.

The envelope was sealed, rather theatrically Hudsucker thought, with red sealing wax, traces of which still adhered to the small ring on the little finger of Underling's tremulous hand. 'The royal seal, eh?' Hudsucker said as he looked at the spidery writing on the front, which merely said, 'Confidential – for Karl Hudsucker's eyes only.'

'Very dramatic,' Hudsucker said. '100,000 dollars worth of electronics and you couldn't send me an email?'

Despite his outward appearance of confidence, however, Hudsucker was less concerned about the envelope in his hand, than the almost identical one, still lying on Underling's desk. The envelope was indeed identical in all respects, with the exception that the name, for whose 'eyes only' this one was addressed was that of Sir Patrick Wellington.

Patrick Wellington was the chairman and owner of Insignia; the British based computer games giant, who, until Hudsucker found Medusa, was the World's number one.

Hudsucker's company, Medusa, renamed after the phenomenally successful game that had seen his company rest the number one spot in the industry from 'Insignia,' owed its success to one thing: the brilliance of the AI technology behind it, and it had taken the strange world of online video gaming by storm.

Within months of its launch, it had sold in its millions and dwarfed all other games, including the also highly successful, but distantly second, 'Troll' from Insignia.

Medusa was unique.

On the face of it, it was just another extremely violent shoot 'em up cum adventure quest game with a simple premise of the gamer fighting and thinking his way through numerous tasks, fights and challenges to set up a final confrontation with the all-powerful dark Lord known as Medusa.

Defeat him, and that was the end of the game.

The unusual thing was, however, that to date a year after its launch – no one, not one single person from the millions of players, had ever defeated Medusa.

Even more unusually, there were no 'cheats' or 'back doors' to the game that anybody had discovered.

Initially, as a testing mechanism and subsequently as part of the strange world of computer games, cheats and back doors were used to make progress through the game easier. By simple means of increasing the power or quantity of weapons, reducing the impact of hits by the enemy on the player, increasing the number of lives available before the player 'died', etc.

This strange industry was predicated on a generally accepted commercial principle that, whilst problems and conflicts needed to be increasingly difficult to negotiate as the player worked his way through the game - once a challenge had been overcome or a puzzle solved, the player would lose patience if he was forced by later failure, to revert back to repeat those known earlier challenges, sometimes with great difficulty, before being able to progress further in the game.

If a player was constantly forced to repeat already solved problems and tasks just to get back to the stage where he had ultimately failed, then they would lose interest in the game – affecting its commercial longevity.

Games designers solved this problem, generally in two ways. Firstly, they typically allowed the player to save the position at the end of a section or particularly difficult challenge, and secondly, by access to so-called 'cheats'.

This, effectively, allowed the player to continue from the last save, rather than to have to fight his way all the way back through the game from the beginning again.

Gamers were typically persistent but not patient; very little stimulation came from constantly having to repeat problems that had already been solved intellectually, just to get back to the point where they could pit themselves against the new challenges.

This semi-secret world of cheats and solutions spawned an entirely separate marketing opportunity, as gamers traded methods of passing certain challenges in the game, or magazines offered access to the secret key combination presses to access the cheats, which increased their ability to progress.

But Medusa was different. It ran contrary to the conventional wisdom usually employed in that there were no saves. 'Die' and you started again from the beginning.

Additionally, no one had ever found access to a cheat to increase the gamer's survivability. Weapons and tactics were either inherent in the game or evolved from the fertile brain of the player.

These apparent anti-commercial constraints were, of course, fiercely resisted by Hudsucker and his Board; but no amount of threats, bribery or persuasion could move Underling, who had total control over Medusa and stubbornly refused to compromise in anyway.

At first the conventional wisdom seemed to hold true and feedback suggested gamers were frustrated and angry that progress through the game was so slow, and challenges apparently already overcome had to be repeated from the beginning.

But then, a unique thing emerged about Medusa. It became apparent you could not solve a problem or defeat an enemy in the game the same way twice.

It was as though it learned from its mistakes and protected itself from suffering defeat by the same mechanism or tactic again. Previously used methodologies didn't work, and every time a player re-started the game, he had to find new ways, new tactics to progress.

Medusa effectively became harder to play each time, and of course, without having recourse to a complete list of previously used tactics by all other players, the chances of an individual finding a unique solution plummeted.

Of course, less skilful players were discouraged, but for

others it became a cult. This status was further enhanced by a clever marketing strategy thought up by Hudsucker himself.

The simple idea was to create an online 'club' of players who contributed their successful solutions to various stages of the game, not as was usual, to help others advance, but to warn of previously used tactics that would not work a second time!

Normally, the competitive nature of gamers would encourage them to keep solutions to themselves or to impress others with their skill. But now they were encouraged to share their tactics in return for thousands of others, which, by definition would fail and therefore should be avoided.

The complexity of the database searches to identify previously used tactics to avoid, were almost as impressive as the game itself.

Add to this a 10 million dollar prize to the first person to defeat Medusa and Hudsucker had an unstoppable commercial winner.

Despite the incredible success of Medusa, Hudsucker had a few serious problems, most of which related to the complete unpredictability and unreliability of the genius behind the game, Seamus Underling.

Apart from the minor irritation of Underling's insistence of living outside of any semblance of civilised society, like a recluse in the middle of nowhere, more serious challenges faced Hudsucker.

Key amongst these was the fact that, before Medusa, he was on the verge of bankruptcy. Even now, after the incredible financial success of the game, his profligate lifestyle and highly leveraged company was vulnerable to powerful rivals, like Insignia and its owner Wellington.

Neither he, nor his Company, owned the game.

His perilous financial state at the time of his desperate meeting with the strange genius Underling had led him to agree that the game remained the intellectual property of the programmer.

A combination of pragmatism and desperation at the outset had led Hudsucker into believing that this would not be a particular problem. He had no doubt he would be able to outmanoeuvre the unworldly Underling at some appropriate time and take ownership by fair means or foul.

He doubted Underling even knew a lawyer, let alone have access to the type of corporate legal expertise to maintain and win an intellectual property battle with him.

No, his real problem was he did not have access to the code. The detailed description and unassembled computer code and the obviously incredible AI programming techniques used in the game were not available to him.

Frighteningly, he suspected that they may not exist outside of Underlings head, but assuming they did, any attempt he had made to negotiate with Underling into securing this commercially sensitive information had fallen on deaf ears.

He had even considered getting thieves backed by the best IT people he could hire to steal Underling's computers, to seek and hopefully disassemble or reverse engineer code.

But the consequences of failure, and the subsequent total alienation of Underling that would certainly follow any failure, was unthinkable.

No, he could not risk jeopardising his, albeit fragile, relationship with Underling until he was absolutely sure he could secure the code.

He also needed a follow up, a sequel.

A 'Medusa II' would secure his future and rescue him from his current, precarious and highly leveraged position. For that, he needed Underling, or more reliably, access to the technology behind the game.

He could not be reliant purely on Underling who was too unstable.

Who knew when he might poison himself by eating amongst the filth and contaminated water in the conditions he chose to live under, or fall down a ravine in the wilderness or get so depressed he shot himself?

Not having to rely on Underling would be a blessed relief – but not until the means to continue without him was within

Hudsucker's grasp.

Another problem was that he had no idea how they would know when someone beat Medusa, if they ever did!

Underling had simply said that he would know when the game had been completed.

Despite Hudsucker's attempts to get more information, not least because he would have to authorise a 10 million dollar payment on the strength of this proof, he had not managed to sway Underling to provide any further details.

Now, he found himself summoned to the middle of nowhere by a lunatic with, who knew what kind of crazy agenda, which seemed not only to involve Hudsucker, but also his greatest rival, Sir Patrick Wellington.

'So, what do I do with this?' he waved the envelope towards Underling, 'Do I just open it, or do I have to wait until midnight and read it under the light of a full moon or something?'

Despite the apparent confident sarcasm of his tone, his eyes were still focussed on the worrying envelope addressed to Wellington on Underling's desk.

The recluse seemed unaware, or at least totally disinterested in Hudsucker's tone.

'You can open it now; it is up to you,' he whispered.

Hudsucker angrily tore open the envelope and unfolded the sheet of paper inside; leaning to one side, he held up the sheet to read the spidery scribble in the light of one of the ancient lamps.

His face darkened as he read.

'You can't do this...,' he said. 'Who else have you sent this too?' He continued staring suspiciously at the envelope addressed to Wellington.

'Nobody,' Underling answered. 'That is your copy; this one,' he paused to pick up the other letter, 'is for Patrick Wellington.'

'It's the same as this?' Hudsucker said as he held up his copy of the letter.

'Identical.'

'Well, Wellington clearly hasn't got his, yet.' Hudsucker

said.

'He will be here tomorrow. I will give it to him then.' Underling placed one shaking hand protectively on the other envelope.

'No copies? No emails? Have you mentioned this to anyone else?'

'There are two copies, you are holding one. This one.' Underling tapped gently on the envelope. 'This one,' he repeated, 'I will give to Patrick Wellington tomorrow.'

Hudsucker read the letter again.

'I, Seamus Underling, have been unfairly deprived of the credit for the success of my creation, Medusa.

Before I die, I intend that rightful credit for my creation shall be acknowledged.

Because I can trust no one and I have no family to inherit or benefit from my work, I have detailed everything, all my unique secrets and techniques and placed these on a remote server.

The IP address of this server, along with the necessary codes to access this data, have been stored within Medusa.

Only by defeating Medusa can this information be accessed.

Anyone who defeats Medusa will automatically be connected, via the Internet, to the remote server and once they have entered the access code, they will be able to download all my secrets.

I hereby bequeath to whoever enters this code, all rights to these secrets in perpetuity.

I am passing this information to two people. The two most powerful people in this ungrateful industry.

It will be amusing to see if these two self-proclaimed geniuses can actually access this data before anyone else from the millions playing the game solve the problem.

Personally, I believe my heir will not be either of these two people. I am convinced my true heir will emerge from this

46

unknown mass of players.
     Whoever that is – he will be very rich with my blessing.'

Signed

Seamus Underling.'

'You can't do this,' Hudsucker repeated. 'It's madness. We have done very well from Medusa. You are jeopardising everything.'

'*You* have done well,' Underling said. 'You are driven by money. Without my game you are nothing, and I have decided I will take control of what is mine.'

Hudsucker's mind was racing.

He knew that if anyone, particularly Wellington, got hold of the secrets to Medusa before he did, he was finished.

Despite the huge financial success of Medusa, his perilous financial state was only secured by massive loans based on the revenue from the game and the value of the Intellectual Property rights in it.

Hudsucker had obtained enormous funding against Medusa; these attracted massive interest repayments. Fortunately, the immense success of the game meant that revenue was more than sufficient to finance the debt. But that wouldn't last forever.

He had to come up with a replacement, a 'Medusa II', to keep his backers satisfied that there was revenue to replace the current game when, as inevitably it would, sales began to decline.

They were already asking about the future, and so far he had found it relatively easy to convince the backers blinded by the huge returns they were currently getting, that R & D in Medusa II was well advanced.

In fact, he had even taken the opportunity to borrow even more on the pretext of hiring three of the most talented game designers in the world to work on Medusa II.

Only two people were more talented than the men he rather disparagingly referred to as 'The Three Stooges'. One was of course Underling himself, the other, Hudsucker's bitter rival, Wellington.

The Three Stooges, Banowski, Yen and Carlton, had been working for months on cracking Medusa. In reality, the progress they had made had been greatly exaggerated for the benefit of his backers. But they did seem to have managed to progress through the game quite far.

Unfortunately, due to the nature of the 'self learning' capabilities of Medusa, progress slowed the further they went.

The implications of failing at any given stage were huge, and so every new step was discussed, considered, argued and backed by massive support from ever more expensive computing power, busily analysing the options, possible outcomes and most importantly the complex searches of the ever growing list of previously used tactics.

What he couldn't of course know is how much progress Wellington was making. He was the big risk. He was a true genius, technologically, as well as being a sound businessman and properly rich.

He did not need external finance; if he borrowed money it was because it was cheaper than using his own well invested wealth. When he did borrow – he dictated the interest rate.

No, if Wellington got to the secrets of Underling's software first, Hudsucker and Medusa the company would be dead in months, when Insignia came up with the equivalent of Medusa II.

Not only that, but Hudsucker would inevitably end up in jail.

His backers had required, apart from rights over the revenue, additional collateral, and he had produced it. Collateral in the form of the Intellectual Property rights to Medusa.

The document that now sat in a bank somewhere, securing the loans, was a forgery. A cleverly produced document allegedly proving Hudsucker's rights to the product that he didn't actually own, complete with the forged signature of Underling, apparently transferring the rights to him.

He had obtained the funds through straightforward fraud,

and once the secrets were out, should someone other than him access them then the fraud would be uncovered.

His life was on the line. He might as well commit suicide – he would rather be dead than be in prison and broke!

The anger welled inside him. Well, if he was finished, he would make dead sure the cause of his misery suffered, too. Hatred shone in his eyes as he looked at Underling through the gloom.

For a moment, he considered dragging the bastard across the desk and wringing his scrawny neck like a chicken.

Then it struck him - suicide. What had put that idea in his head? Hadn't that always been a risk? Not for him but for Underling?

True, in some respects, Underling's letter read like a convoluted suicide note, perhaps that had triggered the thought.

After all, there were two things that everyone knew about the reclusive programmer. Firstly, he was a genius; secondly, he was as mad as a box of frogs.

What if Underling had killed himself or simply died out here in these woods by some tragic accident? After all – the thought had often occurred to him. Not out of any real concern for the madman, but only from the perspective of what would happen if he died before Hudsucker had secured the secrets of the game.

What if Underling were dead? Was that the biggest risk to Hudsucker now? He had always thought it was a danger; but an unavoidable one, as long as he just stayed alive, long enough for Hudsucker to secure his secrets.

But now, Underling's death was clearly not the most pressing danger to Hudsucker.

The biggest risk came from someone, especially Wellington; getting their hands on the secrets before Hudsucker, and in less than 24 hours, unless he prevented it, Wellington would know as much about Medusa as Hudsucker did, but with the money, expertise and infrastructure to get to the solution before him.

He needed time. A little more time to let the Three Stooges find the answers before Wellington.

No. It was clear to him now. His best chance was with

Underling dead. It didn't stop Wellington getting to the answer faster – but it was clear to him that would take longer to achieve than the swearing out of the arrest warrant that Wellington would immediately organise, the minute he understood that Hudsucker had defrauded the banks, some of which his rival sat on the Board of.

As Hudsucker languished in a prison cell, Wellington would have the time, expertise and money to develop the new generation of Medusa games.

Hudsucker turned away from Underling and walked to a window facing out onto the clearing where his car was parked. The glass was so covered in filth it was difficult to see out, but he could make out the shining, highly polished paintwork of his car, glinting in the pale moonlight that illuminated the clearing.

'Why do you live out here?' he said finally, without turning to face Underling.

'It's clean,' Underling replied.

A half cough, half laugh started in Hudsucker's throat as he contemplated the filth around him, but he choked it off.

'What about rats and other vermin?'

'There are far fewer vermin out here than I met every day in New York; the only difference is that out here they don't lie, cheat and steal.'

'What about other things, bigger things, I don't know. What lives out here, bears, wildcats, snakes?' He shuddered slightly at the thought of creatures he had never encountered before, other than safely behind bars in a zoo. He had no idea what animals were indigenous to these woods. Actually, he preferred not to think about it.

'I can protect myself. Nothing bothers me much here. I have a gun. Never had to use it, though; apart from the odd shot into the air to frighten off scavengers.' He spun slightly in his chair, looking at an ancient old shotgun leaning in a corner behind him.

Hudsucker's eyes settled on the ancient gun. 'That thing loaded?' he said quietly.

'Not much use for a gun that isn't,' Underling responded.

Hudsucker turned back to the window.

'There must be something you miss, stuck out here,' he continued.

'Decent scotch. Not much else,' came the reply.

'Well, that can be remedied,' Hudsucker said, 'Got some in the car, I'll get it. Got some glasses out there too, not sure I fancy drinking out of anything you have in here.'

Hudsucker walked out to his car, his mind racing. Wellington was apparently going to be here tomorrow. Underling must be dead before then; it seemed the obvious solution.

Perhaps Wellington was coming, hoping to persuade Underling away from his arrangement with Hudsucker and to join him. If Underling was dead, perhaps it would convince Wellington to move on to another tack, another way to compete with Hudsucker without pursuing further the difficult task of cracking Medusa.

From a small refrigerator housed behind the armrest in the back of his car, Hudsucker took an ice bucket, and lifting the padded lid on the armrest he took out a bottle of single malt, a large bottle of mineral water and two tumblers, and carried them back to the cabin.

He placed everything on the desk in front of Underling. He grabbed a handful of ice cubes, throwing them noisily into one glass. 'Ice?' he said to Underling.

'No ice, no water.' Underling replied, eyeing the scotch hungrily as Hudsucker half-filled the empty tumbler with the whisky, lifting it and handing it to Underling, who grasped it with a trembling hand.

Hudsucker poured a small amount of scotch onto the ice cubes in the other glass, listening to the satisfying crack as the warm liquid cascaded over the ice. He then topped it up with mineral water so that both glasses appeared to be similarly full. Of course, Underling's was pure scotch, Hudsucker's mainly water.

He sipped at his glass as he watched Underling swallow half his whisky in one gulp and close his eyes appreciatively as the warm liquor travelled down his throat and warmed his stomach.

'You know, sometimes we never take enough time to enjoy the good things in life, Seamus,' Hudsucker said as he held up the bottle to Underling who stretched his arm out to receive another generous measure.

Underling took another large swallow. 'You won't get me to change my mind,' he said, 'I have thought this out, this is my inheritance, this is my wish.'

'No more business tonight, Seamus, forget business. When did we ever just have a drink together?'

He already knew the answer to that question. Never. Why the hell would he ever spend a minute longer in this lunatic's presence than he had too?

He threw some more ice in his own glass and splashed a little more of the scotch onto it, before once again topping up Underling's.

It was obvious to Hudsucker that Underling had not been eating properly; in fact he looked thoroughly emaciated. The scotch, drunk too quickly on an empty stomach was visibly taking its effect.

'My inheritance' he mumbled, 'I will secure my inheritance.'

'Your inheritance is safe, Seamus, don't worry.' He poured yet another huge measure into the programmer's glass, watched as he once again took a huge swallow, and noted with satisfaction as his head lolled back against the headrest of the chair, eyes closed, and mouth open.

'Your inheritance is safe with me, Seamus.' Hudsucker said as he watched the glass in Underlings hand slip, spilling some of the amber liquid into his lap as he passed into unconsciousness.

The smile left Hudsucker's face as he looked at the unconscious Underling.

'Your inheritance is safe with me,' he repeated quietly.

TWO

'You've got a week.'

Hudsucker sat at the end of the long, highly polished mahogany boardroom table, a glass of scotch over ice in his hand as he sat looking at the Three Stooges; Banowski, Yen and Carlton sitting to his left and right.

'A week is not enough, we are one or two steps away from the end of the game but we can't afford any slip-ups now.'

The Russian, Banowski, was invariably the spokesman for the three. Yen, the Chinese programmer, brilliant as he was in AI, did not have anywhere near the same degree of language skills. In fact, Hudsucker thought he deliberately exaggerated his Chinese accent as an excuse for not talking to other humans. His thick-lensed glasses were indicative of his terrible eyesight, no doubt aggravated by his semi-nocturnal habits, spending as he did, hours on end in darkened rooms with only a computer screen to relate to.

Carlton, the Englishman, was even worse; Hudsucker thought he was pretty well autistic.

In fact, none of them looked like they ever ate anything other than pizza, and from the paleness of their skin it would seem they never saw daylight or sunshine.

'The computers are running the options on the current state of play, which in itself could take a couple of days. We have at least one more set of options after that – if we are lucky and there are no more surprises another few days computing there. It can't possibly be done in a week.'

Hudsucker waved a dismissive hand. 'If you worked on alternatives, rather than just waiting for the computers to do all the work, it would be quicker. That's why Underling's computers are being delivered today. You can start looking through those, immediately. For all we know, the answers may just be sitting on his disks.'

'How did you get them released so quickly? I thought it

would take weeks before they released Underlings property.'

Hudsucker slammed the glass down on the polished surface of the table. 'It is not Underling's property, it is mine. The lunatic shot himself out there in the woods. I produced all the receipts for the hardware, the generators, power supplies, antennae, everything. They had no reason to hold onto *my* property after they worked out what happened.'

'What exactly did happen?' Banowski and his colleagues had been told Underling committed suicide, but the details were sketchy.

'What difference does it make?' Hudsucker was dismissive. 'The madman killed himself. That's all there is to it. Now we need to find out how this damn program works, before Wellington at Insignia does. Or we are all out of business.'

Banowski persisted. 'What was Wellington doing out there with Underling?'

It was clear that the Stooges were not going to fully concentrate on the importance of cracking Medusa whilst they could happily distract themselves with discussion of Underling's death.

'Look. From what I can gather between me going up there and Wellington visiting him, he stuck the barrel of a shotgun in his mouth and pulled the trigger with his toe. Took his shoe off, apparently, sat in his chair and blew the top of his head off. Seems he had been drinking heavily. In fact, his system was so full of alcohol, if the shotgun hadn't have done the job, the booze would have anyway. I went up to talk to him the day before. Trying to get some information out of him to help you idiots. He was already drunk then. There was no point trying to get any sense out of him. I just turned around and drove back again. He obviously just kept on drinking after I left.'

Hudsucker shuddered slightly and took a swallow of his scotch.

Funny. Pushing the barrel of the shotgun into Underling's drunken mouth and pulling the trigger, seeing the bloody mess caused by the shotgun blast, was in his mind less distasteful than the unpleasantness of having to handle the stinking, fetid sock on the unwashed Underling, as he took it off to give the appearance of Underling having pulled the trigger with his foot.

He returned his gaze to the Stooges. 'Anyway – he clearly blew his brains out soon after I left. It seems Wellington turned up the next day and found him dead. He called the police.'

'What was Wellington doing up there?'

'Who knows?' Hudsucker responded, 'I assume he was struggling like you clowns with Medusa and he'd gone up there to try and get information out of Underling. Maybe offer him money. I don't know.'

'Anyway, looks like his visit was about as useful as mine was. Once the police had decided it was suicide I got my lawyers to explain the commercial sensitivity of the equipment in Underling's cabin. Or more precisely - the commercial sensitivity of data that might be *on* the equipment. I don't think the New Hampshire Police were willing to risk a multi-million dollar lawsuit if anything went missing. Especially, after we had explained that if Wellington had removed anything and we didn't find out in time to protect our position – we would be holding them liable. I've had some of our people go up there and dismantle it all. It will be delivered here this afternoon. I want you working on it immediately.'

'You have access to an account with 3 million dollars in it. I don't care how you use it. Buy more computer power, get in more people, bribe someone. I don't care. The only condition is, I want the solution in a week.'

'Now – is there some reason you guys are still sitting here?'

THREE

It was 7.00 pm when Banowski, Yen and Carlton found it.

To be precise, Yen found it and brought it to the attention of the others.

At first, they were not sure what it was. Well, actually it was obvious what it was, they were just struggling to understand what it meant.

The computer equipment from Underling's cabin had been delivered to the basement office they shared at 2.00 pm that afternoon and they had immediately set about setting it up for examination.

The basement had no external windows, and the working area fronted a pretty old fashioned type of computer room sealed off from the rest of the area by glass panels with a central door protected by a key lock that required a 4-digit code to enter.

The air-conditioned computer room contained banks of rack-mounted servers linked through metres of cable haphazardly streaming out of the back of the racks into patch-panels.

The semi-darkness was broken only by the myriad of small; mostly blue lights flashing as the servers slavishly processed millions of possibilities, crunching their way through options of potential next moves provided by the software the Three Stooges had written especially for the purpose.

One screen sat on a desk close to the door outside of the computer room. It displayed streams of meaningless digits as it ploughed through calculations.

When it finished its computations, Carlton had, totally gratuitously, programmed an alarm that caused the screen to flash red and a dramatic siren sounded, like he had seen in a dozen movies when a security cordon had been breached, or a radioactive leak was occurring, or there was a dramatic countdown prior to some huge technical complex exploding in a fireball.

The siren hadn't sounded for the last seven days.

They had separated Underling's computers into two groups, and whilst Banowski and Carlton worked their way through the directories on the servers and assorted networked computers, seeking to understand the structures and thereby the areas that might provide quickly useful information – Yen had set himself up on the other side of the room with the two laptops which were part of the collection of assorted technology.

It was on one of these laptops Yen had discovered the scans.

The scans were of two hand-written letters. Yen read them both over twice, before calling to Banowski and Carlton.

'Take a look at this,' he said.

Yen connected the laptop to a large screen so he could bring up both letters, side by side for comparison.

They seemed at first glance to be identical.

'I, Seamus Underling, have been unfairly deprived of the credit for the success of my creation, Medusa.

Before I die, I intend that rightful credit for my creation shall be acknowledged.

Because I can trust no one and I have no family to inherit or benefit from my work, I have detailed everything, all my unique secrets and techniques and placed these on a remote server.

The IP address of this server, along with the necessary codes to access this data have been stored within Medusa.

Only by defeating Medusa can this information be accessed.

Anyone who defeats Medusa will automatically be connected, via the Internet, to the remote server and once they have entered the access code, they will be able to download all my secrets.

I hereby bequeath to whoever enters this code, all rights to these secrets in perpetuity.

I am passing this information to two people. The two most powerful people in this ungrateful industry.

It will be amusing to see if these two self-proclaimed

geniuses can actually access this data before anyone else from the millions playing the game solve the problem.

Personally, I believe my heir will not be either of these two people. I am convinced my true heir will emerge from this unknown mass of players.

Whoever that is – he will be very rich with my blessing.'

Signed

Seamus Underling.'

The three men read through the letters twice before Banowski broke the silence.

'The words are identical, but they are not the same document. Same words, same handwriting but not copies. Both have been written out in long-hand.'

'Yeah, and its Underling's writing if you compare it with the handwritten notes in the files we got with the equipment,' Yen said.

Yen checked the properties of the two files.

'No dates on the document, but the file record suggests they were both dated the same day, two days before Underling killed himself. One was scanned 10 minutes before the other. Looks like he hand-wrote two identical letters and scanned them one after the other.'

'Who do you suppose they were for?' Yen continued.

'Seems obvious to me,' Carlton offered. 'Who would you say were *'the two most powerful people in this ungrateful industry?'* Must be Hudsucker and Wellington.'

'Yeah,' Banowski said. 'Bit of a coincidence also that he should write them a couple of days before he died. Hudsucker was up there straight after they were written, or at least scanned; then Wellington is up there the next day and finds Underling dead. '

'Too much of a coincidence for me,' Yen said.

'Looks like he wrote these intending to give them to Hudsucker and Wellington. Probably why the two of them went up

58

there. He says he wanted credit before he died. So he planned to hand them over and then he committed suicide,' Banowski said.

'That makes no sense at all.' Carlton was re-reading the letters.

'It says it will be amusing to see which one of the self-proclaimed geniuses cracked the game first. How was he expecting to be amused at the outcome if he was going to kill himself first?'

'Yes, but...,' Yen began.

Carlton cut him off, 'And, if we assume he gave a copy to Hudsucker, why the hell would he kill himself before he gave Wellington his copy?'

Banowski stood up straight, pushing his hair back with both hands, in a familiar gesture he repeated whenever he was trying to concentrate.

'So, Hudsucker goes up to see Underling and Underling gives him his copy of this letter. The next day, Wellington arrives, presumably to receive his copy, and finds Underling dead. This is crap.'

Yen looked at Banowski. 'So, what are you saying?'

'I'm not saying anything. Except, how do you think Hudsucker would react if Underling handed him a copy of this letter, particularly knowing that within 24 hours the man he hates more than any other in this world, Patrick Wellington, was going to get a copy as well?'

Yen stared at Banowski in silence, taking in slowly the implications of what he was saying.

'Well, I'll tell you one thing,' Carlton broke the silence.

'I sure as hell wouldn't want to be the one giving Hudsucker that message. Especially if he had a loaded shotgun in his hand'

'Shit. You think Hudsucker killed...' Yen never got to complete his sentence as suddenly the room was filled with a flashing red light and the deafening noise of a siren sounding from the terminal attached to the servers in the computer room.

FOUR

It was 2.00 am by the time Banowski, Yen & Carlton finished analysing the output from the latest computer runs, and they sat in the battered old settee and unmatched easy chair which served as their conference area.

Banowski pulled out a pile of computer printouts from under an open pizza box that slid off the small table it had been resting on, tipping the box and half eaten contents onto the floor. He brushed at a smear of barbecue sauce on the listing, spreading it further rather than removing it.

The paper was covered with scribbled notes in multi-colours where they had all added comments as they examined the data from the latest output.

'Well, seems as conclusive as anything with this damn game,' Banowski said. 'Question is: do we tell Hudsucker now, or just go ahead and make the play?'

Yen was sitting next to Banowski on the settee, chewing nervously on a pencil. He leaned forward and opened his mouth, about to speak and then seemed to think better of it, shrugged and leaned back into the settee in an almost horizontal position.

Carlton, sat opposite in the easy chair, was clicking the top of his pen nervously.

'Do either of you guys trust Hudsucker?' he said, ignoring Banowski's question.

A dismissive noise escaped Banowski's lips, half laugh, and half grunt, 'You're kidding. I wouldn't trust him as far as I could spit.'

Yen looked worried. 'We never really finished our conversation when the alarm went off. Hudsucker wouldn't really have killed Underling, would he?'

'Scares me just thinking about it,' Banowski replied. 'I wouldn't put anything passed him. I'm certain he's capable of it. Shit, I think he'd kill his own grandmother if it meant getting answers to Underling's methods.'

'But to kill someone, that's so...,' Yen's response tailed off as if he couldn't quite think of a suitably dire conclusion.

'I think he did.' Carlton suddenly stopped clicking his pen and leaned forward. 'I've been thinking about it. Nothing else really fits. Nothing you can call proof but I'm damn sure he's capable of it.' He paused. 'Thing is. If he thinks we know, or even suspect he might have killed Underling; I think he'd do anything to keep it covered up.'

'You think he'd kill us?' Yen looked terrified.

'I don't know. But I don't want to take that chance, do you?' Carlton replied.

Banowski was beginning to comprehend the enormity of what Carlton was suggesting. 'So what do we do? Go to the police?' he said.

Carlton's laugh was humourless. 'And tell them what? We think Hudsucker killed Underling and we need protection because we think he is going to kill us, too? They have already written this off as a suicide and we have no real evidence.'

'Perhaps they will take another look.' Banowski said hopefully, 'Perhaps they can find some evidence if they think there is a reason to believe the death wasn't a suicide. I'm sure they probably didn't look that hard for evidence.'

'Why would they?' Carlton said. 'A drunken lunatic alone in the woods with a loaded shotgun. It's an accident waiting to happen. They'll think we're paranoid.'

'I'd rather be paranoid than dead.' Yen was beginning to sound panicky. 'So what do we do?'

'I've been thinking about that, too.' Carlton said.

'We've been working to solve Medusa, to understand it, to see if we can work out how Underling has made this software so damn clever. It now seems from Underling's letter, we won't have to work it out – he's going to give it to us on a plate – posthumously.' Banowski paused then continued, 'Look, supposing this latest strategy works and we beat Medusa. If we run this strategy with Hudsucker's knowledge, then he'll know as much as we do. We won't control the code – he will. Do you think he is going to give us anything like what it's worth?'

'We know now from Underling's letter that we will have access to the code, so why don't we give ourselves a little insurance?'

'What kind of insurance?' Yen was still looking nervous.

'Right. My idea is this. We run the latest strategy without telling Hudsucker. If it succeeds, we have access to the Underling data and therefore something to bargain with. If it doesn't, then no one is any the wiser.' He paused to order his thoughts.

'If we get the answer, we hand it over to Hudsucker after he has paid us for it. He has made some vague promises about shares of profits and so on, but do you trust him to come through? 'Cos, I sure as hell don't!'

'So what are we talking here?' Banowski asked.

'I don't know, I'm not greedy, let's say six million dollars. That's two million each and we can walk away, rich, but mostly - alive. We can leave Hudsucker to hire some more drones and let them worry about getting paid.'

'And if the strategy doesn't work?' Banowski said.

'Well, if it fails, it fails in one of two ways. We either get through to the next round and have to run another computation, or it fails and we are out of the game.'

'Hudsucker is not going to give us any more time. If we have to run another computation it is going to take longer than Hudsucker is prepared to wait, and if we fail we are out of the game anyway; it would take months, maybe years to get us back to this stage.'

Yen looked deflated. 'And so we accept we have just wasted our time here and walk away with nothing.'

'I'm not suggesting we leave with nothing. I say we run. We have access to the three million dollar Medusa slush fund Hudsucker set up. I say we take that and run.'

'He'll kill us.' Yen was wide eyed and was beginning to shake.

'I thought of that. That's why I said we give ourselves some insurance. I say we contact Wellington, tell him what we know. If we tell him about Underling's letter, maybe he would pay us for a copy of it. What do you think that might be worth to him - a couple of million?'

'Hold on.' Banowski's mind was racing, 'you're going too fast.'

'Look. What I'm saying is, unless we have the Underling data to negotiate with; we run. We take the three million, maybe five million if we're lucky. In any event, we let Wellington have the Underling letter and we tell him our suspicions about Underling's death. Wellington has powerful friends. If he wants the case re-opened it'll get re-opened.'

Banowski considered for a moment. 'Yeah, and if we can figure it out, Wellington can and he has the money to back it up. If he gets the Police to re-open the case, Hudsucker will be too busy keeping his ass out of jail to worry too much about us.'

'Exactly.' Carlton leaned back triumphantly. 'So?' he said finally.

'I'm in,' Banowski said as he and Carlton looked expectantly towards Yen who stared first at Banowski then at Carlton and back to Banowski, before nodding his head in agreement.

Carlton stood up. Okay, let's run the strategy. See if we can't kick Medusa's ass.'

FIVE

Paul Grimes was 6 foot 3 inches tall and weighed over 300 lbs. His massive frame was encased in a light blue two piece suit which was in need of pressing. A large double chin hung over the unfastened shirt collar, and the red tie hanging untidily from it looked like it was an after-thought rather than a conscious addition to his attire.

His face sagged, with puffy eyes which suggested too much liquor and too little sleep. He ran a hand through blonde, tousled hair that was beginning to encroach over his ears and was clearly in need of cutting.

But Wellington knew that he had the sharpest investigative mind in the business, and as a police detective he had no peer, which was why Grimes now sat in a comfortable leather chair opposite Sir Patrick Wellington in his impressive wood panelled office.

Wellington wanted the best, and the best was Grimes.

He reached over the large mahogany desk to hand over two documents to the huge policeman.

One was a single sheet of paper, clearly a photocopy or scan, the other a formally bound document consisting of 10 pages. This was an original document.

'Whisky okay?' Wellington said as Grimes began to scan the documents.

'Fine. Good scotch,' Grimes answered, holding the large crystal glass up in acknowledgement to Wellington, without taking his eyes off the two documents.

'Okay. Let me see if I've got this right,' he said. 'These three guys, Banowski, Yen and Carlton work for Hudsucker, and they phoned you today, out of the blue, offering to sell you some information about this computer game, Medusa, for two million dollars, is that right?'

'Well, to be precise, it was information about how I could

get my hands on the information, if that makes any sense.'

'And this information is worth two million?'

'It's worth a lot more than that – assuming they actually can give me access to it.'

'And you wanted a bit more proof than just their word that they could get it for you, and this document is what they sent you?'

'Correct.'

'Well, seems to me that if this document is to be believed, this tells you and them how to get the information. Now you know what they know, why would you pay that amount of money?'

'I have already been working on Medusa. I think I'm pretty close to the end, anyway. But it seems so are they. I'd rather pay two million and do a deal with them than risk them getting to the data first and deciding to give it to Hudsucker or sell it to the highest bidder. I've agreed to pay them the two million dollars, and if they get to the end of the Game before me, 10 million, free and clear, just to hand it straight over to me – no questions asked.'

'So, what's to stop them just getting you and this Hudsucker into a bidding war if they get there first?'

'Nothing, really,' Wellington said. 'But these guys are computer hacks, very good computer hacks, but hacks all the same. They are not business men. They probably realise they have no real hope of exploiting the commercial opportunities without help. That help really means doing business with me, or Hudsucker, anyway.'

'That's where I come in.' Grimes said.

'Precisely. These guys think Hudsucker killed Underling. I don't know whether he did or not, but I think he is perfectly capable of it and that letter suggests a motive and opportunity.'

'I agree,' Grimes replied. 'I also checked with the morgue. It seems Hudsucker enquired about the body. Says, he feels obligated to pay for 'his friend's' funeral and wanted to know when the body would be released. He's planning a cremation.'

'Interesting,' Wellington said.

'That's what I thought,' replied Grimes. 'Hudsucker doesn't strike me as being the thoughtful type who worries about his 'friends'. I doubt very much that he's got any, and if he has, this

Underling seems like an unlikely candidate. Always bothers me when people want bodies burnt in a hurry.'

He swallowed the last of his whisky and held it out to Wellington who recharged his glass.

'Anyway, I have put a stop to that. I'll get the body properly examined. There are too many bodies passing through the morgue for the Medical Examiner to take a huge amount of trouble with every sudden death and suicide. I'll make sure it gets a proper autopsy, I doubt it's had more than the most cursory one.'

'What about this other document?' He held up the bound papers.

'Be careful with that, it's the original. It is the document assigning ownership of Medusa to Hudsucker and registering it with the bank as collateral for Hudsucker's loan. I sit on the board of the bank, that's how I managed to get my hands on it. It seems Underling is accusing Hudsucker of cheating him in the other letter, so...'

Grimes interrupted, 'So you want me to check this out too, see if it is kosher. Okay, I know just the man - if it's a fake he'll prove it.'

Wellington stood up; effectively suggesting the interview was at an end. 'Just keep him busy. I am close to completing Medusa anyway. With luck, I'll get there before his guys, but if not I want Hudsucker worrying more about staying out of jail than battling with me.'

'Don't worry,' Grimes said as he finished his scotch. 'I'll keep him busy. I'll be in touch.'

SIX

It was two days after the initial meeting with Grimes that Wellington received the call from the detective to give him the news.

From Wellington's perspective, it couldn't have been much better. Grimes had Hudsucker in custody, and it seemed the evidence against him was conclusive.

'First off, he killed Underling, no doubt about that. A proper examination of the victim's mouth showed damage to teeth and gums caused by the barrel of the shotgun. It must have been rammed into his mouth quite hard to have caused the damage, and it would have been painful. No way a suicide, however drunk, would have done that to himself. If you want to kill yourself, you just put the barrel in your mouth; you don't smash in your teeth and gums to do it. Secondly - Underling's foot. The bare foot he allegedly used to pull the trigger on the gun. It had nothing on it except athlete's foot and corns. No blood, no brains, powder residue, bone, tissue - nothing. On the other hand, the shoe and sock that had been removed and was found a couple of yards from the body did.'

Grimes paused to let the facts sink in.

'Underling was shot before the shoe and sock was taken off. Never seen a suicide yet who killed himself and then undressed! The pattern of the residue is conclusive, it was not sprayed where the shoe and sock were thrown; there is even a line of blood on the sock which was caused by the splatter while the shoe was still in place.'

'It gets better,' he continued.

'The document, the one assigning the rights to Medusa to Hudsucker is a fake. Underling's signature is definitely his, but it is not ink. It is a very clever copy that has been superimposed on the document after the event. It was a good job, but a computerised fake, so are the apparent witness signatures, they've been added after the event as well. I haven't followed up with the witnesses yet, but I'm pretty sure they knew nothing about witnessing the document. If they had, it would have been simple enough just to get them to sign the document for real. Why fake their signatures as well if he didn't need to? I'm going to interview him now. A confession would be nice, but I don't think we need it. I'm pretty sure he won't get bail, either, so it looks like you get a free run at this game of yours. I guess, technically, it still belongs to Underling, or more precisely his estate; he hasn't got any relatives so it will no doubt be sold to the highest bidder. Can't see Hudsucker being in a position to enter into a bidding war with you from jail, though.'

'Thanks Paul,' Wellington said, 'I owe you one.'

'No problem, just remember me in your will,' Grimes said as Wellington replaced the receiver.

Wellington stood for a moment, looking across at the screen on his desk. It showed a picture of what appeared to be an underground cavern, lit by flaming wooden torches. The view was across the dimly lit chamber to a dark tunnel entrance, a deep threatening blackness. Two words flashed across the screen: 'Game Paused'.

He knew that when he returned to his seat and pressed continue, that from that tunnel entrance would emerge the Medusa.

He needed to compose himself, before embarking on the final stage of the game. He realised how much was at stake, and he needed to be totally focussed.

But, despite Grimes' welcome news about Hudsucker, he was concerned.

He had tried to get hold of Banowski, Yen and Carlton twice since they had sent him the Underling document. He had been unable to get hold of them.

Had they cracked the game? Had greed got the better of them, and had they suddenly decided that maybe 10 million dollars was not enough?

Maybe he would get Grimes to track them down. But in the meantime, the only sensible thing was to continue. To beat the game himself. One way or the other that was the key to his next decision.

If they hadn't cracked the game and he did, he would pay the two million; if they came forward to collect it and he would be free to pursue the next generation of Medusa games.

If on the other hand, they had beaten him to the answers; he had no doubt he would persuade them to honour their agreement. 10 million dollars free and clear would, he had no doubt, be preferable to a commercial battle with him.

He needed to focus.

Wellington buzzed through to his butler.

'I want no calls, no interruptions, nothing, until I contact you. If I need anything I'll let you know – in the meantime I want no disturbances of any kind until I come out of this room. I don't care if the place is on fire. Stay out until I call you.'

He walked to the heavy dual doors and locked them, throwing a bolt across as an extra measure to ensure no one could walk in and disturb his concentration. He then checked that all the windows were shut and locked, before closing the electronic drapes, sealing out the daylight.

The room was plunged into semi-darkness, lit only by a small desk lamp alongside the computer on Wellington's desk and the eerie, electric flashing of the message on the computer screen.

Wellington sat down at the keyboard, closed his eyes and inhaled deeply, composing himself before opening his eyes again and pressing 'continue'.

SEVEN

The interview with Hudsucker had lasted four hours, before he had finally confessed to Grimes that he had murdered Underling.

The final clincher was two sworn statements from the alleged witnesses to the transaction transferring ownership from Underling to Hudsucker. Both these Wall Street financiers' initial reaction was to call lawyers and refuse to talk to Grimes. They smelled money.

Their reluctance to talk, however, pretty quickly dissolved when Grimes showed their respective lawyers the evidence against Hudsucker, and rather than be implicated in a murder and major fraud, they quickly, on advice, cooperated and signed statements confirming they had never seen the document before and they certainly were not party to any discussions nor did they sign it as witnesses.

This final nail in Hudsucker's coffin seemed to end his resistance, and he confessed both the fraud and the murder.

Having first ensured he had a verbal and written confession, Grimes went on to ask Hudsucker about Banowski, Yen and Carlton.

'Have you any idea where they are?' Grimes asked Hudsucker, 'There is no sign of them at the offices or their home addresses. Got any idea where they might be?'

'One of two places, I would guess,' Hudsucker said bitterly. 'Either they have cracked Medusa and are busy trying to sell the information to Wellington or they are on a beach in Rio spending my three million dollars.'

Hudsucker explained about the slush fund; he had been in the process of trying to track down the Three Stooges when Grimes had arrived to arrest him. He had not had the opportunity to check the bank account, but he was expecting the money to be long gone by now and them with it.

'Well,' Grimes said, 'What do you need to check the bank

account?'

'Just a phone,' Hudsucker replied.

'Well, that's not a problem.' Grimes looked towards the uniformed police officer standing, arms crossed, by the door. 'Get Mr Hudsucker a phone in here.'

It took just a few minutes for Hudsucker to confirm his identity with the bank and get the information he needed.

As he hung up the phone, he looked at Grimes, a puzzled expression on his face. 'The money is still there, all of it. The stupid idiots have left it too late. I've just put a hold on the funds; they should have got it out while they had the chance.'

'So, where does that leave us?' Grimes said.

'Only other suggestion I have is that they are busy doing a deal with Wellington. They must have beaten Medusa and want to sell the information to him. Can't think of any other reason they wouldn't have just cleared out with the money.'

'Perhaps they are just honest,' Grimes said.

'Yeah, and maybe pigs can fly. Check with Wellington.'

Grimes tried to phone Wellington, but his call went straight to voice mail. He left a message for him to call him back and then phoned the main number. The phone was answered by the butler.

Wellington's butler explained the orders he was under, and nothing could move him to go against those instructions and disturb him. He offered to let his employer know as soon as he contacted him, but until then he was not about to risk his job by trying to speak to his boss.

Grimes was about to hang up. 'Oh, by the way, has anyone been to see him in the last 24 hours?'

The butler confirmed that Wellington had had no visitors and if he did, they would be wasting their time. They would not be allowed in.

'Looks like we'll have to wait until Wellington phones me back. In the meantime, Mr Hudsucker, you might as well get your head down.'

Grimes rose to leave, talking to the uniformed officer as he went. 'Take Mr Hudsucker to the custody suite and make him comfortable.'

As the uniformed officer took Hudsucker out of the interview room, Grimes' mobile rang. The caller display showed 'Wellington', and Grimes answered the call.

'I've just sent Hudsucker down to the cells; we've got statements from....,' Grimes' explanation tailed off as Wellington interrupted.

'Two. It says it's two.' Wellington seemed agitated, confused.

'What do you mean, 'two',' Grimes said, but Wellington seemed to be rambling, not listening to him.

'It says it's two,' he repeated, 'But there isn't a two. I've beaten it; it says it's two.'

'You need to calm down, Mr Wellington.' Grimes had never known the man to be this way before. 'I don't understand what you are saying, what does 'two' mean; what are you talking about.'

Wellington continued rambling. 'There were three of them, three Medusas. It came in as one, then split into three and attacked me. But I beat it. I beat all three of them.'

'But how could it be two?' Wellington asked, but the question did not seem to be directed at Grimes.

'Look, Mr Wellington, I have no idea what you are talking about. You need to calm down, are you okay?'

'Two,' Wellington said and the line went dead.

Grimes tried to call back three times, but each time the call went straight to voice mail.

He thought for a moment and then rang Wellington's office and spoke once again to his butler.

'Have you spoken to your boss? He's just phoned me in one hell of a state, is he okay?'

'I haven't spoken to him. He's still locked in his room. I can't disturb him he gave me strict instructions...'

Grimes cut in impatiently. 'He's in trouble, I'm telling you, I've just spoken to him. Get in there, check he's okay.'

'But he gave direct instructions he was not....,' Grimes cut in again. 'I don't care what he said. You need to get in there now.'

'I can't, I...'

'Shit!' Grimes cut off the call. Then, thinking for a few moments, he suddenly strode out of the interview room and hurried to the dispatcher.

'Get a car out to Sir Patrick Wellington's house, you've got the address. I've just had a call from him, and he seems to be in some kind of trouble. I want some officers in there, break in if you have to, but be quick.'

As the dispatcher made the call, Grimes sat down heavily on the corner of a desk.

'What the hell is going on?' he said to the dispatcher, who looked at him in puzzlement.

EIGHT

Grimes sat in the interview room, reading over the notes he had made on the telephone conversation with Wellington. It had been very strange, and it was difficult to remember exactly what the obviously disturbed man had said, but he thought he had the gist.

He then read the report from the police officers who had gone, on his instructions, to Wellington's home.

It seemed the officers had faced a little opposition from the butler who had tried very hard to keep them out. It seems he had taken his boss' instructions to heart, refusing to let them in.

After a few minutes arguing with him and a call in to Grimes they had gone in, anyway.

The door to Wellington's office was locked from the inside. They hammered on the door, but had no response.

They had told the butler that they were going to go in one way or the other; they would take responsibility for the intrusion, but unless he gave them a key, they would break the door down.

The butler had relented and given them the key. Unfortunately, that hadn't helped; they unlocked the door but it was still secured by a bolt on the inside. After several more attempts to raise an answer from Wellington, they had finally smashed their way in.

They found nothing. They checked every inch of the room, the en-suite bathroom, cupboards - there was no trace of Wellington.

They drew back the drapes. All the windows were intact, closed and locked.

Wellington had gone.

When they reported back to Grimes, he assumed they had obviously missed something, so he had driven out there himself, repeating the inch by inch search of the room, even tapping the wooden, panelled walls. The only explanation he could come up with was some kind of secret door.

Still, he found nothing.

'I want photographs,' Grimes said, 'Get a photographer out here and tell him to cover every inch now. I want them developed and in my hands this evening.'

With one more look around, Grimes turned to leave.

There was only one person he could think of who could throw some light on this, and he was sitting, locked in a cell, back at headquarters.

He needed to talk to Hudsucker.

NINE

Grimes and Hudsucker sat facing each other across the table of the same interview room they had used earlier, as Grimes systematically related everything to Hudsucker, occasionally stopping to answer a question or to produce some notes in the folder before him.

After an hour, an officer knocked and came in with a pile of colour photographs taken in Wellington's office.

Grimes went through them carefully, one at a time, handing each one to Hudsucker as he finished with it.

There was not anything, not one single thing that seemed unusual or out of place.

Finally, Grimes piled the photos up tidily and placed them in the folder with the other notes and papers.

They sat in silence for a moment, before Grimes said, 'What the hell was he talking about when he kept mentioning 'two' - he mentioned it a couple of times, then he started talking about 'three', three Medusas, something about 'there was one it became three but he beat them all'. Something like that.'

'There is only one Medusa,' Hudsucker said emphatically. 'There are not three of them, only one. He must have been sitting in that room too long. He must have been hallucinating.'

'It makes no sense,' Grimes said.

'If the Three Stooges were here it might help; they spent most of their life playing the game. Maybe they might think of something. Have you found them yet?'

'No sign,' Grimes said. We've checked all their known haunts, train stations, bus stations, airports. Nothing. They seem to have disappeared off the face of the Earth.'

'People don't just disappear without a trace - do they?' Hudsucker said.

Grimes thought, 'People disappear more often than you would think. Usually, they choose to disappear but, if someone is looking for them, usually they leave some kind of trace. Most are people who just want out of a relationship. Not a police matter, really. The trail will go dry, sometimes, but usually there is the beginning of a trail - a visit to a bank or cash machine, a bus ticket bought with a credit card, a CCTV camera sighting – something.'

'Never heard of four people disappearing in one night, though, especially when one is from a locked room; it's like a bad Agatha Christie plot.'

'Wellington had no reason to disappear; he had the World at his fingertips. He had the key to Medusa II. The Three Stooges, well, maybe they thought they could come up with Medusa II on their own.'

Grimes sighed, 'I'm getting tired of listening to numbers - two, Medusa two, the Three Stooges, three Medusas. Maybe it means nothing. Just the ravings of a man having a breakdown.'

Suddenly, Hudsucker sat forward. 'Medusa two?' he said. 'Perhaps he was talking about Medusa TWO!'

Grimes looked completely baffled.

'Let me see those photographs again,' Hudsucker said, and Grimes took them out of the folder and handed them to him. He looked through them rapidly. Casting aside one after another, until he finally settled on one. He sat staring at it, his mouth open.

'My God!' Hudsucker said quietly. 'My God!'

'What?' Grimes said.

'Look at this picture, what do you see?' He handed the photo to Grimes.

'I see Wellington's desk, his computer, his chair, books, papers, nothing interesting.'

'The screen, man, look at the screen! The game is right at the beginning, it is waiting for someone to start playing it. '

'Yes, I see that, but why is that important? It looks like Wellington had failed, didn't get to the end. If you fail, the game sends you right back to the beginning - that's the way it works, right?'

'Yes,' Hudsucker said impatiently, 'But he didn't fail, did he - he defeated the Medusa, he told you. 'One became three but I beat them all!"

Grimes had no idea what Hudsucker was getting at.

'Two, he said 'It says it's two', he beat it, but it says it's two.'

Grimes still looked confused.

'Look, there is only one game. It is called Medusa. Medusa II is the sequel, the follow-up game we were planning to develop, once we knew how Underling's AI code worked.'

"AI', wasn't that a film?' Grimes replied.

'AI – Artificial Intelligence. It is the holy grail of computing. Intelligent computers that can learn, infer, make random intuitive leaps of what we would call inspiration or instinct, based on experience and knowledge. Trouble is - nobody really understands what 'human' intelligence is, so how you define intelligence in a machine is pretty much impossible.'

'Look, AI research is as old as computing, older in fact. There is a famous test, 'The Turing Test', devised by a British mathematician, Alan Turing, over 60 years ago – it is still valid today. Basically a human talks to a machine over a terminal, and if the human cannot detect that there is a machine at the other end, then that machine is intelligent. There is a bit more to it, but that's the general idea. Underling was the world's leader in AI programming; he used that expertise in Medusa. That's what makes it so unique.'

'I'm not sure I understand what you mean.'

'Seems to me we humans have been a bit complacent, a bit arrogant. Anything that we think of as 'intelligence' that does not come from us we dismiss as 'artificial'. Maybe intelligence exists and just needs a vehicle to exist in, human or machine. Then, machines would not necessarily serve us; they might start serving themselves, using people for their own purposes. I don't think the Three Stooges ran away. I think they were taken. I think they defeated Medusa. I think they did it before Wellington. By beating Medusa, they became part of the game. They became part of Medusa II.'

Grimes' mouth was hanging open, as Hudsucker continued,

'Because the Three Stooges became part of the game, part of Medusa II, instantly Wellington was suddenly playing Medusa II, that's what he meant. It says it is Two. One Medusa became three. That's what he said. He was playing Medusa II with the addition of the combined intellect of the Three Stooges. One Medusa becoming three.'

'How could the game just suddenly change? How did it know to change?' Grimes was struggling to keep up.

'It's an online game. Everyone plays online. Everything everyone does, anywhere in the World, impacts in real time,' Hudsucker explained, 'When Wellington beat Medusa, he did not beat the original Medusa, he beat Medusa II. The cycle repeated itself.'

'You're saying Wellington became part of the game just like Banowski, Yen and Carlton. That's impossible, that's crazy!'

'Crazy or not,' Hudsucker replied. 'Take another look at the photograph; look at the title - the name at the top.'

Grimes studied the photo once more. In bold letters, across the top of the screen, was the game title which for some reason he had not taken in before.

Grimes' mouth fell open.

Clearly visible on the screen, in white and red, were the words 'MEDUSA III'

The Cottage

ONE

'Again, we see that most things we put down to some kind of supernatural activity can be explained much more satisfactorily in a perfectly logical way. So, don't worry about ghosts and sleep tight. That noise is probably just the wind, or the natural creaking of ageing beams... that strange light some perfectly natural phenomenon.'

Steve Finding eased himself in his chair as he continued to speak into the microphone.

'I'd like to thank our friends in Norfolk for this week's fascinating tale, even if we were able to show that the ghostly lady in front of Barry's car was simply mist from low lying water.'

'Well, that's all we have time for tonight on 'Finding Ghosts'. Join me next week for another expedition into the world of the paranormal.'

He slid the fader button cueing the closing music and leaned back wearily in the chair, pulling off his headphones and hanging them on the microphone.

Kneading his knuckles into tired eyes, he sighed, swivelled in his chair to look through the glass panel separating his sound-proofed studio from his producer who also removed his earphones, smiled and gave Finding a 'thumbs up'.

The signal confirmed they were 'Off Air', and Finding climbed painfully out of the chair, stretched, yawned and, picking up his script and coffee mug, walked out of the studio.

'Good show, Steve,' John Wilson, his producer said, 'Fancy a pint?'

'Not tonight, John,' Finding said, 'I'm absolutely knackered. I think I'll just go home to bed. What's on for tomorrow?'

Wilson rifled through the papers in front of him, before selecting a couple of sheets of A4 stapled together in a corner, and handing them to Finding.

'Here's the briefing. We have this couple coming in for a preliminary chat - maybe a piece for a few weeks time.'

Finding scanned the typed notes, whilst Wilson continued, 'Young couple in their twenties, married three years, Brian and Julie Palmer. Recently moved out of a rented flat into their first house, a cottage in the main street in Grove in Oxfordshire.'

'It says here they have experienced some strange activity. Like what?' Finding asked.

'Nothing dramatic, apparently there is a measurable 'cold spot' in one room, some kind of physical manifestation in the same spot. Just a bit of mist, by all accounts, noises, bumps in the night, that sort of thing. No headless horsemen or ghoulies.'

'Do you think there's enough interest for our listeners? Doesn't sound hugely fascinating,' Finding replied.

'I agree,' Wilson responded, 'although it seems to be causing tension between the couple, and it's a pretty ordinary cottage in the centre of a main street. Not your typical scary hovel in the middle of nowhere.'

'Anyway, thought it might combine a 'Finding Ghosts' story with a bit of human interest. Might be an angle on how paranormal experiences can cause stress in relationships.'

'Okay. Guess it's worth an initial chat anyway. What time they in?'

'They'll be here at 11.00 am tomorrow.'

'Okay John, see you in the morning. I'm off... my bed is calling.'

TWO

The following morning, Finding arrived at the studio a little late and helped himself to a plastic cup full of the stewed, luke-warm black liquid that passed for coffee, in the reception area.

Standing at the front desk, Amanda the receptionist handed him his mail, and he quickly shuffled through it, without identifying anything that prompted him to open it immediately.

Amanda smiled. 'Your visitors are in the meeting room, Steve. John is with them; he said to send you in as soon as you arrived.'

'Right,' Finding responded, throwing the pile of unopened letters back onto the counter. 'Keep those for a while will you? I'll pick them up later'.

Amanda pressed a button concealed somewhere under the desk, and a buzzer sounded to indicate the adjoining door into the studio was unlocked to give Finding access.

In the meeting room, a young couple sat together on one side of a pine coloured table, opposite John Wilson; before them, plastic cups of the same dark liquid that Finding was drinking, sat on the table, together with a small plate containing a rather unappetising selection of assorted biscuits.

John immediately stood up, 'Ah, morning Steve,' he said brightly, 'This is Brian and Julie Palmer - Brian, Julie, this is Steve Finding.'

Finding stepped forward, holding out his hand as he greeted them.

'Sorry I'm a little late, very rude of me; a combination of the perils of a late night radio show and the traffic on the Banbury Road. It's nice to meet you both.'

'Okay,' he said, taking a seat at one end of the table, with the Palmers on his right. Wilson returned to his seat to his left.

'I'm not sure whether John has explained, or whether you are regular listeners to 'Finding Ghosts', but the radio programme goes out in the evening once a week and is an hour long show where we discuss and sometimes investigate stories of paranormal activity or other strange events. Sometimes, it takes the form of a phone-in, other times we do pieces on stories of interest that might have made the news or that listeners tell us about.'

He sipped his now almost completely cold coffee and grimaced.

'Now, I understand you have experienced some strange events in your home, is that right? Can you tell me a bit about it? When did they start?'

The Palmers looked at each other, and then Brian Palmer spoke first.

'Look, if you want my opinion - it's a load of nonsense. Julie is convinced there is a ghost in the house. Me? I think it's a dump we should never have bought, and it eats money.'

Finding looked at Julie Palmer, who had turned to face her husband as he spoke, but then immediately turned away again and lowered her head, her face colouring with embarrassment.

'Not a good start,' Finding thought. The aggression in Brian Palmer's voice was palpable, and the topic was obviously a source of friction between the couple.

He decided to try and put them at their ease a little.

'I know the feeling,' he said quietly. 'Bought an old place, myself. I moved out of a modern apartment in London, always thought it would be great to have a place in the country, with a bit more character. Took an absolute fortune just to get it warm and dry in the winter. Character can be a very expensive commodity, sometimes.'

'So,' he continued, 'how long since you moved in?'

'We got married three years ago. At first, we lived together in my flat - it was rented. Julie found this place and we decided to get a mortgage.'

'She always wanted an older cottage; personally, I liked being in a modern place in the middle of things in town, but... anyway, we bought it and moved in about six months ago.'

'How soon afterwards did you start feeling something

wasn't quite right?'

Brian Palmer continued, 'Depends what you mean by 'quite right'. The place was a mess, really, every floorboard moved and creaked, especially at night; at least it seemed worse at night when we were trying to sleep.'

'Lots of bumps and banging, probably the dodgy plumbing. The main thing was the dining room, though. There is this cold spot in one corner. Frankly, the whole house gives me the creeps; but that room – I just can't wait to get out of it. But Julie insists on sitting in there all the bloody time.'

It was clear that Brian was pretty angry, as he kept looking accusingly at his wife as he spoke.

'How about you, Julie? How do you feel about it?' Finding smiled reassuringly, as Julie Palmer once again looked rather sheepishly at her husband, before answering.

'Brian's right, of course - it does need a lot of work, but I just fell in love with the place the minute I walked into it. It felt somehow – right, if that makes any sense?'

'Makes perfect sense, Julie,' Finding said, 'I'm sure, we've all experienced that. Some places seem warm and comforting immediately you go in, other places the complete opposite.'

He looked at her husband who still seemed to be suppressing his anger with some difficulty.

'Clearly, you don't feel the same, Brian?' Finding said.

'The complete bloody opposite, frankly,' Brian responded, 'I felt uncomfortable the minute I walked into the place.' He paused, clearly anticipating the obvious question as to why, if he felt that way, did they buy the house in the first place.

'Look, I thought maybe it was just because it had been empty for a while; it had no furniture and needed 'tarting' up a bit. Especially, as Julie seemed so keen on it. Trouble is, if anything, the atmosphere has got worse. I just can't warm to the place.'

Finding was beginning to become intrigued. Not really by the paranormal aspect; what he had heard so far was not particularly unique, in fact in many respects it was a lot less interesting than many of the cases they investigated.

What really interested him was the fact that, whilst it was common for people to detect an 'atmosphere' in a building, either good or bad, whatever caused that feeling, it was generally consistent. Very rarely were two otherwise compatible people so diametrically opposed on the subject.

Finding turned back to Julie. 'There are lots of theories for the causes of so-called 'atmospheres' in buildings. What do you think causes it in your cottage?'

Julie seemed to steel herself, expecting to be challenged, then she straightened in her chair before answering firmly, 'It's a ghost.'

Finding looked from Julie to Brian who blatantly raised his eyes to the ceiling in an obvious sign of frustration.

'You seem very sure, Julie?' Finding said.

'I'm sure,' Julie said defensively, again glancing nervously at her husband. 'I can't tell you, why. I just... I don't know how to explain - I just feel it. I know she's there, especially when I'm in the dining room.'

'Where the cold spot is?' Finding asked.

'Yes,' Julie said

'You said 'she', Julie - how do you know it's a she?'

Julie looked as if she had not really thought about what was clearly an obvious question for someone to ask.

'I don't know,' she said, 'I just know she is; somehow I just feel it. It's like, when you are sitting with a close girlfriend, someone you trust and share things with. It just feels right. It feels like she is looking after me. Sorry, that sounds stupid, I know.'

'No, no, not at all, Julie,' Finding was reassuring, 'If it was easy to explain then there wouldn't be any mystery about it, would there? The fact that it is not easy to explain is why it is called '*super*-natural.'

Brian Palmer was clearly embarrassed and wanted to distance himself from what his wife was saying.

It seemed a common male response, Finding knew, many men found it so hard to accept this kind of emotional response to atmospheres and feelings. Somehow, it seemed 'unmanly'.

'Well, if it is a ghost, it doesn't surprise me it's a bloody woman. She clearly hates me!' he said sarcastically.

Finding looked at the notes, before continuing. 'It says here that there has been some kind of apparition, who saw it?'

'Me,' Julie said, 'Not an apparition, really, more of a shape; half shadow, half... I don't know, a mist, no real shape to it.'

'Not a woman?' Finding asked.

'No, just this shape, really, but it was her, I know it was.'

'Where did you see it?' Finding inquired.

'It was in the dining room. It was only there for a second. It seemed to be hanging over my chair.'

'Your chair?' Finding said.

Brian Palmer interrupted, 'She has a bloody armchair in the dining room. She's put it in the corner, directly where the cold spot is. She sits there reading or sewing rather than sitting in the living room with me.'

'I just feel comfortable there,' Julie said defensively, 'I can't relax with the television on. We don't talk, anyway. I might as well sit and read where I'm comfortable, rather than trying to concentrate while you watch football.'

'Is it not uncomfortable sitting there if it is a real cold spot? By the way, have you measured the temperature there? Is it really any colder?'

'It doesn't really feel cold or uncomfortable to me,' Julie said, 'I like it.'

'Feels bloody cold to me,' Brian said, 'and yes - I have actually stood a thermometer on the chair; it is a good degree, sometimes more, lower than the rest of the room.'

'That's interesting,' Finding said, 'In my experience, whilst cold spots are quite common - I've even felt them myself, very rarely is there a real, measurable difference in temperature. Usually, it is the result of air movement of some kind, acting on the skin. It feels colder, but the ambient temperature is not actually different.

Finding thought for a moment and then looked at his watch.

'Look,' he said, 'I think this is worth further investigation.

I'd like to visit the house, maybe bring one or two people with me to take a look. Would that be okay with you guys?'

'If you think it's worth the bother?' Brian Palmer shrugged.

'I would like that,' Julie said, 'It would be nice to find out whether I'm going mad or not.'

'I'm sure there is no need to worry about that, Julie. Look, I'll get John here to sort out a time with you when I can come along and take a look, and we'll take it from there.'

Finding stood up, offering his hand to Julie first and then to Brian.

'Sorry, I've got to rush off, but hopefully I'll see you again soon, in the meantime I'll leave you with John to make the arrangements.'

Finding turned to John Wilson. 'John, could I just have a quick word outside about tomorrow's schedule?'

He smiled at the Palmers and left with John following him out into the corridor.

Once out of earshot of the couple, John said, 'Well, what do you think?'

'I'm not sure the ghost is the real story here, but the couple interest me. I think it's worth a follow up. At least it's worth a visit'.

'Okay, I'll sort it,' John said as Finding walked off down the corridor.

THREE

Three days after the meeting at the studio, Steve Finding pulled up outside 'Jennings Cottage' in Main Street, Grove, the home of Julie and Brian Palmer.

He wasn't sure exactly what he was expecting, but the cottage really didn't strike him as a likely candidate for a ghost.

Built in 1860, according to the date in the masonry above the centre upstairs window, the cottage was a detached two story, double fronted brick house with a grey slate tiled roof.

The central, white painted, wooden front door was flanked on either side by large, wooden sash windows. Three similar windows were evenly spaced across the front of the cottage on the first floor.

A garage, attached to the right of the building as Finding looked, had a pair of rather dilapidated, part glazed, wooden doors, painted the same colour as the front door.

The garage doors didn't quite close properly, and a number of the panes of glass were cracked, with one missing completely.

A dirt path led down the side of the garage, presumably to the rear garden.

The house was close to the road, with only a couple of metres of front garden which was quite overgrown with mature bushes; the window on the left, as he looked, was almost totally obscured by an elderberry bush.

Actually, other houses in the vicinity seemed better candidates for a ghost, with an array of both modern and older houses, including some, obviously much older, thatched cottages.

Almost directly opposite was a bustling, modern precinct with the usual array of local shops and small supermarkets around a central car parking area.

Jennings Cottage looked in need of a bit of TLC, but nothing that a little enthusiastic DIY and a coat of paint couldn't fix.

Finding pushed open the small, creaking iron gate and approached the front door, knocking directly on the wood, there being no sign of a bell or knocker.

A few seconds later, the door was opened by Julie Palmer.

Her blonde hair was tousled, and she had clearly been crying, as she turned sideways-on, lowering her head slightly as she let Finding pass her into the front corridor of the cottage.

The dark corridor, lit only from the daylight coming through the clear glass panels at the top of the front door, gave way to a small central hallway with stairs heading up to the first floor.

Three doors led off the hallway. The one to the left that clearly led to a room to the front of the house was closed; the other two, one off to the right and one directly ahead, were ajar.

Julie ushered Finding into the kitchen directly ahead of them.

It was quite a large room, with the usual selection of cooker, washing machine, fridge and cupboards, and a large window over the sink, looked out on quite a large and beautiful, but overgrown back garden.

'Can I get you tea, coffee?' Julie asked, as she busied herself with cups and saucers - clearly, Finding thought, avoiding making eye contact with him, because of her obviously distressed state.

'Coffee's fine. Black, no sugar,' he responded.

'This is lovely, Julie,' he said, 'I can see what Brian meant, it needs a bit of re-decorating, but it is - will be - absolutely beautiful.'

'I think so,' Julie said, 'If only Brian felt the same.'

'Please, sit down,' she said, I'll make your coffee.'

Finding sat in a wooden chair at the small breakfast table.

'No Brian?' he asked

'I'm sorry,' Julie replied, 'He had to go out at the last minute. I'm sorry, it must seem so rude, we knew you were coming, but we...,' her voice trailed off as she was clearly struggling to explain her husband's absence. Finding saw that once again tears were filling her eyes and threatening to burst out and flow down

90

her already pink face.

'No problem, Julie.' Finding's voice was reassuring. 'This is just a preliminary visit, really to see whether there is a story here for our listeners. I just wanted to have a look around, and also get a little more information from you, so we can research everything properly. A couple of colleagues will be here shortly, they are the ones who will investigate any physical evidence. I just want a little more background from you. Is that alright?'

Julie pulled a sheet of kitchen roll from a holder on the wall, dabbing at her tear-filled eyes, before blowing her nose.

'Very elegant,' she said, smiling briefly, 'I'm sorry, this must be very embarrassing for you.'

'Not at all, Julie. Don't worry,' Finding said as he took the coffee that she handed him, whilst she collected her own and sat down opposite him at the table.

Finding sipped the coffee. 'Brilliant,' he said brightly, 'Better than that dish water we get at the studio. Great to have a proper cup of coffee for a change.'

Julie smiled, looking slightly more relaxed.

'Look,' she said, 'There's no point in beating around the bush here. The truth is, Brian and I have had an almighty row, and he stormed out half an hour ago in a rage. I'm not sure where he's gone. Or when he'll be back, so if you would prefer to forget about it... well, I'm sure you have better things to do with your time than getting involved in stupid domestic disputes.'

Finding smiled. 'Don't worry, Julie, I've had my share of domestics myself. No need to be embarrassed. Was it about the house again?'

'It's never about anything else at the moment,' Julie replied.

'We were up most of the night. There is just so much anger in Brian at the moment. It's really not like him. He was always so laid back. Before we moved here, I could hardly get him to change a light bulb. Now he is relentless; spends every minute at home, hammering nails into floor boards to try and stop them moving and creaking, oiling doors, sanding down paintwork. But because he is so angry all the time, he goes at it like a bull at a gate, ends up making it worse than it was before.'

She sipped her coffee, before topping up Finding's cup and continuing, 'At two o'clock this morning, he was still upstairs, hammering nails into floorboards. I went up to tell him how late it was, that it wasn't fair on the neighbours, but he just yelled at me; said if he didn't get it done we would be living in this hovel for the rest of our lives. Because he was so angry, he smashed his thumb with the hammer. I've never seen him act like it before, he threw the hammer across the room, smashed the bedroom mirror to pieces. It was frightening.'

'It must have been,' Finding said, 'And you've never seen him like this before?'

'No, never. If anything, I've always had to push him to get excited about anything. It's not like him at all. Anyway, I went back to bed but couldn't sleep. He eventually came to bed around five o'clock in the morning; he was tossing and turning so much that I got up. Didn't seem much point in lying there, so I thought I'd read for a bit.'

'Which is your room?' Finding said, 'Perhaps you could show me around, if that's okay with you?'

'Oh yes, of course,' Julie said, getting up. Finding followed her out of the kitchen and up the stairs.

At the top of the stairs was another corridor which mirrored the one on the ground floor, but was shorter as it culminated in a door to a front bedroom which spanned two of the three windows that Finding had seen from the front.

There was nothing special about the room. A large double bed, built-in wardrobes, a dressing table and an old pine dresser.

'This is our room,' Julie said.

'It's a nice bedroom, plenty of light from the two windows,' Finding remarked.

'Yes, it's fine – we get a little noise from the road sometimes, unfortunately there's a take-away across the road, can be a little noisy when the pub turns out, but it's not too bad.'

Finding stood and looked out onto the main street below.

He spoke to Julie without turning away from the window.

'Your lady ghost - do you feel her here or is it in one particular place?'

He turned to see Julie's reaction. She lowered her head slightly in embarrassment, before answering.

'I sense her everywhere, but I don't *feel* her here, if that doesn't sound stupid.'

Finding didn't respond, as Julie was obviously trying to clarify her thoughts.

'I suppose, it's like when someone is in the house with you, but not actually in the same room, do you know what I mean? Only when I'm in the dining room do I feel that she is actually there with me. Everywhere else, it's... well, it's like I know she is around and I can find her just by going into the dining room.'

She lowered her head again, 'I expect you think I'm completely mad. Brian does.'

'No,' Finding said, 'Look, let me be completely frank with you. I am fascinated, like many people with stories about ghosts and the paranormal in general. Since I've been doing 'Finding Ghosts', I've investigated dozens of incidents. Some are totally fraudulent, but not by any means the majority. One thing I have come to appreciate is that a lot of people, maybe even a substantial majority, believe they are experiencing something real, something tangible.'

'However, in almost every single incidence I, that is to say me and my team, have usually come up with some rational explanation for the occurrence.'

'But that doesn't mean the experience is any less real for those experiencing them. In fact, I believe there are things humans are capable of, that we don't understand, in fact we are not even aware that we can do, let alone explain it.'

'I'm an atheist. I don't believe in God, angels, the Devil or supernatural beings, whether religious based or otherwise. But I do believe in the incredible power of the human mind.'

'I also believe, as we have become increasingly secular in our outlook, which I personally approve of, and as science unlocks mysteries previously not understood, we have also lost something.

Something that is inherent in us, but no longer needed, as we rely more and more on science and technology.'

'We sense things. We read people without realising we are doing it; we understand how people are feeling, sometimes what they are thinking. Some people know some of the secrets and make a living out of it, but most of us aren't even aware we are doing it.'

Julie listened intently as Finding continued. Clearly this was a passion of his.

'Animals pick up on things. They know instinctively when danger is present, before any human picks up on it; they are known to be able to predict epileptic fits in their owners in time to warn them, to put themselves in a safe place before the attack is ever felt; they can even detect cancers or the impending death of people.'

'This is not *super*-natural,' he said, emphasising the 'super', 'It's natural. We are animals, too. I believe we also have these powers, but we have lost control of them.'

'Our world, our science, our technology, our lifestyles are like noise. Picking up on these abilities is like picking up a whispered conversation in a crowded, noisy room. We can't hear anymore, we have too many distractions.'

'So you think it is in my mind?' Julie said.

'Not exactly, I think you are sensitive; you are picking up on something, some kind of energy that is not actually supernatural but is not understood yet. Some people think buildings can retain atmospheres, energy from past events, sometimes it may be temperature, damp, draughts that our body and mind try to interpret from past experiences. Like a whole body equivalent of an optical illusion.'

'Optical illusions work in the brain, if the eye sees a picture that doesn't seem to make sense, the brain will try and rationalise what it is seeing into something it has experience of and make a wrong, but logical, assumption'.

'I think, perhaps our bodies are capable of doing that as well. It tries to make sense of something illogical and tries to interpret it in a way it understands.

'Hear a voice, there must be a person even if there isn't;

94

feel a touch, there must be someone there but you can't see them; feel cold, there must have been a drop in temperature, even though a thermometer can't record it.'

'So you think there is no ghost, and my mind and body is picking up on things in the house,' Julie said.

'Possibly. When my colleagues get here we will let them check things out and we'll see what happens. I'm not ruling out anything, Julie, honestly. I would love to find some evidence of something, but I haven't encountered anything yet that suggests to me ghosts exist.'

There was a bang on the front door.

'Speak of the Devil! – That will be my colleagues.' Finding said, smiling at the contradiction of beliefs in his statement.

FOUR

Finding's two colleagues were Darren Masters and Sue Williams. They were both in their early twenties and both extremely bright Physics graduates, taking Post Graduate Degrees in Oxford.

Paranormal investigation was their hobby rather than an occupation, and the small additional income they were given as researchers on 'Finding Ghosts' was extremely useful.

They brought great research skills, logical thinking and practical knowledge of the laws of physics to Finding's more lay investigative abilities.

They had both worked on many of Finding's investigations and, like him, so far were still to be convinced of the presence of ghosts in particular and other paranormal activity in general.

Julie let them in.

Both where carrying large aluminium equipment boxes which they dumped in the hall, as Julie and Finding led them through to the kitchen.

Finding summarised the conversation so far, looking occasionally at Julie who, from time to time, nodded in agreement.

He briefly explained the strain that the situation was causing in the couple's relationship, but only enough to suggest that the activity might be influencing behaviour (both Julie's and Brian's).

'So where do we start?' Finding asked.

Darren responded first, 'Well, the centre of the activity seems to be in the dining room. I suggest we get the full layout of the place first, leave the dining room until last.'

Sue nodded in agreement. 'We'll probably need to focus mainly on the dining room with the equipment, but we should check out everything else, make sure we don't miss anything.

The four of them repeated the route earlier taken by Finding, starting upstairs in the Palmer's bedroom at the front of the house.

'While we are walking around, Julie,' Sue said, 'If you feel anything, let us know. For example, if you feel the presence changing, getting stronger or weaker anywhere, it would be helpful if you could point it out.'

Finding and his two colleagues followed Julie from room to room. After the front bedroom, they passed back down the short corridor to a second bedroom, smaller than the first, off to the right, with a window overlooking the garden, then into the bathroom, also at the rear.

As they entered the third bedroom at the front of the house, directly over the dining room, Julie spoke.

'I can always feel her stronger in this room than any of the others, apart from the dining room. I can now, but she's not here, she's downstairs, I know.'

'I think we should mount a thermal camera up here to see if we can detect anything, particularly any change in temperature. It doesn't feel any different to me in here. What about you guys?'

Both Finding and Sue confirmed that they really couldn't feel anything different in the room.

'Okay, let's go downstairs,' Finding said, and Julie led them back down to the ground floor.

They had already checked out the kitchen and hall. The living room which ran the complete length of the house, with windows both front and back, was equally unremarkable, with a large open fire in the side wall and the usual assortment of furniture, television, music centre, three piece suite, bookcases and other odd pieces of furniture.

Again, there seemed nothing unusual to any of them.

'Okay,' Finding said, 'Only the dining room left.'

As they congregated at the closed dining room door, Julie rested her hand on the door handle and then turned to them, before opening it.

'I'm afraid it's a bit of a mess,' she said as she opened the door.

What greeted the investigators was totally unexpected.

'A bit of a mess' was an understatement.

The entire room was covered in a layer of dust, and lumps of plaster which spread over everything, the dining room table, chairs, sideboard and an upright piano against the right hand wall. Dust even clung to the curtains.

It looked at first like the building was in the first stage of demolition, before the cause of the problem became apparent.

The entire ceiling, at least the plaster, had collapsed into the room. As the three colleagues looked up, wooden slats and beams were completely exposed.

On closer inspection, there was only one small area of the ceiling that had not collapsed - the area in the right hand corner by the window, directly above an upholstered, wing-backed armchair with a small occasional table next to it, on which stood a reading lamp.

A paperback novel lay open, cover up beside the lamp, where obviously someone had been sitting reading.

Only this small area seemed to have escaped the plaster.

'What the hell happened here?' Finding said.

'It happened this morning, before you arrived. I told you, Brian had been up all night, and when he came to bed around five, I couldn't sleep, so I got up and came down here to read.'

Tears were beginning to well up in her eyes again, and Finding placed a comforting hand on her shoulder.

'It's alright, Julie, just take your time,' he said.

'Well, I suppose I was tired and I was feeling shaky after the hammer-throwing, and well - I always feel safe here. I suppose I just fell asleep.'

'I must have been asleep for about an hour when the door slammed open and Brian came bursting in, waking me up.'

'He was still so angry, he was standing there, in the middle of the room, shouting and swearing, saying the place was a slum, a complete waste of money. He frightened me so much.' Julie began to shake, tears began to run down her cheeks, and Sue put an arm around her.

'Anyway,' she continued, 'He kicked out at one of the dining room chairs. It flew across the room. You can see where it took a chunk of plaster out of the wall.'

'Then suddenly, the ceiling just fell in. It fell on top of him. He was absolutely covered in white dust and plaster. I got up to see if he was okay, but he just pushed me away, told me to leave him alone. He stormed off upstairs, washed and changed and then he came back down, and without saying anything he just left the house. I heard the front door slam. He hasn't been back since.'

Finding looked across at the corner by the window.

'You were sitting there?' he said, pointing at the chair.

'Yes,' Julie replied, 'It missed me completely, the dust and the plaster. It missed me. I think that made Brian even angrier. He obviously felt a fool, covered in all this dust and mess and I wasn't touched.'

Darren had walked over to the chair and stood in front of it. He turned to the others.

'Sue,' he said, 'Come over here.'

Sue walked across and stood next to Darren in front of the armchair.

'Feel that?' he said quietly.

Sue nodded. 'It feels cold,' she replied.

FIVE

It was three weeks later when Finding returned to Jennings Cottage.

Darren and Sue had set up various pieces of scientific equipment, primarily in the dining room; with an additional camera, triggered by temperature changes or movement, in the bedroom above, where Julie had suggested she felt a strong sense of her ghost.

Finding had had several discussions with his producer as to whether they should actually air the programme, and they still had not fully reached a decision.

The story was interesting enough, but Finding was determined that 'Finding Ghosts' should remain an investigative journalism programme, and he was concerned that there was a serious danger in this potential episode turning into the worst kind of voyeuristic, exploitative exposé, with them being party to the broadcasting of a marriage breakdown in full glare of the public.

On the other hand, the paranormal aspects had certain interesting elements, and the stresses and strains this apparent visitation put on an otherwise apparently healthy relationship, did have quite a strong public interest element.

Unable to finally come to a conclusion, they had decided to postpone a final decision until after his visit to the cottage and the Palmers.

They were, after all, obliged to provide the couple with the results of their investigation, and during this process Finding could evaluate the current state of the Palmer's relationship and whether any airing was likely to be compelling radio or the audible equivalent of the 'Jeremy Kyle Show'.

So, at 11.00 am, Finding knocked once again on the front door of Jennings Cottage, carrying an opaque, plastic wallet containing the results of Darren and Sue's investigations.

Once again, the door was answered by Julie, who looked

pale and tired but did not, at least, seem to have been crying.

She ushered him into the dining room, and he was surprised to find a woman sitting in Julie's chair.

Julie introduced her. 'This is my friend Mary; I wanted her to be here. She has been a great help to me since all this trouble started with Brian.'

'Things are no better then?' Finding said, 'Between you and Brian, I mean?' This didn't bode well for the programme.

'No. In fact, Brian and I are unable even to talk to each other anymore. I am going to live with Mary. I'm not sure exactly what the future holds, but whatever it is, I know it does not involve Brian.

'I'm sorry,' Finding said, 'It's sad when relationships break up. You're sure that it is not just the pressure concerning the house? Maybe if you moved...?'

Julie cut him off. 'No. I have been so frightened these last few weeks. The incident with the hammer, his behaviour in here with the chair and the ceiling. It seems it is only a matter of time before that violence is directed towards me.'

Hearing the mention of the ceiling, Finding realised he hadn't looked. Clearly, the mess, the dust and rubble had been cleaned up, but the ceiling had not yet been repaired and re-plastered.

'Well. I'm sorry, Julie. I really am. I hope you don't feel our presence has in anyway been a catalyst for all this.'

'No, not at all,' she replied, 'If anything, it has helped me come to terms with things. No, Brian and I are not meant to be.' She smiled resignedly at her friend Mary who moved out of the chair and sat Julie down in her place; sitting beside her on the arm of the chair, she put a reassuring arm around the young woman's shoulder and hugged her briefly.

'Okay,' Finding said, opening the folder he was holding, 'You okay if I read this in front of Mary?'

'Of course,' Julie replied, 'I have no secrets from Mary.' She smiled at her friend and placed a hand on her knee, shaking it gently.

'Right. Well, Darren and Sue's report is basically in two parts. The first part is the research that they have done on the property, its history, occupants etc.; the second part is their investigation of the physical evidence, the cold spot, sightings, noises and so on. I'll start with the history, if that's alright?'

Julie nodded. Mary held her again around the shoulders as they listened.

'Okay, I'll just give the highlights. I have a full copy for you. You can read it in detail later if you want.'

'The house was built in 1860 by a Thomas Jennings, hence the name. He was the local builder and not only built this cottage, but a lot of others in the village, as well; but this was his own home and he lived here with his wife, Isobel.'

'They had 3 children, all boys who worked for their father's building business. We can assume, he was relatively well off; there is evidence of a couple of live-in servants at one time.'

'Anyway, it also seems he was a bit of a tyrant - not that that was unusual in Victorian times, but it seems he had a bit of a reputation as a drinker. He apparently spent a lot of time at the pub down the road, The Bell and, as was quite common, laid into anyone in the house who got in his way when he got home - wife, kids, servants, whoever.'

'Even sober, he seems to have been a particularly bad-tempered man and not someone to get on the wrong side of.'

'He had no daughters, and it seems his wife outlived him by twenty years. He died at the age of 62, of some kind of lung disease it would seem, in a sanatorium near Wallingford.'

'After his death, Isobel sold the house and went to live with her sister in London. She died there at the grand old age of 84.'

'Only other piece of local gossip at the time was a suggestion that he, or possibly one of his sons, impregnated a maid who lived in the house. The maid, a local girl by the name of Rose Jenkins, died in childbirth – the baby died, too, so nothing was ever proved, one way or the other.'

Finding paused to let the information sink in, before continuing to the two women who seemed fascinated by the tale.

'The house has been bought and sold a total of 12 times since then. All the details of the owners are listed here. Darren and Sue are incredibly thorough. They paid particular attention to any females that might have died in the property and therefore be a candidate for your female ghost.'

'Unusually, the only female who seems to have died actually in the property is this maid, Rose Jenkins. So, she appears to be the only candidate, unless the alleged ghost pre-dates the building of the cottage, but that seems unlikely, as prior to that it was farmland.'

Finding paused again, considering if there was anything vital that he might have missed.

'Well, I think that's pretty much it on the history. The upshot of all this is Rose Jenkins, the maid who died in 1871; appears, as I said earlier, to be the only candidate for a female ghost.'

'Is it possible that Brian was somehow influenced by the spirit of Jennings? His anger and violent behaviour only seemed to start when we moved in here?' Julie asked.

'It's a theory,' Finding said, 'But unlikely, it seems to me. We now come to the second part of the report, the - shall we call it - haunting?'

'Unfortunately, the physical evidence doesn't seem to back up your theory about Jennings but, moreover, it seems to call into question the whole idea of ghosts, male or female, at all.'

He turned over the page and studied it for a few seconds, before continuing.

'Okay. Let's start with the upstairs bedroom. The guys left thermometers and cameras in the room for a week. They were not triggered once, and they would have been by any sudden or uneven temperature change; nothing other than a normal and gradual falling and rising of temperature associated with the outside weather, the heating and natural changes between day and night.

Also nothing moved at all in that room for the whole week; nothing, not even a mouse.'

'Now, the dining room was different.'

'As we know, most cold spots are, in fact, not 'cold spots' at all, at least not in any measurable sense compared with the ambient temperature in the vicinity.'

'They are usually due to unusual air movement, draughts, hot air rising and falling in a particular place – this movement of air across the skin triggers a cooling reaction on it, just like a breeze in the sunshine. It reacts to it and feels cool, although there is no actual drop in temperature.'

'In this case, there is. I mean a measurable drop in temperature that can not only be detected by our bodies, but more importantly, by a thermometer.'

'So Darren and Sue set out to account for it – and they did.'

'It seems, there is an underground water course that runs directly under that corner of the room. At some stage, it seems likely that someone drilled down into it to create a well. It was never really filled in, just covered up and built over.'

'Water vapour and air circulating up through the floorboards is cooling the air above it, not by much, and it fluctuates. But enough to create a detectable and measurable difference to a sensitive thermometer, as well as to that equally sensitive thermometer, the human skin.'

He paused, before continuing, 'It also seems that the air above this spot is high in humidity; basically, it is full of water vapour.'

'It is constantly condensing, causing damp and then, through a combination of sunlight, concentrated through the window and the radiator below the window, evaporating again, effectively exaggerating the temperature change effect on the skin.'

'This almost certainly also accounts for the 'shape', or as you described it, 'mist' that you saw.'

'If the condensation had been particularly heavy, followed by an extremely hot concentration of sun through the window, it could well have been enough to create a cloud of water vapour. Darren and Sue have actually been able to reproduce it in the Lab.'

'What about the ceiling?' Julie asked.

'I was just coming to that,' Finding said. 'You remember

you said Brian was going crazy trying to stop the movement and the creaking of these very old floorboards. He was hammering in nails all over the place.'

Julie nodded.

'Look up at the ceiling,' Finding said, 'You can see, the whole lot has come down, except for a small section in your corner, over your chair.'

'About a foot in front of you, there is a water pipe. Brian nailed straight through a floorboard and into that pipe. It was leaking for weeks.'

'The slope of the floor naturally ran away from the outside wall, the water dripped into the space between the floorboards and the plaster and it tended to run away in that direction.'

'The plaster is porous; it soaked up the water until it just became too heavy to stay up and collapsed beneath its own weight. It could have gone at anytime, but it was probably triggered by the shock of the chair hitting the wall when Brian kicked it. It was the last straw; it just gave way like an avalanche.'

'Had it stayed up longer, it would have eventually leached like blotting paper into the plaster above the chair as well, but as it collapsed before that happened, the dripping from the pipe had no plaster beneath it to drip onto.'

'If you look carefully, you can see the slight discoloration of the battens up there; they are absorbing the water at the moment, but eventually, until it's fixed, it will start coming through into the room and onto anything beneath it.'

As if for emphasis, he added, 'In short, you need a plumber as well as a plasterer.'

'Oh, and while you're calling in tradesman, I should call a pest controller. We found evidence of rats. That probably also accounts for some of the noises in the rafters.'

They sat quietly for a minute or two, before Finding broke the silence.

'Conclusions,' he said with an air of finality. 'No ghosts, of either sex; no apparitions, no ghostly noises. Nothing that can't be explained by science and natural phenomena.'

SIX

Finding, Julie and Mary sat quietly for a few minutes. Occasionally, Julie asked a question and Finding responded, sometimes referring to the notes, but nothing dramatically altered any of the conclusions.

Finally, Finding stood up. 'I should go,' he said as he placed a copy of the report on the dining table.

'I'll leave this here,' he said, 'If you have any questions give me a call. I need to get back to the studio. I need to talk to my producer; decide whether we want to put this out in a future edition of 'Finding Ghosts'.'

'If we do, then that can only happen if you and Brian are agreeable. So, you will need to discuss this with Brian. We can't go ahead, unless you both agree.'

'That's not likely, I'm afraid,' Julie responded, 'Brian and I are just not talking anymore.'

'Well, I'll leave it with you. If you change your mind, let me know. It wouldn't go out for a few weeks anyway. We have our schedule confirmed for at least the next two shows. Give me a call.'

Finding left the dining room and started down the corridor towards the front door, Julie and Mary following along behind him.

Suddenly, he saw the shape of the top of a head through the glass and heard the lock on the door turn and click, as the front door opened and there, standing in the doorway, was Brian Palmer.

He looked dishevelled and unshaven, and Finding immediately smelled the unmistakable odour of alcohol as Palmer staggered slightly. He braced himself against the corridor wall, his eyes settling on Finding.

'Shit!' Finding said beneath his breath, realising that Palmer was seriously drunk.

'What the hell are you doing here?' Palmer slurred, 'How the hell did you get in?'

'I came to bring you the results of our investigation.' He

tried to speak calmly. 'I've explained it all to your wife. She has a copy of our report, I'm sure she can tell you...'

He was cut off in mid sentence as Palmer lunged forward, grabbing Finding by the collar with both hands, pulling him forward until his face was inches from Finding's. The alcoholic stench of Palmer's breath was almost unbearable.

'What the hell are you talking about, you sick bastard. What gives you the right to break into people's houses?'

'I didn't break in, Brian.' Finding was trying to sound calmer than he felt.

'Your wife let me in, ask her, ask her friend Mary, they both...'

'Who the hell is Mary?' Palmer was shouting directly into Finding's face. 'My wife's name is Julie, not Mary, what the hell are you talking about?'

'I know, I mean your wife's friend Mary - I've just been talking to them both, explaining the results of the investigation, you can ask them, ask them now!' He turned, struggling in Palmer's grasp, towards Julie and Mary who had been standing behind him immediately before Palmer opened the door.

They were nowhere to be seen.

'Listen, you sick bastard. Julie has no friend called Mary and she didn't let you in. I've just got back from the undertakers. Three years, that's all we were married for... three years! She was only 27, for Christ's sake. Now I've got to bury her.'

'I'm drunk, does that surprise you? This house - it's this bloody house! I should burn it to the ground. If we hadn't come here, she'd still be alive.'

He dragged Finding by the collar with one hand, opening the front door with the other.

'Get out, get out you sick vulture, go and dig up your stories somewhere else and leave me alone! Get out!' he screamed again, as he threw Finding out onto the path and slammed the door behind him.

SEVEN

Finding said nothing to John Wilson or to Darren and Sue about his return visit to Jennings Cottage, except to say that he had dropped off a copy of their results.

As they sat in the conference room, Finding unusually had a glass of scotch, and he listened to the others as they discussed this and other upcoming stories.

'So, have we decided what we are going to do with the Jennings's Cottage story?' Sue said.

'Nothing much we can do. Julie Palmer is dead, following a car accident on the M40, and her husband has been charged with causing death by dangerous driving. He looks to be going down for a while, and he won't cooperate with the programme, anyway. We could try going with it anyway – but not sure our lawyers would sanction it.'

'Bloody shame,' Sue said, 'We put a lot of work into that report. If we had only known Julie was already dead, just hours after we removed all the measuring equipment, we could have avoided all that typing.'

'Still, it was an interesting story anyway. The only one where the history really backed up the science.'

'It was interesting that Julie said she knew the ghost was female, and Jennings's maid was the only female who had died in that house.'

'Still, not hugely significant I suppose. Not sure what the mix of male to female was back in the 1870's, but it must have been roughly 50-50. I guess she had at least even odds of getting the sex right.'

Sue nodded in agreement.

'Shame, though. Still think it would have been nice to investigate Mary a little more. I doubt anyone much mourned the death of a maid in those days - dying in childbirth was pretty common.'

Finding had been staring into his whisky glass, not really contributing to the conversation, deep as he was in his own thoughts.

'Mary?' he said suddenly, staring at Darren, 'You said Mary? – But the maid's name was Rose.'

'Yeah, not that it matters much I suppose, but not really. Her real name was Rosemary. When we checked the 1871 census, she was recorded as living with another maid at Jennings's Cottage. Given the size of the place, they must have shared a room. The one over the dining room was smallest.'

'Seems logical that Thomas and his wife Isobel shared the front room, and the three boys shared the long room, leaving the smallest for the servants.'

'According to the census records, she was down as 'Rose' Jenkins, but her birth certificate says her birth name was 'Rosemary''

'In the 1861 census, she was six years old, living with her Mum and Dad. In that census, she's recorded as 'Mary Jenkins'.

'I'd always go with Mum and Dad when it came to names. I think she was born 'Rosemary'.'

'But I'd bet next week's wages, if I was getting any,' he smiled, 'that everyone else called her 'Mary'.'

Shark

ONE

Gary Bowler considered himself a very lucky man.

He had his own business and he was doing very nicely, thank you.

True, he did have to spend a good proportion of his time dealing with clowns, but then he made a lot of money out of them, and even the clowns could be entertaining in their own way.

He looked at his watch, a beautiful gold Rolex, and realised he had an hour or so to kill before seeing his next client.

Sharon Porter was one of his better punters, and having given her an ultimatum to come up with a 100 quid by 8.00 pm this evening, he didn't want to be unfair to her by turning up early.

Besides which, he understood the power of the fear he induced in the punters, and the terror Sharon would be feeling right at this moment fed him in a tangible way. It really was like food and drink to him, and he felt that familiar warm glow in the pit of his stomach, knowing the respect through fear she would be feeling for him right now. Fear was good for business.

He stood by his black 6 series BMW which glimmered brightly under the street lights in this derelict area of London's East End.

The amber lights flashed and the alarm beeped briefly, in response to the pressing of the remote door lock on his car key fob and he pulled open the driver's door. He stood for a moment, looking across at the welcoming lights of the Butcher's Arms pub across the street. He looked again at his watch - yes, he had time for a quick one before he needed to leave to see Sharon Porter. He slammed the car door shut again, reactivated the alarm and strode across the road into the Butcher's Arms.

It was early, so there were only a few of the more hardened drinkers in the bar. They looked up as Bowler walked in and he smiled to himself as they recognised him and immediately turned their eyes away. Yes, he thought, fear was certainly good for business.

The barman poured him a large single malt, no ice, and placed it in front of Bowler, nodding politely and making no attempt to ask for payment as he immediately returned to the corner of the bar where he had previously been engaged in conversation with one of the drinkers, resuming the conversation and pointedly trying not to look in Bowler's direction.

He sipped the whisky appreciatively as he scanned the room, before his eyes settled on his reflection in the dusty, mirrored wall of the bar.

Again he smiled and nodded almost imperceptibly as he admired the carefully cultivated image he cut.

His 6 feet 5 inch muscular frame was dressed in an expensive, dark blue tailored suit, above a crisp white shirt and blue silk tie. The long, black mohair coat he was also wearing was clearly expensive, too. Clean shaven, his sleek black hair brushed straight back, glistening with gel, with cold, dark brown eyes above a scarred face and broken nose gave him, he imagined, the classic East End look synonymous with the Kray twins – a look he aspired to; they were, after all, his role models.

The only concession to modern times was the diamond stud in his right earlobe that glistened as brightly as his professionally whitened teeth.

Image was important, he thought; half the battle was looking the part. Most punters were not stupid enough to get on the wrong side of him. Mind you, even if they did, he knew he was more than capable of putting them straight, very quickly.

Yes, life was good for Gary Bowler. He made money, lending small amounts of cash to idiots who, he knew, would struggle to repay, often consolidating those borrowings with further loans until they ended up owing thousands to him, for the outlay of a few hundred quid.

Collecting the money weekly in cash was fun and far more lucrative, financially, than the measly amounts of interest he'd earn if he stuck it in the bank. There was something about a cash business that made it all real to him; there was no substitute for the feeling of that huge wedge of cash he invariably carried around with him.

It could get complicated. Often he had to take possession of the punter's pension book or family allowance book, which meant he needed to meet them at the appropriate post office, give them their book, before taking the money and the book back, after they had signed for their money. But that was a small inconvenience; better than risking them spending any of the money before he had taken his bit of it.

He never took it all. After all, they did need to eat - a dead punter wasn't going to pay him anything. Mind you, a badly injured one, occasionally, was good for business; it kept the other punters in line and, sometimes, as well as their child benefits, they might actually find themselves entitled to disability payments.

Actually, as long as the money kept coming in, the odd default was good – he enjoyed the violence; he didn't mind admitting it, and not only was it fun, but it kept the other punters honest. Keeping them in fear was important, and Bowler was very, very good at that.

Enough of reminiscing, he thought, as he glanced once again at his watch, before swigging back the remains of the whisky.

Time to visit Sharon.

TWO

Bowler parked the BMW outside the shabby tenement building which was 4 stories high, with a concrete walkway at the front on each floor; with identical flats, save for the varying colours of the front doors, the walkways gave access to the 2-bedroom council flats behind.

They had certainly seen better days, and it seemed to him that the local council had as little interest in their upkeep as the tenants who lived in them. 'How could these animals live in this filth?' he thought as his mind wandered to his spotless docklands apartment. Still, he had class; the idiots who lived here, he was sure, didn't deserve any better.

He glanced up and down the dark, damp street to see if there were any obvious signs of any stupid young idiots who might not know who the car belonged to and try to nick something. He was fairly confident that most people around here knew him and would recognise the car. Trouble was, you never knew when some little chancer might come along and think that heaving a brick through the window might be a good idea.

He also knew that, if they did, he would know exactly who to lean on to find the culprit, and the toe-rag responsible would be lucky if he still had hands to pick a brick up with, after Bowler had finished with him.

He climbed the concrete stairs to the left of the building. He screwed up his face as his nose was assaulted by the smell of stale urine in the stairwell. 'Filth!' he muttered under his breath, as he made his way up to the third floor and out along the walkway, pausing outside the peeling, blue wooden door of number 34, the flat where Sharon Porter, single mother of this parish, lived with the three snot-nosed little tearaways she called children.

Time for a little amateur dramatics, he thought, just to keep Sharon on her best behaviour. So, without knocking, he turned the door handle downwards gently, testing to see if the door was locked – it was. So, still holding the handle down, Bowler stepped back from the door and then powered forward, shoulder first, against the flimsy panel.

The cheap Yale lock and security chain were no real contest against Bowler's bull-like strength, and the door flew open inwards, a crack spidering across the frosted glass panel at the top of the door as it crashed back against the hall wall.

Bowler's huge frame almost filled the open doorway as he stood, legs astride, looking into the hallway and smiled at Sharon Porter who was physically shaking, her arms folded across her chest as she held herself desperately trying to steady her trembling body, a look of desperation and fear on her tear-streaked face.

'Knock, knock,' Bowler said sarcastically as an evil smile spread across his lips, and he savoured the look of absolute terror on the face of his victim.

'I hope you have my money, Sharon. You already look a mess. I would hate to have to work on your face. Let's be honest, you already have enough problems.'

'I have some here... I... couldn't... I got as much as I could... it was... I've got it here...,' Sharon pulled a crumpled bunch of assorted bank notes from her jeans, struggling to sort it in shaking hands, 'I've got £80... a bit more.' She held out the crumpled notes with one hand, the other returned to her pocket as she pathetically pulled out a few coins and held them out in her other hand, 'A bit more... about three pounds... I couldn't... it was all I could get together... please... I'll get the rest... I just need a bit more time... I...' Her voice tailed off as her eyes filled with tears which burst out, streaming down her terrified face.

Bowler's face darkened and his eyes bore into hers, all of his contrived humour instantly erased as he moved deliberately forward.

He slapped the hand containing the change upwards viciously, and the few coins flew up into Sharon's face, before bouncing off the walls and clattering noisily on the bare floorboards of the hallway.

'Do I look like I need your loose change?' he hissed as he

grabbed her face from under her chin and pulled her violently forward, until her face was almost touching his.

'Please,' she begged, 'It's 80 pounds. I can get the rest; I just need some more time... please... I...'

Bowler tore the notes from her hand, shoving them into his pocket without counting them.

'You've had time,' he whispered, his breath warm on her face. 'What are all the sad punters in this filthy hovel going to think if it gets out I'm a soft touch, that you can just get away without paying what's due. It's not good for business, Sharon. You must understand that, you pay or you hurt – that's the rules. You know that.'

Sharon closed her eyes and sobbed uncontrollably, shaking as she lost control of her bladder.

Bowler, still squeezing Sharon's face tightly, stepped back, stared down at her jeans and watched as a dark stain spread at the top of her thighs.

The look of disgust on his face was palpable, as he withdrew his hand from her face and struck her viciously with the back of his hand on her cheekbone, knocking her backwards, her head cracking painfully against the wall as she fell.

'Filth!' he repeated quietly through clenched teeth.

He stood over the prostrate woman, and his hand went to his inside jacket pocket, pulling out an old-fashioned cut throat razor which he flicked open expertly. Some of the thugs around here used Stanley knives, but Bowler considered that unsophisticated. He eyed the razor lovingly - he liked tradition.

He squatted down next to the helpless woman, holding the blade against her cheek and pressing just hard enough for a small drop of blood to pool around the sharp point.

'Please...,' Sharon pleaded, 'please, I can give you something else, please don't hurt me any more, please.'

'What could you possibly have that I would want,' Bowler said.

'I know this old man, he wants some money, he wants to borrow some money, I can give you his address – you can get some money from him. He wants to borrow some money for himself, and he said he could make up for the shortfall – you can get the 20 pounds I owe you from him, and he'll be a new customer for you... please...,' she pleaded.

Bowler thought for a moment. 'Why would this old man pay what you owe?' he said quietly.

'He was talking to me in 'The Butcher's'. He told me he needed money to buy his grandchildren Christmas presents. He was asking me if I knew someone. I told him about you, said I'd put him in touch if he paid you the extra 20 pounds I owed you.'

'Another loser,' Bowler whispered almost to himself, 'So you want me to pay what you owe with my own money – I lend it to him and he gives it to me – are you joking?'

'No, no, he wants a few hundred, it seems like he used to be quite well off, lives on a couple of pensions, apparently; has a big house, it must be worth millions, in Hampstead. I don't know, says he wants to sell the house, but hasn't got enough money to buy his grand kids presents, needs the money now.'

'So, if he owns a house, why doesn't he just borrow some money against it? Sounds like a load of old moody to me.'

'I don't know, honestly, I'm just telling you what he told me, he's an old man, maybe he's mad or something, I don't know. Even if the story about the house is rubbish, he has his pensions; you can get your money from him.'

'More bloody pension books I've got to look after. Still...' Bowler paused, his mind going through the options.

After a few minutes he turned back to Sharon, looking her up and down, his eyes resting on a small wedding ring she still wore, despite her husband having left years before. He grabbed her hand, pulling the ring off her finger.

'I'll take this as interest, it's probably junk - but, what the hell, might get a fiver for it. Right, this is what's going to happen - you give me the address of this old man and I'll go and see him. If what you are telling me is true, then you have until this time next week to come up with 150 quid – an extra fifty for all the trouble you've put me to. If it works out with the old man, then - provided you come up with the money you owe next week - no problem. But if you're lying to me, well, let's say you wont need to worry about how much money you owe me. You won't need to worry about anything, ever again.'

He wiped the small smear of blood on the razor on her jumper, before standing up slowly, closing it and returning it to his inside pocket, patting his chest as he felt the comforting hardness of the razor beneath.

'Now,' he said, 'Give me the old fool's address.'

THREE

Bowler parked the BMW three streets away. It was best his car wasn't seen directly outside the old man's house until he had sussed it all out.

There was something odd about all this. He had driven past the place slowly but couldn't see much, as the expensive houses in this leafy North London suburb were set back from the road, in their own grounds, with mature trees ensuring privacy for the obviously well-heeled owners of these multi-million pound properties.

It had occurred to him not to stop – to return to Sharon Porter and make a proper example of her for taking liberties. The fact was she had probably just made this all up to get him out of her flat. She was probably packing bags now, preparing to run, before he realised he'd been conned and came back for her.

'Stupid bitch,' he whispered under his breath, 'If she thinks I won't find out where she is in five minutes...'

Still, it was a long drive through London from the East End to Hampstead; he might as well check it out, who knows? Maybe she's right; maybe he is a mad old rich nutter he can squeeze some money out of. No harm in seeing what the hell it was all about - it might not be a complete waste of his evening.

Better play it carefully though, the neighbourhood was filled with the kind of punters who would have their own security cameras; better to park a few streets away and walk back.

He arrived at the house a little after 9.30 pm and was pleased that his quick survey of the area revealed no cameras, private or public, that might record his arrival. Pausing for a last, brief sweep of the area with his eyes, he crunched his way around the curved gravel drive to the front of the house, noticing that the trees that had previously obscured the front of the house from the street, now satisfactorily obscured him from anyone who might be passing in the quiet street outside.

The huge, double-sided Victorian house was well lit. Whoever lived inside was clearly not worried about his electricity bill, lights seemed to be burning in most rooms, including in the hallway, as he climbed up the tiled steps to a wide, dark brown hardwood door with two leaded glass panels with multi-coloured panes, which cast light onto the steps as Bowler used the large brass knocker, a lion's head with a metal ring in its mouth; the two firm knocks echoing through what was clearly a substantial hall inside.

Several minutes and a second, louder series of knocks from Bowler passed, and just as he was turning to leave, he caught sight of a dark shadow inside, slowly moving towards the door, until the shadow took the shape of a small figure, and the lock clicked as the large heavy door swung slowly open to reveal a short, frail, thin old man who looked to Bowler to be 80 if he was a day.

Dressed in baggy grey trousers, a long green cardigan and a frayed old checked shirt which, judging by the gap around his scrawny neck was several sizes too big, the old man had watery, grey/blue eyes, snow white hair and a pallid complexion that seemed to suggest he was very ill. Bowler noticed a tremor in his hand, and every movement he made seemed to take a huge effort.

'Ah, you must be Mr Bowler. Mrs Porter described you to me, and very accurately it seems, besides I don't get many visitors. In fact, I don't get any visitors.'

The old man's concentration seemed to drift off for a moment or two as he contemplated what he said. Until Bowler shook him out of his revere.

'What's this about?' Bowler asked brusquely, 'I'm a busy man, what is it you want from me.'

The old man started, as if he had forgotten where he was. 'Ah, yes, sorry, I'm forgetting my manners. Old man, you see; my mind wanders, please, please do come in.' He opened the door wide and stepped back against the wall to let Bowler pass into the corridor.

'Look, I told you, I'm a busy man, I was told you would pay what the Porter woman owes me and that you needed money.'

Bowler looked around the huge hall. The place was full of antiques, any one of which could easily pay off the few grand Porter owed him. 'You don't look as though you need money to me.'

'Oh yes, forgive me, Mr Bowler, you must forgive an old man. I have so few visitors, you see. When I get one, I tend to make the most of them, but yes, I do want to pay off Mrs Porter's debts and I do want some money from you. I promise, I am not wasting your time - please come this way. Perhaps I can offer you a drink?'

Bowler followed the old man through the hall and down a long corridor as he turned off left into a large room packed with furniture. Bowler was not an expert on antiques, but he recognised good stuff when he saw it. His eyes took in the floor-to-ceiling bookshelves stuffed with books, old books; the place must have been full of first editions. Tapestries and paintings hung on the dark wood panel walls. This room alone was an Aladdin's cave of treasures.

Bowler's mind raced. Whatever happened, tonight was not going to be a waste of time. He knew just the people to move this stuff for him. The old fool was mad to have let him in – he needed to think, to plan how and when he was going to come back.

If it was true that the old fool was alone and had few visitors, he could pick his time. Lock the old man in a cellar - a place like this is bound to have a cellar, then take his time removing everything.

No, this evening was definitely not going to be a waste of his time.

'My name is William DeVere.' The old man had spoken from behind a real old bar, in front of glass-backed shelves stocked with more bottles than 'The Butcher's Arms'. 'What can I get you to drink, Mr Bowler?'

'A decent single malt, if you've got one,' Bowler replied.

'I think I can manage that,' the old man said, and Bowler watched as DeVere, too frail and shaky to hold a crystal decanter in one hand, had to concentrate as he carefully poured a large measure into a matching crystal whisky glass, with two hands.

As he carefully replaced the decanter and dropped in the stopper, Bowler was amused to see that the old fool seemed exhausted from the effort required simply to pour a drink.

'Shall we sit here?' DeVere indicated two comfortable, leather-bound armchairs, either side of a fire that was set, but not alight. Bowler, ignoring his host, sat in one of the chairs and waited for the old man to struggle across with his drink, taking it from him abruptly and swigging at it without comment.

DeVere took the chair opposite, lowering himself slowly into the seat, his weight on his arms until he dropped the last few inches, breathing heavily with the effort.

Bowler's mind was racing. He sensed enormous opportunities here, but it all seemed to have fallen into his lap too easily, there must be something wrong, this old fool could not be as naïve and vulnerable as he appeared to be, someone must be looking after him. He could hardly pour a drink by himself, let alone look after this enormous house, which was obviously cleaned regularly. The fire was set even if it was not alight, who was doing that? Obviously not this frail old man.

'You really live alone in this huge house? You must have some help – who cleans for you? - feeds you?'

'I have a cleaner, Mrs Williams; she has a key and can let herself in. She's actually a friend of Mrs Porter's – she and her daughter come every Thursday and tidies the place up, set the fires. I don't make much mess, you see. It doesn't take much. If I need food, I order it to be delivered from the supermarket; you can get wonderful ready-made food now, even I can work a microwave oven. If necessary, it is delivered when Mrs Williams is here - she puts it away for me. But I'm rarely here, so she comes, lets herself in, does what's needed and leaves. It's been that way for five years. In fact, I have hardly even seen her in all that time.'

Bowler sipped at the whisky, his mind racing - this was all too good to be true. 'But how do you pay her? What happens if you have a leak or a light needs fixing? How does that get sorted?'

'I have an agent who looks after the property for me. I pay them a monthly management fee, by direct debit, they also pay

Mrs Williams. If she needs something, she contacts them and they sort it out for me; they just add it to my bill. Same applies to the utility companies, everything is paid by direct debit – if anything needs to be done, they have keys. It all works very well – I am very lucky, I suppose. Everything just happens automatically. I never need to be involved. It has to be that way.'

'Why does it have to be that way? I don't understand?' Bowler was still desperately looking for what had to be the flaw in this incredible opportunity; there had to be one, or had he just been incredibly lucky? The old fool's cleaner knew Porter, Porter knew him, perhaps it was just plain, old-fashioned good fortune that this obviously demented old fool had been sent his way.

Then, something occurred to him. 'You said you are rarely here? What did you mean?'

'Can I get you another whisky, Mr Bowler?' DeVere said.

'I'll get it,' Bowler replied. By the time this crippled old man manages to get out of the chair and over to the bar he would have died of thirst. He got up and walked over to the bar, pouring himself another generous measure from the crystal decanter.

DeVere continued his story, 'I have other houses, in other parts of the world. I share my time between them. I have the same arrangement everywhere; I can just drop everything and leave as I wish. I could be away for a year or two at a time. With this arrangement, I know I can leave at a minutes notice, a taxi, a plane ticket, I can just go. I don't even need to pack, I have all I need, wherever I go and because of the arrangements. The houses are always ready for me.'

'You can just disappear for a year or two and nobody cares?' Things seemed to be getting better and better from Bowler's perspective. 'But what if the agent needs you for something they can't handle?'

'They can email me. But, actually, there is very little that ever happens where they need me personally. In fact, it hasn't been necessary for several years.'

Bowler looked around the room again. 'This is some house,' he said eventually. He needed to get the lay of the land, so to speak, suss it out properly, if he was going to plan this efficiently he needed as much information as he could get. 'Any chance you could show me around?'

DeVere smiled politely. 'You are most welcome, Mr Bowler, but would you mind showing yourself around? I'm afraid I don't walk well, and stairs are a real problem. I suppose, I could have had lifts fitted, but actually I tend not to use many of the rooms, so it didn't seem really necessary. But please feel free to go anywhere you like. You are most welcome. I'll wait for you here if you don't mind.'

'Better and better,' Bowler thought. The demented old fool was giving him a free hand to case the place!

'I'll just take a look around and I'll be right back,' he said as he left the old man who's obviously fragile mind had once again drifted off somewhere as he sat staring into an unlit fire.

FOUR

Bowler spent an hour, wandering around the great maze of a house. Each room he entered, like the first, was full of what clearly were valuable antiques, paintings and books. One huge bedroom had obviously been a woman's, judging by the furniture and the décor. A large four-poster bed with floral drapes and matching bedding was complimented by a soft, deep carpet. Long, heavy velvet red drapes dropping from ceiling to floor were closed across a large bay window at the front of the house.

He caught his breath, though, as he inspected the large dressing table with three mirrors and a padded stool that matched the fabrics on the four-poster.

The dressing table was covered with an assortment of crystal bottles, some with little tasselled pumps, containing various creams, perfumes and powders, hand mirrors, combs, clips and hairbrushes. But what really caught Bowler's eye were the jewels. Delicate little filigree trees, heavy with gold, diamond and multicoloured stone chains and necklaces.

His eyes widened as he stroked his fingers across the hanging chains, watching them glint in the light from the tasselled wall-lights.

Then he gasped audibly as he noticed a large, padded jewellery box, on one side of the table top. The lid was open and the box was filled to the brim with bracelets, rings, earrings, bangles of all kinds.

He picked up one small silver-coloured ring, but which contained a single, flawless white diamond, larger than any Bowler had ever seen – and Bowler knew his diamonds. It was at least three times the size of the one in his own ear lobe, and he knew how valuable that was.

There seemed to be no order at all, they were all just piled in the box. He could just close this box and walk out right now with valuables that were probably worth more than his flat in

Docklands.

He cautioned himself – no, this had to be done properly. It needed to be handled carefully, and he knew what that meant.

The old man needed to be taken care of, permanently, so that once Bowler had helped himself to the almost limitless wealth he had stumbled upon, there would be no come back, no possibility of the old fool implicating him or the police tracing anything back to him.

That probably meant getting shot of Porter too. But she had outlived her usefulness anyway, and she was the only person who could make the connection between him and DeVere. Yes, she would need to go as well.

Despite his caution he could not resist pocketing the diamond ring. He had still not completely worked out how he was going to maximise this opportunity, but whatever happened, the ring on its own was going to turn a good evening into a great year.

Bowler continued his inspection of the house, and having started at the top, he eventually had worked his way back down to the ground floor where, at the back of the house, he discovered a wide corridor flanked on both sides with floor-to-ceiling bookcases; once more the shelves were full of ancient looking books.

He ran his hand along the spines of the books as he walked down the passage towards the rear of the house.

Then he noticed something extremely odd. The shelves on the left came to an abrupt end and there was a gap of around six feet, before the shelves continued beyond the gap.

Set in the centre of the wall was what Bowler could only describe as a steel vault door, the kind of door you might see in a bank, safety deposit facility or high class jewellers.

He stroked his hand across it, feeling the cold hardness of the metal, before testing the levers to find them securely sealed.

With what looked like millions in jewels and antiques filling every room of the house, what else possibly could be so valuable as to need a vault in this private house?

FIVE

'It's what they call a 'Panic Room', apparently'. DeVere seemed completely unperturbed by the question when Bowler had rushed back to the living room to ask him about the vault door.

'What the hell is a panic room?' Bowler was helping himself to another whisky. DeVere seemed not to have moved in the hour or so Bowler had been showing himself around what he was now consciously beginning to think of as his 'Aladdin's Cave'.

'It was built by my elder brother some years ago. My brother Charles was not at all like me, he was forever worrying about being robbed or kidnapped; he was also obsessed during the 'Cold War' that there might be a nuclear attack. So, strictly speaking it started out as a kind of 'Fall Out' shelter in which he could sit out the radiation, if the Russians ever attacked. He filled it with everything you could possibly need - medicines, food, filtered water, a generator, fuel, heating, cooling, everything he thought he would need to live for years until it was safe to go outside again. A pathetic obsession actually. He spent, I was going to say, a small fortune on it, but actually it was more like a large fortune frankly.'

'Nothing valuable in there, then.' Bowler looked disappointed.

'No, not really,' DeVere replied. 'Well, a small amount of gold. Charles' paranoia extended to banks as well – he converted some money into gold. He was a little, shall we say, eccentric, but even Charles realised money wouldn't help much in a post-apocalyptic England, but he was convinced gold would still be valuable; in fact, given the breakdown of the banking system that would clearly follow such a disaster, gold was likely to dramatically increase in value. I never moved it out again. I don't have much use for cash really; as I explained, everything I do is done electronically pretty much and it's not like gold earns interest, it really doesn't matter where it sits, its value rises and falls based on external influences. It might as well sit down there as anywhere else.'

'Are you crazy?' Bowler just couldn't believe what he was hearing. 'How much gold is down there for God's sake?'

'Well, they are in 1kilogram bars. Much too heavy for me to move; another reason for leaving it there. I believe there are about 100 of them.'

'You have 100 kilos of gold bars sat in your basement? Are you mad? How much is it worth?'

'No idea really, 3 or 4 million pounds, not an expert I'm afraid. It's not really important. I'm too old to spend a fraction of it and I have no relatives, no one to leave it to. Neither I nor my brother had children you see. I am the last of my line. Whatever is left will go to charity when I die.'

'Not if I can help it,' Bowler thought as he sat back, trying to consider his next move. 'Would you mind if I looked at it?' he said finally, 'I've never seen real gold bars before, and I'd quite like to see this room of yours.'

'Of course,' DeVere smiled, a look of pain crossed his face as he struggled to push himself out of the chair and hobbled towards the door. Bowler following impatiently behind, frustrated by the irritatingly slow progress of his host.

After what seemed like an age to Bowler, they arrived in the corridor outside the steel vault door.

'You called this a panic room,' Bowler said, as DeVere fiddled with an electronic control panel mounted on the wall to the left of the vault.

'Yes.' DeVere seemed to be pressing buttons randomly as far as Bowler could see. 'Yes,' the old man continued, 'When the Soviet Block collapsed; it took a while, but even my brother Charles finally realised that the likelihood of a nuclear attack from that direction had become rather less likely. But it didn't really help much with his paranoia, he just transferred his fears to the threat of being kidnapped, tortured and robbed in his own house. He had been reading about wealthy Americans who were building these things called *panic rooms*, basically a secure, self-contained place that a householder could retreat to, safe from attack, that

128

would be impenetrable and would keep you safe until the attackers got bored and went away.'

DeVere tapped at the electronic keypad without success. 'Sorry, I seem to have got the numbers wrong, let me try again.'

Bowler's patience was wearing thin, and he needed all his self-control to prevent himself grabbing the old fool by his scrawny neck and throttling him, but he realised he had no choice but to wait for the old man to get the door open.

'So Charles spent even more money adding a few more refinements to change a fall-out shelter to a panic room. Computer connections for email, secure telephone lines to the emergency services, huge panic buttons to automatically seal the room up with a single press if the house was invaded. He also installed this.' Bowler watched as DeVere pressed a button that was simply marked 'Conceal'.

Immediately, Bowler heard an electric motor kick in and he stepped backward quickly as he realised the whole wall-to-ceiling bookshelves began to slide to the right. As he watched, the steel door was slowly concealed by the bookcase, and a loud click could be heard as the bookcase obviously clicked into place, the electric motor cut out and silence returned to the corridor.

'Amazing,' Bowler said quietly while he inspected the wall. As the bookcase had slid across, what he had expected to be a blank wall behind where the bookshelves had originally been positioned, there was a door to another room, with two large pictures hanging either side.

DeVere opened the door of the previously hidden room and reached for a light switch inside. It was some kind of a store room, quite small but with rows of shelves which were full of assorted household items, cleaning products, mops, buckets and bowls, toilet rolls, light bulbs, in fact just about anything that might be needed to keep the rest of the house habitable.

Bowler realised how clever this set-up was. Once the bookshelf was locked in place, there was no long blank expanse of wall. The room and the pictures gave a completely natural look to the corridor, and there was absolutely no indication that the bookshelf concealed the panic room.

'Once inside,' DeVere continued, 'the bookshelf slides into place automatically. Not only are you safe and secure inside the room, but actually anyone coming down this corridor would not even know there was a room here.'

'How do you get it open again?' Bowler said.

DeVere hobbled slowly to the bookshelf and traced his bony hand along the fourth shelf, apparently looking for a particular book.

'Ah, here it is - *'One Thousand and One Nights'*, you are familiar with the story of *'Ali Baba and the forty thieves?'*

Bowler looked blankly at DeVere.

'Never mind, never mind,' the old man said as he pulled the old leather bound book out, slid his hand in the gap left behind and felt around the back of the shelf. 'Open Sesame!' he said quietly, as again the electric motor started up, and he pushed the book back into the space as the bookshelf slid back once more, slowly concealing the store room and exposing the steel vault that led to the panic room.

Hobbling back to the now visible electronic panel and, once again, with trembling fingers, began typing in a code. As he finished he stepped back. For a second or two, Bowler assumed the old man had once again typed in the wrong code, but suddenly another electronic whirring started up, accompanied by flashing green lights on the panel. The entire centre of the circular vault door slowly slid outwards, stopping with a solid clunk. A small steel handle, which had been lying flush with the cold metal surface, popped out from the left hand side of the door, which seemed to click open slightly.

DeVere clasped the exposed handle, but was clearly having difficulty pulling open the heavy steel door. 'Can you help?' he said to Bowler who grabbed the handle and pulled; the door was clearly thick and heavy, but it swung open quite easily on well lubricated hinges.

As the door swung open, neon lights inside the room flickered into life, and Bowler looked down half a dozen concrete steps that led down into the cellar-like panic room.

DeVere gingerly led the way down into the cellar, holding tightly to a chrome banister embedded in the steps, with Bowler following him in.

SIX

DeVere, who seemed to be totally exhausted by the efforts of the last 30 minutes or so, shuffled slowly across to the far left-hand corner of the room, a corner that seemed completely incongruous in the high-tech surroundings of glass, chrome and electronics.

A large, predominantly deep red, patterned Persian carpet had been laid out there and it was surrounded by clear glass walls with a glass door. In this space, like a Victorian island, preserved in some kind of modern day electronic display case, was a collection of antique furniture, vases and ornaments that created a kind of facsimile of one of the living areas in the main house.

Two padded leather antique wing-backed chairs, similar to those in the living room, stood in one corner, before a ceiling-high set of bookshelves once again filled with ancient looking books. Each chair had beside it an antique table upon which stood green-shaded glass reading lamps. An open volume laid on one table, alongside a glass decanter containing an amber liquid, which could have been brandy or whisky, Bowler couldn't tell, next to a couple of crystal glasses.

It was to one of these chairs DeVere hobbled, lowering himself into it and sighing thankfully.

'Please look around, Mr Bowler,' he said, 'I will rest here if you don't mind.'

DeVere sat in his little Victorian oasis, as Bowler wandered around the room. Three doors led off at the far side of the cellar, furthest from the entrance; one led into a storage room-cum-kitchen, probably twice the size of the hidden room upstairs. This contained a sink and a fully fitted kitchen on one side, whilst the opposite side was row upon row of shelves stacked with tinned foods, dry goods, oils, candles, matches and medicines of all kinds. A huge water tank filled one corner; another shelf contained hundreds of packets of water sterilisation tablets. Also alongside the tank were pallets full of bottled mineral water.

Bowler went to the sink and turned on the taps, hot and cold running water was available, so the room was obviously connected to the mains water supply. Presumably, the water tank and bottled water were for emergencies, should there be some disruption to the supply outside of the room.

Behind the second door was a fully fitted bathroom, with toilet, shower and bath, again all obviously connected to the mains supply.

The third and final room seemed to be some kind of utility area. A large diesel generator was fitted, and surrounded by stacks of Jerry cans full of diesel; water pipes and electrical connections all seemed to be piped through this room, as were telephone and computer network cables.

It seemed that even if electricity and water were cut off externally, anyone living in the room could survive for probably years, without any need to go outside.

Bowler returned to the main room and inspected a modern desk upon which sat two computer screens and three telephones. One of the screens seemed to be permanently connected to the Internet.

Bowler returned to the glass room and helped himself to a drink from the decanter alongside DeVere and took his seat opposite.

'Impressive,' he said quietly, as his smile disappeared and his dark eyes bore into those of the frail old man sitting opposite him.

He was now sure of his plan as he sipped at his glass which contained the same, excellent malt whisky he had enjoyed earlier. Just one more thing he needed to know before he put his plan into action.

'Where's the gold?' he said quietly.

'Right here,' DeVere responded by turning slightly in his chair and picking up a small remote control device which he pointed at an antique sideboard nearby.

Bowler watched as a wooden panel made of thin slats rolled

sideways from the front of the cabinet and round into the frame of the sideboard to reveal a glass case inside. Lights inside the case flickered on and Bowler couldn't suppress an audible gasp as, stacked in neat piles on shelves, five high, in the cabinet behind the glass were gold ingots which shone brightly in the internal light, pile by pile, shelf after shelf. Bowler started to count but gave up. The old man had said there were a hundred of them, a kilo each.

The old man might have had difficulty shifting them, but not him. This would be the easiest three or four million he would ever make.

He just needed to give himself plenty of time. Not only to move the gold, but it would take days to empty the house out properly, catalogue everything, get it properly valued.

But DeVere's lifestyle was going to make that easy for him. He needed to take his time, make sure that all angles were covered.

He crossed his legs and leaned back in the chair, sipping appreciatively at the single malt. He had, in his earlier days before learning his trade as a loan shark, amongst many other things, been a burglar. But never had he had the opportunity to take all the time in the world, with the best food and drink whilst he emptied out his 'Aladdin's Cave' completely.

But one thing still bothered him. He had pushed it to the back of his mind as he had allowed himself to be distracted by the incredible wealth that had fallen into his lap.

Okay, the old man was clearly on his last legs, probably totally gaga by now, but it still bothered him as to why he was here; what was this 'cock and bull' story about him needing to borrow money.

He had time, plenty of it. He needed answers to these last few questions.

SEVEN

'Okay,' Bowler said, 'I've seen enough, but I'm not sure why I've seen it. Why am I here, DeVere? And none of this moody about you needing money. You may need a lot of things, for example a bloody nurse to look after you, and probably a bloody shrink as well. But what you sure as hell don't need is my money.'

'Oh no, Mr Bowler, you are quite wrong. I do want money from you, and I certainly do want to pay Mrs Porter's outstanding debt to you. I do hope you don't think I have got you here under false pretences. I believe Mrs Porter was £20 short this week. I would like to make sure that is paid, and she is obviously very frightened of you, so I want enough to pay off what she owes you in total so she doesn't have to see you any more. She tells me she took a number of small loans from you, apparently it all totalled up to £450, but she says you expect her to repay £14,000. I must say, that does seem an extremely high interest rate, but never mind. You need £14,020, that's what I want from you, Mr Bowler.'

Bowler looked incredulously at the frail old man before him.

'Let me get this straight - you want me to lend you £14,020 so you can pay off Porter's debts? Are you crazy or what?'

'Sorry, Mr Bowler, you seem to be under some misunderstanding, I don't think, at any time I said I wanted to 'borrow' money from you. Perhaps Mrs Porter didn't explain things properly. I suppose it is understandable. You did frighten her terribly, you know. Far be it from me to criticise, Mr Bowler, but I'm not sure it is very gentlemanly to frighten a nice lady like Mrs Porter so, even if she does owe you money. I'm sure you must know how horrible it is to be frightened like that.'

Bowler was completely speechless for a moment as he stared at this insane old man.

'No Mr Bowler,' DeVere continued. 'I'm not looking to borrow any money from you, I want you to give it to me so that we can clear Mrs Porter's obligation to you. I'm very old fashioned, you see, I believe debts should be honoured, so you will give me £14,020. I will deposit it in the bank and I will set up a standing order. As you know, I like doing business that way. I will repay the money to you at the rate of £400 per month, for 3 years. You will have your money back. That is a total of £14,400; you will make a profit of £380. Very generous, I would have thought, given the rather dubious legal nature of your business methods.'

The huge loan shark jumped to his feet, his eyes blazing and his face a deep red as he moved towards DeVere, grabbing him with one huge hand by the collar and lifting him bodily out of the chair.

'Please, Mr Bowler, please! You are hurting me. I can see why Mrs Porter is so frightened of you. You really do need to do something about your temper.'

Bowler raised a fist, threatening to punch the old man in the face, but seemed, with an enormous effort to restrain himself.

'No, no,' he said between clenched teeth, 'If I hit you I'd probably kill you. You're half dead already. I've had enough of you, you mad old fool. No, I'll tell you what you are going to do. You are going to start by sending an email.'

Bowler dragged DeVere by the collar, out of the glass room and over to the computer desk, throwing him down into the chair in front of the keyboard.

'You will send an email to this agent of yours. Tell him you are leaving tonight, going abroad to one of your other houses. You have no idea when you will be back, but you'll probably be gone a year or two.'

'This wont work, Mr Bowler, please be reasonable.'

'I'll show you reasonable, you stupid old fool!' he hissed as he hit the old man a glancing blow on the side of the head, splitting his lip, which started to bleed immediately. His bottom lip seemed to be swelling as he spoke.

DeVere leaned on the desk panting, his trembling hand reaching gingerly to his lip, withdrew it, and looked at the blood on his fingers.

Meanwhile, Bowler took the cut throat razor out of his inside pocket, flicked it open and held the sharp edge a centimetre from one of DeVere's watery eyes.

'I hope you can still type with one eye – because if you don't start that email now you're going to lose this one.'

The old man began to shudder uncontrollably, 'Alright, please, please be reasonable, Mr Bowler.'

'Type!' Bowler shouted directly into DeVere's face, warm spittle hit DeVere's face and the old man swallowed, took a deep breath and clicked open the email program, entered the agent's email address and started typing.

When he was finished, Bowler read it carefully. 'Right, send it,' he said.

'But, Mr Bowler, I think you are making a mistake, can we talk about this, please...'

'Send it you old fool!'

DeVere sighed as he pressed 'send'.

Bowler checked the outbox to make sure it had gone.

'Good, now come with me.'

He dragged DeVere by the collar back to the glass room and threw him down in the chair. The old man was breathing heavily as one hand went to his chest as if trying to calm his dangerously thumping heart.

'Right, this is what is going to happen. I'm going to start by taking the gold. I'm going to get my car, bring it around to the front and then load it up. I'm going to tie you up and leave you here. I'll be back tomorrow, so if you behave yourself I might even feed you. Then I'm going to make a few calls. I don't see any rush. You said the cleaner comes every Thursday, today is Friday, so I've got best part of a week to clear the place out, before anyone notices anything. By next Thursday, she'll be coming in to an empty house.'

He thought for a few seconds. 'Or I may just get you to order the agents to sack the woman, tell them you've found somebody else who's going to live in. Christ, I could move in myself for a while – it's perfect!' His mind raced from one

137

possibility to another, 'Still, no rush, got plenty of time to think about it.'

'You mustn't take the gold, Mr Bowler! Please, I must warn you that would not be a good idea.'

'Shut up and tell me how I open this case? Is it alarmed?'

'No, no alarm, it's not even locked. It opens with the button on the remote. But I am asking you not to take it. Please, Mr Bowler, you still have the chance to do the right thing. Don't take the gold.'

'I'm doing the right thing – for me – you have to look after number one in this world.'

'I warn you, Mr Bowler, do not take the gold, take my offer.'

Bowler ignored the pleading of DeVere and pointed the remote control at the cabinet, 'Which button...' he said.

'Please, Mr Bowler, please don't...' His sentence was cut off as Bowler struck him across the face with the back of his hand, knocking the old men backwards into the chair. 'Which button...' he repeated.

DeVere looked resigned. 'The yellow one,' he said as he closed his eyes and bowed his head, breathing heavily from the shock of the blow.

Bowler stepped closer to the cabinet and slowly and deliberately pressed the yellow button, his heart racing as he heard a low hum and the glass panel lowered, tantalisingly slowly, exposing the piles of burnished gold that seemed to Bowler to be so bright they were almost luminescent.

'Just sit there and behave,' Bowler said to DeVere, without once taking his eyes off the piles of gold bars that seemed to be hypnotising him. He knelt in front of the cabinet, gently lifting out one of the bars, surprised by the unexpected weight of the relatively small block. 'Beautiful,' he whispered to himself as he turned the embossed ingot in his hands. 'Beautiful,' he repeated.

Bowler looked around the panic room, deciding on his next move, and his eyes fell on a small-wheeled trolley on the opposite side of the room; presumably this had been used to transport the gold, but if not, it certainly looked perfect for the job. He collected it, wheeling it over to the glass room and positioning it next to the cabinet containing the gold, as he carefully began to remove the ingots and place them on the trolley. He was surprised at the amount of effort required, and he removed his jacket, throwing it onto the chair next to DeVere, before continuing with his task, his face red and beads of sweat beginning to form on his forehead.

Once finished, he leaned back on his heels to catch his breath for a few seconds, before rising to his feet and turning to DeVere who was still sitting, chin forward on his chest, eyes closed breathing erratically.

Should he kill him now? No. He shuddered at the thought of having to spend the next few days with a decaying body, as he would be spending some time in the house while he emptied it out.

Killing was not an issue for Bowler. Killing or grievous bodily harm caused him little concern. But he had always hated filth and decay, hence his almost pathological obsession with personal hygiene and cleanliness in general.

It was unfortunate; so much of his otherwise enjoyable career required him to spend time with filth like Porter and her ilk.

No. He would kill DeVere later, without compunction or remorse. But it was better to keep him alive until he was ready to abandon this house completely, seal this room in the sure and certain knowledge that the rotting corpse of this disgusting old fool would probably never be discovered.

He would then dispose of Porter, and any links between him and the old man were gone and he could enjoy his new found wealth without any risk of being connected.

He should bring her here and kill her with DeVere. The two of them could share their last moments together, and he would have the pleasure of showing them both the stupidity of trying to cross him. Yes, he liked that idea. Neither of them would ever be seen again and social services could look after the kids.

It seemed a perfect solution to him.

But, business before pleasure, he thought – later; first he needed to get this gold out of here and into his car.

Looking across to the vault door, he noticed for the first

139

time a small lift to the right of the steps. Hopefully, this still worked and he could wheel the trolley on to it, take it up to the door level and wheel it along the corridor to the front door.

He would then collect his car, bring it around to the front of the house and under the cover of the mature trees, load his gold into the car and take it away.

He looked back at the old man, who was still slumped in the chair. He looked in a bad way, and Bowler was doubtful he would have the strength to get out of the chair, let alone cause him any other kind of problem. But there was too much at stake. If DeVere could get to the desk, he might phone out or send an email. He considered again killing him immediately, but dismissed it quickly with a shudder as he tried to shake the odious image of a decomposing body from his mind.

No. It was better just to incapacitate him for the time being. He crossed to the storage room, and after a quick search he discovered rolls of Gaffa Tape stacked on the shelves, amongst the myriad other household items. Ripping loose two rolls he returned to DeVere and began to bind him, from shoulder to ankles, into the chair with long strips of the tape. He used most of both rolls before cutting the end off with his razor.

He pushed his fingers down between the tape and DeVere's body and pulled. Even Bowler could not have escaped from this binding, much less this frail old man.

He cut one last small piece of tape and was about to place it across DeVere's mouth, when the old man began to struggle hysterically.

'No! No, don't cover my mouth! I will suffocate, please. There is no need. The room is completely sound-proof, a bomb could go off in here and no one would hear, even if they were standing right outside the door.'

'You expect me to take your word for that?' Bowler said as he pressed the tape across the old man's mouth, ignoring the terrified look in the old man's eyes. Tears now began to stream down his cheeks.

'Breathe through your nose.' he said dismissively.

Walking away from the old man, Bowler headed towards the exit and then stopped, looking at the desk with the computer and the phones.

He glanced back at the old man. He was pretty sure there was no way he could get free, but why take chances?

He once again headed into the storage room, returning this time with a large sledge hammer and crossing to the desk, he swung the hammer above his head, bringing it down with all his strength on the computer screen and keyboard. He then pulled the computer out from under the desk, and with a few further blows, smashed the computers into pieces, before doing the same to the phones.

He smiled. Everything was done. All he had to do now was take his gold and load it in the car.

It was then that he noticed that the solid steel vault door which they had left open when they entered, was sealed shut.

EIGHT

Bowler climbed the concrete steps to the vault door and, placing both hands against it, he pressed with all his strength. It was solid with no give whatsoever, and he ran his palms all over the surface, seeking out any indication of hidden handles or buttons, similar to the one that had sprung out on the other side.

Having failed to find anything remotely like a means of opening it, he also traced his hands around the frame. The door fitted so well, it was difficult even to see the gap between door and frame without really close inspection.

A similar search of the wall around the frame also failed to reveal anything that might indicate a means of opening the door.

Despite the fact that he knew the room had its own independent air supply, the lack of any window to the outside and the perfect seal of the door brought on the beginnings of a feeling of claustrophobia he was not aware, previously, that he might have had. He suddenly felt the need to be out of this room, to step outside the house and take some deep breaths of air that was not filtered to him by machines in this room.

Clearly, the door operated electronically, therefore there must be a control panel somewhere, to open it from the inside. What would be the point of a panic room you couldn't get out of when the panic was over?

The inescapable logic calmed him, and he suddenly realised the wisdom of having not killed the old man. He would know where the switch was.

Of course, it must have been him who closed the door, while he was busy with the gold. The control must be in the glass room, as DeVere had not been out of that room all the time Bowler was recovering the gold from the cabinet.

He returned to the old man and viciously ripped the piece of Gaffa tape from his mouth, causing the old man to cry out in pain.

'Where's the switch, old man?' he said, not waiting for the answer as he searched around the chair for some device that might be an electronic switch. He could find nothing.

Bowler turned angrily to DeVere. 'Where is it, where's the switch?' he said.

'There isn't one,' DeVere replied quietly.

Bowler picked up the crystal decanter and threw it against the bookcase behind the old man's chair. The glass shattered noisily, spraying the expensive whisky across the books, splattering both DeVere and Bowler.

'What do you mean?' Bowler shouted, 'There must be one, it must be here. How could you shut the door, otherwise?'

'I didn't shut the door,' the old man replied quietly.

Bowler took the razor out of his pocket. Flicking it open, he approached the old man, holding the blade once again close to DeVere's eyes. 'You'd better start making sense or I'm going to carve the information out of you.'

For the first time, the old man's expression changed and a look of defiance crossed his face. 'You need to calm down and listen, Mr Bowler. I repeat - I did not close the door.'

'Then, who did?' He shouted, 'Have you got someone outside, that bitch Porter? Are you working together to try and get out of paying me?'

'No, Mr Bowler, Mrs Porter knows nothing about this. You have not been deceived in any way. You will recall, I told you about my cleaner, Mrs Williams? As I told you, I have hardly seen her in the five years she has been looking after me. That's not to say I have never seen her, in fact I saw her a couple of months ago. She let herself in on her usual Thursday visit, but she was surprised to find me here. She was late you see, she was upset; she thought I might be angry by her tardiness, and she was most keen to explain why she was so late. I think she felt I might dismiss her.'

'Is she out there?' Bowler shouted, pointing at the vault door with his open razor.

'No. Please, Mr Bowler, let me finish. She told me she was late because she had been with her friend, Mrs Porter who had

143

recently had a visit from you, Mr Bowler. She was terrified, apparently, hysterical. Mrs Williams thought she was so frightened by your visit that she might do something stupid. She has 3 children, you know? What would happen to her children if Mrs Porter had done something silly, harmed herself even? She said she didn't feel she could leave her. Eventually, she told her that she would perhaps mention it to me. She wasn't sure whether I would be able to help. She knows I am a bit of a recluse, but she of course knows I have money. It was in any event the only thing she could think of to try and calm her friend down. This was apparently the reason she was late.'

Bowler was beginning to regret throwing the whisky decanter. He could do with a drink right now as his mind raced, his chest heaving. He knew, he was adept at getting information out of people, but usually it didn't matter much if they lived or died, and the consequences of this frail old man dying on him terrified him more than he could ever remember being terrified before.

He found more decanters on a sideboard across the room and poured himself a large drink - it turned out to be brandy rather than whisky, but frankly at this moment he didn't care as he gulped it back.

DeVere continued his story, 'I told her it was not a problem. I arranged to see Mrs Porter and she told me all about you. Of course, the simple thing would have been for me to just pay what you were asking for and suggest she stayed well away from you in the future, but I have to admit to being a little old-fashioned. I hate to see bad manners and injustice, so I told her to get you to come and see me. I expect, she thought, or maybe hoped, I would pay you off. But that would have left you to repeat this behaviour with all your other victims. I wanted to put a stop to it. So here we are.'

The brandy seemed to have calmed Bowler a little and he forced a laugh, trying to re-assert the upper hand which somehow he felt had suddenly transferred a little to DeVere. This was not good. He needed to regain the initiative.

'I'm not interested in your charity work DeVere; I still want to know how you shut the door.'

144

The old man looked Bowler in the eye with a sense of purpose that unsettled the loan shark. 'I didn't shut the door. You did. Another of my brother Charles' refinements. When you opened the gold locker, the vault door was automatically closed. The idea was to seal any prospective thief in, as soon as an attempt to remove the gold was made.'

'Okay, but what would have happened if he accidentally sealed himself in? He must have had a way of opening it again.'

DeVere nodded. 'Quite right. It's behind the picture there.' Indicating at a family portrait hanging alongside the bookcase behind him.

Bowler hurried over to the painting, inspecting it closely. As he pushed his fingers all around the frame, he finally hit on a small button and with a click, the picture swung away from the wall on hinges on one side, to reveal a control panel similar to the one outside the vault door in the corridor.

Bowler returned to where DeVere was sitting, raised his razor to the old man's face and spoke through clenched teeth, 'I will ask you this only once, what is the code?'

DeVere looked steadily into Bowler's eyes. 'There isn't one. It has been disabled.'

Bowler laughed briefly and then seemed unsure as the old man held his gaze steadily, with no appreciable change of demeanour.

'Disabled? What do you mean *disabled*? How are you going to get out of here?' Whatever the old fool was suggesting did not make any sense.

DeVere's gaze remained focussed on Bowler's obvious discomfort.

'You will remember that Charles built this place originally as a fall-out shelter, he then refined it to make it into a panic room. I have never suffered with the same paranoia that ruined so much of my dear brother's life. I had no need of either a fall-out shelter or a panic room, but its other potential use occurred to me a few years ago. That led me to make my own modifications after Charles died.'

'Modifications? What Modifications?' Bowler had no idea what the old fool was talking about.

'A little while ago, you accused me of being half dead, Mr Bowler. Actually, you dramatically underestimated the position. I am well beyond half dead, I have terminal cancer. Six months ago, my doctors estimated I had somewhere between a year and a year and a half to live. Of course, this is not an exact science - I could go tomorrow or last another year or even two, but that is at the, shall we say, optimistic end of the scale. I wonder if you might cut me out of these tapes, Mr Bowler, and perhaps we can share a drink? I am in no position or condition to threaten you, I'm sure you realise that. On the other hand, treating me harshly is likely only to shorten my time on this Earth and I have precious little of that to waste.'

As if in a daze, Bowler found himself cutting through DeVere's bindings with his razor. When he had finished, he poured himself and DeVere a large brandy and returned to the old man who took the proffered glass in his trembling liver-spotted hand and sipped it gently.

'You still haven't told me what modifications you made,' Bowler said as he sat down next to DeVere.

The old man continued, 'I have always hated funerals, you know, everything about them, the cars, the flowers, the pious words spoken over a cold grave and I'm afraid I've always had a rather illogical fear of cremation. Perhaps, I inherited a little of my older brother's paranoia. Then, the obvious solution occurred to me. So I made some simple and far less expensive alterations to Charles' panic room. I realised that where I wanted to be was here. Here in the house I was born in and would die in.'

He sipped the brandy, 'You know, Mr Bowler, I'm grateful to you, fine as this brandy is, it always tastes better when shared with someone. So here's to your health, Mr Bowler, or do you think we know each other well enough to be a little less impersonal. May I call you Gary? You are more than welcome to call me William.'

'Of course, had I tried to get approval to simply stay and

146

die here, I have no doubt all kinds of bureaucratic nonsense would have come into play. So I simply decided not to tell anyone. So here we are, Gary. Welcome to my mausoleum.'

'I'm not sure I understand...' Bowler's voice trailed off.

'It's so simple, Gary. You see, there was no need for you to force me to send that email to the agent. I had already sent one earlier, saying much the same thing. If everyone thinks I've left the country no one is going to be looking for me. My money is in trust, the upkeep of the house will continue without me. No one alive, apart from you and I, know of the existence of this room and, as you know, once the door closed the bookcases hid it completely and it is sound proof. Life goes on out there. Mrs Williams cleans, the agents deal with everything else, the bank pays the bills. I am surplus to requirements. I disappear and my life goes on without me. Perfect, really.'

'These modifications you made, what were they?' Bowler asked.

'This room,' the old man said, looking around him, 'my furniture, carpets, books, the occasional wine or brandy, watch this.' Taking the remote control from the table where Bowler had left it, he pressed a button and ceiling-to-floor, red velvet drapes slowly closed around the room, separating the little glass room from the high-tech equipment outside. 'Just like the rest of the house. I have everything I need here.' He smiled, a clear look of contentment settling upon him.

'The other modifications were very small. Disconnecting the panel that opens the door. Oh, and by the way, smashing the telephones was also unnecessary, they were already disconnected and the computer, well... you dealt with that, didn't you.'

'But me...' Bowler said, 'What about me, how do I get out?'

DeVere smiled. 'You don't, I'm afraid. There is no way to get out of here. It was your choice. I did warn you not to take the gold, and to take my offer. You had the opportunity to do the right thing. A man must take responsibility for his actions, Gary.'

Bowler stared at DeVere as the full horror of the situation began to sink in.

'I have to admit, I suppose I get the best of this deal. A little company until I die. You, I'm afraid though, Gary, you have the worst of it I regret. It will, I'm sure, be rather unpleasant, living with my decaying corpse, but I'm sure you will get used to it, and there is plenty of food and drink. No television or radio of course, but then I never cared much for them, books have always been enough for me.'

Bowler screamed, and jumping out of the chair, rushed out of the glass room, grabbed the sledge hammer and smashed it with all his strength against the vault door. After a few minutes, in which time he had not managed even to raise anything other than a pathetic scuff mark on the impenetrable door, he turned to the walls, slamming the sledge hammer against them until he collapsed, exhausted, sobbing quietly.

'The walls are two feet thick, solid steel and backed by concrete. You must accept, Gary, there is no way out.'

He raised his brandy in a salute to the prostrate loan shark.

'You have made your tomb, Gary! It's time to lie in it.'

The Thief
in the Waiting Room

ONE

Terry Bannister had always thought that this town was unlucky for him.

As a professional thief, he accepted arrest as an occupational hazard and didn't rely on luck or superstition – but, what the hell – it's better to be safe than sorry, and as on the last two occasions he had been 'given a tug', as the expression went, by your friendly neighbourhood 'filth' - it had been in this very town.

On both occasions, he had been driving a stolen motor enroute to 'Cut & Shut' Eddie who regularly disposed of stolen vehicles for him.

The first occasion he had been pulled over by an over-officious 'plod' who claimed he had run a red light in the Jaguar he was driving.

If there was one thing Terry hated - it was a bent copper. But his argument in court that he was highly unlikely to have brought attention to himself by running a red light in a stolen vehicle didn't seem to wash with the magistrates who committed him to Crown Court for sentencing, anyway.

As usual, it was one law for 'Plod', who could obviously lie with impunity, another for a hard-working grafter who was just trying to make a living.

The second time was even more irritating. A bloody woman driver ran a red light and crashed into him as he was driving a nicked BMW M5. It was her fault, entirely, but all she got was a caution, while he got banged up again. Is there no bloody justice in the World?

So, the point was, whilst he didn't really believe in luck, good or bad, he had decided that it was better to be safe than sorry, and he was not going to pull any stunts in this town anymore.

Unfortunately, you couldn't rely on the punters, could you? Sometimes, they were asking for it and what was a bloke supposed to do? He was a professional, after all, and what sort of a geezer would he be if he ignored an opportunity that was staring him in the face? He'd never be able to hold his head up again.

So, that was how he came to be sitting in the waiting room of the local Kwik Fit tyre centre, waiting for a flat tyre to be repaired on the BMW M5 he had 'acquired' a couple of hours back.

He had been minding his own business, having a steak lunch in the local carvery, with absolutely no intention whatsoever of getting involved in any naughtiness in his unlucky town.

But then, £12.95 was £12.95, wasn't it? So, having it away on his heels without paying seemed almost a duty. After all, it wasn't even a particularly good steak, so paying for it would have been silly, wouldn't it?

So, when he went to the gents', intending to climb out of the window which he had noticed open during an earlier trip to the bog, the rather nice, expensive-looking leather jacket hanging on the coat hook by the toilet door was just asking to be nicked, wasn't it?

What idiot leaves an expensive jacket like that just hanging about asking to be lifted? He would be doing the idiot a favour, really - teaching him a lesson about looking after things properly.

So he had taken it, and after trying it on in the gents' to find it was an almost perfect fit, he climbed out of the window into the rear car park.

Then, things seemed to get better and better.

In the car park was one of his favourite cars, a brand-new BMW M5.

The couple sitting in the car were obviously in the middle of a huge domestic as the woman, tears and make-up streaming down her cheeks, her face red with anger, jumped out of the front passenger seat, slammed the door and stormed off, up the road. Her partner jumped out of the driver's seat and hurried after her, calling out to her as he went.

Terry smiled as he noticed the guy had left the door open, ignition keys dangling invitingly.

Surely, this was fate and an indication that his luck in this town had finally turned, and it was a clear case of 'third-time lucky'

A free meal, a lovely new leather jacket which included the owner's wallet with 50 quid in cash and a nice assortment of credit cards, and now a beautiful M5. Things couldn't get much better!

Mind you, there's no point in pushing your luck, so he took off the leather jacket and hid it in the boot. He would recover it when he got to Eddie's and had sold his new acquisition.

M5s were ten a penny, but someone might recognise a nice coat like that.

Feeling, life couldn't get much better, he drove off, remembering to be especially careful at the traffic lights, even slowing down on green, just in case!

Unfortunately, he had not gone more than a mile or so when the front, offside wheel started playing up and he pulled over to find the M5 had a flat tyre.

Now, this might, under different circumstances, have suggested that his phenomenal run of good fortune had suddenly and abruptly come to an end, until he noticed that, by sheer chance, he had pulled up outside a Kwik Fit tyre centre.

All he had to do was pull into the garage, under cover and out of the way of prying eyes, get the tyre fixed, and he could be on his way in less than an hour.

Mind you, these tyre people were thieving bastards, and he had no doubt they'd try and tell him he needed a new tyre for some horrendous price, rather than fixing the bloody thing. After all, it only had to last long enough to get to Eddie's, and he would be shot of the car with a nice, tax-free three grand in his pocket.

Terry was ready for a battle with the grease-monkeys if they tried to do him for a new tyre; so he sat in the waiting room while the M5 was put up on the ramp and examined.

Whilst he sat there, drinking some bloody awful coffee from a vending machine, its only merit being that the bloke behind the counter had given him a token so he hadn't had to pay for it, he considered how he was going to pay for the flat.

152

'D'yer take plastic?' he said to the bloke behind the counter.

'Yep,' came the reply. 'Trouble is, our machine is down at the moment, so we can't do chip and pin, so we'll have to do it the old-fashioned way and you'll need to sign for it.'

Terry couldn't believe his luck. Without a pin number it was difficult to use a stolen credit card, except over the phone, on the Internet or in one of the old fashioned places still not using the new machines.

Here he was, with the perfect opportunity to use one of 'Leather Jacket's' credit cards, hopefully before he had the opportunity to put a stop on it.

Terry was still pondering his continuing run of good luck when the guy who had been checking over the M5 came into the waiting room.

'Sorry mate,' he said, 'the tyre is not repairable and will need to be replaced, but we do have them in stock so we can do it straight away, if you like. By the way, the nearside one is a bit dodgy, not illegal yet but will need replacing soon.'

Terry chuckled. He wasn't going to be paying anyway, and with two brand-new tyres on the car he might be able to squeeze an extra couple of hundred out of Eddie.

'Change them both,' he said, still unable to believe his luck.

Terry sat in the waiting room, smiling quietly to himself as the engineer disappeared back out into the garage to return 30 minutes later to say the job was done, they had re-balanced the wheels as well and his car was ready to go.

Terry handed over 'Leather Jacket's' gold visa card. 'Put them on there' he said nonchalantly.

The guy behind the counter took the card, looking at it briefly, before looking back at Terry.

'You know what, mate?' he said to Terry 'I reckon I must be the luckiest guy in town right now.'

Terry wondered what he meant as, still holding the visa card, the guy at the counter turned to a huge bloke in overalls, covered in grease and with forearms like tree trunks, who was standing by the front door behind Terry.

'Lock the door, Charlie,' said the guy behind the counter to the huge mechanic who obediently turned and locked the outside door before turning back to face Terry, massive arms folded across his equally massive chest.

Terry turned again to face the guy behind the counter, still not sure what he was talking about, 'Lucky?' he asked.

'Yep,' the guy said, 'How much luck do you need to have, to find your wallet stolen while you're having lunch, only to have the toe-rag who stole it, walk in a couple of hours later and try to buy a couple of tyres off you, with your nicked credit card?'

Terry's mouth fell open as he saw the huge mechanic moving menacingly towards him.

'Okay,' said the man behind the counter, 'So where the bloody hell is my jacket?'

Long Alley

ONE

Steve Finding hadn't expected to see Mary again.

It had been six months since his first and only encounter with her at Jennings Cottage in the village of Grove in Oxfordshire, and he had not returned to the place since.

Of course, it was possible he might, under normal circumstances, have expected at some time to bump into her. Oxfordshire isn't that big a place and as a radio presenter, he spent a good chunk of his time visiting local towns and villages for his radio show.

But the main reason he did not expect to see her again was because she died in 1871.

His radio show 'Finding Ghosts' was, it seems, under a little pressure from the programme commissioners.

Ratings, which had been good until recently, were slipping; as it seemed listeners were beginning to lose interest in a show that, whilst ostensibly investigating incidents of ghost sightings and other paranormal activity, tended to very quickly dismiss them with a more rational explanation than a restless spirit.

But it was probably, he thought, more a case of him taking his eye off the ball and forgetting that the main objective of his programme was to entertain rather than inform.

It seemed a good proportion of his listeners did not want rationality. They wanted spirits, ghoulies, blood and guts, not a simple explanation for why these things didn't really exist.

The irony of it all was not, however, lost on him.

Before Mary, he had never believed in ghosts.

Every investigation, every sighting, every single so-called occurrence of supernatural activity he and his researchers, Darren Masters and Sue Williams had examined, had proven to be explainable with logic and science.

Every single one that is - except the Jennings Cottage incident and his first encounter with Mary.

The irony being that this had been precisely the one story that he had been unable to broadcast.

Firstly, because the only person to see the ghosts (there had been two) was Finding himself, and he was not about to make himself a laughing stock by going 'public' with no supporting evidence - and secondly, the couple who owned the cottage and originally reported the incident were unable or unwilling to provide consent and support for the story.

Julie, the wife, was dead and her husband Brian was in prison serving two years for causing her death by drunken driving.

Since that time it seemed, somehow, Finding's enthusiasm for the job had waned and he had clearly just been going through the motions.

After all, there seemed little point in continuing, if he couldn't even tell the truth when the truth was really worth telling.

But now, here she was again - unexpected, uninvited and definitely unwanted.

He had awoken from a deep sleep made deeper by one or two more drinks than had been good for him after last night's show, and seen her.

She was sitting quietly in the armchair by the window, observing him.

A startled cry escaped his lips, and he shot up to a sitting position, clutching at his chest as his heart threatened to burst through his rib cage.

His initial reaction, terror, was understandable; waking, as he had, from a deep sleep in his own bed to find a young woman, dead for close on 150 years, sitting staring at him.

His heart rate dropped slightly from what seemed to him a dangerously high level, as he realised she apparently was not going to attack him, drink his blood, rip out his soul and drag him screaming into Hell, or whatever it was that ghosts were supposed to do to humans.

She was simply sitting there, looking at him.

He sat up in bed wondering what to do next.

Strangely, since he slept naked he was reluctant to get out

of the bed in front of her and then, realising how ridiculous it was to be embarrassed in the presence of a long-dead young woman, he threw his legs over the side of the bed and stood up shakily.

Still feeling vulnerable and not altogether confident, he nevertheless found himself wrapping the duvet around him.

But then, as he turned to her again, she was gone, and he stood staring for a few brief seconds at the empty chair before cautiously approaching it and patting the surface of the seat, as if he was expecting to be able to detect some small remaining trace of her presence.

There was none.

TWO

Finding sat in the conference room of the radio station in Banbury Road with his producer, John Wilson and the 'Finding Ghosts' researchers Darren & Sue, discussing the final details of the next show.

Once again, he was feeling a distinct lack of enthusiasm for the tale of the alleged poltergeist activity affecting two early teenage girls in a council house in Reading.

Despite the absolute assurances of the girls' mother that she had witnessed items of furniture moving of their own accord, or flying across the room as well as screaming and hysteria from the girls who were, clearly in her view, possessed by demons; once again the story had come to nothing.

These 'absolute assurances' had become somewhat less absolute when a motion-activated camera and recorder, fitted with night vision and planted secretly in the girls' room by Sue, whilst Darren and Finding kept the occupants talking in the kitchen, revealed the truth.

Later, the girls were filmed discussing when the next poltergeist experience should occur, apparently deciding that, as already long delayed homework was due to be handed in, in a few days, *that* might be an appropriate time.

After all, even the most disciplinarian of teachers could not possibly demand completed homework whilst the poor unfortunate pupils were suffering from demonic possession.

This was further supported by a later filmed conversation involving the mother as well, which indicated that a potential all-expenses trip to a popular daytime TV programme might have been a more powerful incentive for her than any desire to rescue the souls of her offspring from Satan's clutches.

Yet again it appeared to Finding to be just another non-story.

It also seemed that John Wilson was beginning to pick up on Finding's lack of enthusiasm.

'We need a little more punch this week, Steve,' Wilson remarked. 'I know the story is not a great one, but we need to convince 'the suits' that 'Finding Ghosts' can still attract good audiences. I've already had a few snide comments about...'

Steve Finding cut Wilson off with a half-hearted wave of his hand, 'I know, I know,' he said wearily, 'I'll hype it up a bit.'

Wilson looked away looking distinctly unconvinced.

'Okay,' he said, 'we need to guys, I'm telling you! Let's make it a good one.'

'What's on the agenda now?' Darren replied.

'I'm going home. I'll work on the script for, 'Exorcist: just when you thought it was safe to go back to Reading,' Finding muttered sarcastically, linking the council house poltergeist story to the classic horror film, 'see if I can't find a new twist on it, spice it up a bit.'

He sat, fingers drumming nervously on the table as he watched the others trail out of the room.

Frankly, he wasn't sure how he was going to 'spice up' the story.

In truth, he found it hard to get his early morning encounter with Mary out of his head.

Had he seen her at all? Had he just had one of those dreams where he was dreaming he was awake? Or was he hallucinating?

As he left the room he tried to reassure himself it wasn't the latter.

Hallucinations were all he needed right now, but was that really worse than seeing dead people?

THREE

Finding didn't go home straight away.

He called in at a favourite haunt of his, a small shop in East St Helen's Street in Abingdon, called 'Local Roots' where he could sit, drink coffee and think, or chat with the owner.

The communal tables meant that visitors had to sit together, which encouraged talking, often to complete strangers. Finding had met some interesting people, as well as a few rather uninteresting ones.

Also on the plus side, he had even managed to pick up the odd idea for the show.

Today though, the shop was empty, which for once he was grateful for, as he sat at a large table and turned to face out onto the street and across to the old 'County Hall' which was now a museum.

He was sitting there with his mug of black coffee, trying to take his mind off Mary and focus on the changes he should make to the script for his next show.

Then he saw her. Standing on the corner, outside the pub opposite and directly in front of the museum, stood Mary.

She seemed invisible to everyone else as they bustled by in both directions, as she stood, stock still, looking directly at him.

Finding's mouth dropped open, and he yelped as hot black coffee spilled in his lap from the mug he was holding while he leaned back against the bench.

'Shit!' he said as he grabbed napkins and started dabbing at his trousers ineffectively as the scalding liquid burned through to his thighs.

'You okay?' Chris, the owner, called across from his position behind the counter.

'Spilt my coffee,' Finding growled as he put his mug down on the table, before turning again to look across the street.

She was still standing motionless looking at him. Chris

came across with a damp cloth and handed it to Finding, who wiped his legs and the bench.

'Look over there,' he said to Chris; pointing out of the window, 'Can you see that woman over there?'

'What woman?' Chris replied.

'*That* woman,' Finding said emphatically, 'Blue dress, dark hair tied back, standing in front of the museum.'

'I can't see any woman,' Chris said.

'You must, she's standing right there, looking over here, she's...' Finding's voice tailed off as he noticed the strange look Chris was giving him.

'Never mind,' he said, 'sorry, she must have gone, you missed her.'

As he watched, Mary turned her back and began to walk off in the direction of the front of the museum.

Finding jumped to his feet, 'Look, I'll be back in a minute, want to try and catch up with her.' He hurried out of the shop and across the street.

By the time Finding reached the front of the museum, Mary was standing on the steps to the entrance, under the covered palisade of arches that spanned the façade.

He stopped uncertainly as she looked at him, but as soon as he moved forward towards her, she turned her back and walked into the museum.

Finding followed at a distance, while she climbed the three flights of stairs to the museum's display area. To his right sat a middle-aged woman behind a counter with an assortment of posters and small booklets as well as jars with souvenir pencils and such like, and a till.

She glanced at Finding before returning her gaze to the paperback book open on her lap.

He looked around for Mary. The museum seemed empty, apart from the lady at the counter and a middle-aged man in hiking shorts with a knapsack over his shoulder, who was standing at the far end of the room, staring into a large display case housing a couple of headless dummies dressed in mediaeval costumes.

He scanned the room and suddenly she was there again. She emerged silently from behind a screen, went across to a table-high glass display case and stopped.

As Finding watched, she bent over the case, apparently reading a document displayed there.

'This is ridiculous,' he said out loud, his sudden outburst attracting the attention of both the visitor and the lady behind the counter, who frowned slightly, viewing Finding quizzically.

Realising his behaviour must have appeared odd, he smiled half-heartedly at the woman, raising a hand in acknowledgement; trying to reassure her he was not completely mad.

Mary, who seemed totally oblivious to anything except the document in the display case, continued to study it intently before returning her gaze to Finding who moved slowly towards her.

She seemed to wait, allowing him to come within a few feet of her, before briefly returning her gaze to the display case and then walking off behind the screen from which she had originally emerged.

As she vanished from Finding's sight, he suddenly hurried towards the screen, only to find that Mary had, once more, disappeared.

He looked around urgently, searching here and there, behind any display cabinet capable of concealing someone. She was nowhere to be seen.

'Can I help you?'

The woman at the entrance, obviously concerned by Finding's erratic behaviour, had come out from behind the counter and was approaching Finding cautiously.

'No,' Finding said, then 'Yes, yes did you see that woman? The woman in blue, dark hair...'

'There has been nobody in here today, except you and that gentleman over there.' She gestured towards the hiker in the shorts.

'The only entrance is through the front door by my counter. If a young lady had come in, I'd have seen her.'

Finding noticed the woman was eyeing the front of his trousers suspiciously, and as he looked down he realised his

163

attempts to mop up the spilled coffee with the wet cloth Chris had given him in the shop had only served to create a huge damp patch on the front of his trousers.

'Accident. Coffee,' he said rather inadequately. 'Look, I'm sorry. I'm just a little tired, not much sleep last night. I promise I'll be no more trouble.'

He tried to reinforce the promise with what he realised was a rather weak and unconvincing smile.

Finding thought better of staying any longer in the museum under the watchful gaze of the lady who, he was certain, was not too far away from calling the police.

He slowly walked out of the museum and across the road to 'Local Roots'. His cup was still on the table, but the contents were cold.

'Sorry about that,' he said to Chris, 'can I get another coffee? I'll try to get this one in my mouth, I promise.' While he spoke, he stared once more out of the window in the direction of the museum.

FOUR

Finding managed to finish his coffee without spilling it while he sat, rather half-heartedly responding to Chris' occasional comments on articles in the *Guardian* which was lying spread out on his counter.

What was going on? Why suddenly, after six months was Mary appearing to him? Was she trying to tell him something? What was the significance of the museum?

The questions were coming thick and fast, answers less so.

Then it occurred to him.

He was, of course, embarrassed by his behaviour in the museum and anxious to get away from the scrutiny of the receptionist, curator or assistant, whatever the middle-aged woman was.

Otherwise, he would have realised that, rather than chasing an apparition around the place, he should have taken more notice of why she was there.

What had she been studying in the display case? He needed to go back and take another look.

Fortunately, his trousers had now dried out sufficiently so that he no longer looked as much like an incontinent lunatic as he had before.

He returned to the museum, pleased to note that the woman had been replaced by someone else. Maybe, given the time of day, she had taken a lunch break?

In any event, he was grateful to have the opportunity to see what information he could collect, before she returned.

Nothing in the case appeared to have any real significance to him or Mary.

Most of it seemed to refer to old Abingdon Town Council records dating back to the time of Charles II, orders relating to Oliver Cromwell's obsession with removing so-called 'Popish Recusants' or those suspected of being 'popishly affected.'

165

These dated to around 1658. Whatever Mary was trying to tell him, if she was at all, couldn't possibly have anything to do with this.

It would take an awful lot more than what little celebrity he had, to turn the entire tide of the English Civil War and reverse the dissolution of the abbeys!

Only one item seemed to involve anything of a personal nature, and that related to a woman called Mawyan Duhen who, in 1675, was made the subject of a so called 'Bastardry Order'.

It would seem that this unfortunate woman was made the subject of a complaint laid by some clearly enlightened people called the 'Church Wardens and Overseers of the Poor' for the heinous crime of having an illegitimate child, a boy, apparently born on the 14th May 1675, who was referred to only as 'the bastard child'; clearly he did not rate a name.

The complaint was, on examination, found proven and it seems that one John North, a 'yeoman of Shippon', was identified as the father.

In some kind of early incarnation of the Child Support Agency, North was ordered to pay the sum of three shillings per week for the upkeep of the boy, back-dated to the child's date of birth.

However, this amount was to be paid, not to the mother, but to the church wardens; further the payments would last so long as the child was a charge on the parish.

Mawyan was ordered 'to be forthwith committed to the House of Correction' where she was to be 'set on work and punished during the term of one whole year'.

'No council flat then,' Finding muttered under his breath.

166

FIVE

After returning home at around 6.00 pm, Steve Finding worked half-heartedly on the script for the Reading Poltergeist story, finding it difficult to concentrate on the matter in hand as his mind constantly drifted to the encounter with Mary.

By 11.30 pm, he finally thought he had enough to satisfy the script meeting tomorrow and had, at least he hoped he had, managed to spice up the story a little by including some background information on the association of the instances of poltergeist phenomena with pubescent girls. Perhaps the slight allusion to sexual motivations would prove an interesting angle for listeners disappointed by the distinct lack of wandering spirits.

He stood up from his desk, shutting his laptop and stretching, before crossing to a sideboard and pouring himself a whisky which he carried to the bedroom. He was sitting in the chair by the window where Mary had manifested herself earlier and staring out of the window into the deep darkness as he sipped his drink.

What was Mary trying to tell Finding? Did it have anything to do with Mawyan Duhen? And why him?

His thoughts returned to the Jenning's Cottage incident when he had, unfortunately uncorroborated by anyone else, encountered the long dead maid, Rosemary Jenkins, sometimes known it seemed as Mary.

Nothing appeared to make any sense. As far as he was able to establish, she was a ghost that inhabited the cottage, others had detected her presence there and he had seen her himself. But why had she suddenly taken to following him around?

Finally, he found his eyelids drooping and he realised how tired he was. Perhaps it was a delayed reaction to his experiences and the tragic events at Jenning's Cottage, events that had left a bright young woman dead and her husband in prison.

There had been no upside to this story. He had not even

been able to use it in the Show. Perhaps some post-traumatic episode was affecting him, coupled with the pressure of the falling ratings of his programme. It was not healthy. He needed to focus on getting himself back on track or find himself looking for another means of earning a living if 'Finding Ghosts' folded.

He swallowed the last of the whisky, sighed and stripped off, throwing clothes in the general direction of the wicker laundry basket by the door before going through into the en-suite bathroom and taking a shower. He cleaned his teeth and, leaning on the hand basin, he stared at his reflection in the mirror.

Beneath his eyes were deep shadows, his skin looked slightly grey to him and he sighed as he noticed the increasing presence of grey hair at his temples and even more prominently, in the stubble of his unshaven chin.

He bent down, cupping his hand under the running cold tap scooping water into his mouth, rinsing and spitting it out into the sink.

He stood up, and his gaze returned to the mirror. He jumped, as there reflected behind him and staring directly into his eyes, was Mary.

Finding spun around quickly, his hands rising instinctively to ward off some perceived threat.

There was no one there.

SIX

Sitting at the conference table in the studio, Finding was aware that Wilson, Darren and Sue were eyeing him suspiciously while he stared into his plastic cup as if some underlying explanation as to what was happening to him lay somewhere in the rapidly cooling black liquid.

'You with us Steve?' Wilson said and Finding raised his eyes to the producer who was sat opposite, holding Finding's script notes for the Reading Poltergeist story.

Having got Finding's attention, Wilson cleared his throat and placed the notes on the table in front of him before pushing them to one side and patting them gently.

'Okay,' he continued, 'I think we are agreed that this is an improvement on the original emphasis of the story, so we should run with this as the approach for the next show. However, in my view it's not great and we really need to up our game for the next show. What's next?'

Sue pushed a few sheets of typed A4 paper held together in the corner by a paper clip across the table to Wilson. 'This might be promising', she said, at the same time sliding two further copies to Finding and to Darren before continuing.

Wilson picked up the papers, Finding left his untouched, continuing to stare, apparently uninterested, into his coffee cup. Darren also left his copy on the table but then he and Sue worked together on everything, he was already fully aware of the contents.

'It's a report of a haunting. What makes it interesting is that there seems to have been no previous history, which is unusual. Usually these stories go back a long time. Perceived sightings, probably triggered by historical events and incidents, but this seems to have only started in the last couple of weeks or so.'

'Yes,' Darren added, 'and there have been at least four separate sightings, different people at different times, which is also unusual.'

'Okay,' Wilson said, 'Run it by us.'

Sue glanced at the pages before replying. 'There are some old almshouses in Abingdon, actually there's a triangle of them, three sets, the oldest is called 'Long Alley', dates back to 1446. The other two sets called...,' she checked her papers, '...Brick Alley and Twitty's, were built later in the 1700's. There are some pictures here.' She threw an assortment of photographs into the centre of the table.

Wilson picked them up and went through them quickly.

They showed various angles on a long, low brick and tile building opposite a church fronting onto a well-manicured, grass covered graveyard.

The unusual building had a covered walkway to the front, off which were a number of single, green painted doors; presumably the entrances to the small almshouses. At the front, supporting the roof of the walkway, were a series of wooden arches which ran the length of the building like glassless windows. They were supported by a low brick wall broken in a couple of places by an entrance porch that gave access to the walkway.

Reflecting the obvious religious influences, there seemed to be a number of pious bible readings along the walls of the walkway from which the building, 'Long Alley', had obviously got its name.

Two footpaths crossed, one leading alongside the church and down to the side of the 'Long Alley' building, whilst another cut across between the church and the lawned cemetery, heading down to the river.

Two further sets of brick-built almshouses, far less ornate than the obviously much older building, formed two sides of a triangle with the church where the point of the triangle would have been.

Sue continued, 'The sightings were all by occupants of the almshouses; they are mostly elderly women. Three of the witnesses were old ladies, two live in 'Brick Alley', the other in 'Twitty's'; the old man is the only one who actually lives in one of the 'Long Alley' houses. But in each case the sighting was of a young woman and she was seen in the covered walkway.'

Suddenly Finding seemed to take an interest. He picked up the photos and scanned them quickly before turning to the notes Sue had slid in front of him and reading them briefly.

'I know this place,' he said at last, 'The church is St Helen's, it is at the other end of East St Helen's Street where I have coffee sometimes. What did this woman look like?'

It was a few hundred yards from the Abingdon museum and the place in the street where he had seen Mary.

'Dark hair? Blue dress?' he said excitedly.

'No,' Sue responded, 'All the descriptions were the same. She was wearing some kind of long smock affair, a dirty beige colour apparently, and she had long darkish-blonde hair, but done up in a bun at the back. One of the old ladies who saw her said that the smock reminded her of the kind of thing people were forced to wear in the workhouse when she was a child.'

Finding looked puzzled. 'Two ghosts within a few hundred yards of each other,' he said quietly to himself, 'Do I only see bloody ghosts in pairs...'

'What?' Wilson said, 'What are you talking about, two ghosts?'

'Sorry, nothing', Finding dismissed the comment with a wave of his hand, 'I'm not sleeping well at the moment, not sure what I'm saying half the time. Have we been there? Spoken to these witnesses?'

'Yep,' Darren said brightly, 'All the witnesses are in their eighties, apart from the one who mentioned the 'workhouse smock' and she is over ninety. But they all seemed to have all their marbles, good witnesses really.'

'Yes,' Sue said, 'We also spoke to the vicar. One of the old ladies helps with the flowers in the church. She mentioned it to the vicar, said she thought the girl was a 'restless soul'. She asked the vicar to say a prayer for her.'

'What time of day were the sightings?' Wilson asked.

'All after dark, early to mid evening, apparently. In the case of the old ladies, they all saw her from outside of 'Long

Alley'. It seems she was just walking; at least they described it more as floating along the walkway, back and forth. The old man was different.'

'How different?' Finding said.

'He was actually in the walkway, he added, "she came at him', was how he described it. He had come out of his house, the last one along on the right, and was heading to the pub around the corner, The Old Anchor'. Apparently, as he came out of his door, he looked down to the far end of the walkway and he saw the woman in the shadows. It was quite dark, apparently. She was standing at one of the doors at the far end. He thought at first she was visiting, waiting for the door to open. Apparently, as he was about to lock his door, she turned and looked at him. Then, as he said, 'she came at him'.'

'What did he mean by that?' Wilson said.

'Well,' Sue continued, 'She apparently started moving towards him, he also described it as 'floating', but her hands were outstretched towards him and she was moving fast. He says he couldn't see her face properly, but he sensed she was not happy. He was sure she was going to attack him. He went back into his house, slammed the door. He heard a hammering on the door as he leaned against it. He says it didn't seem like the hammering of a young woman. That was it. He said it terrified him. He didn't open the door again until the next morning. There was nothing apparently unusual the next day. Everything was as per normal. But he was clearly shaken by it.'

'I think I should look into it. I'd like to make a few enquiries of my own down there. Anyone got any objections?' Finding looked around the table.

Wilson spoke, 'Well, I was beginning to wonder whether you were interested at all, Steve, but it's good to see you enthusiastic about something at last. Yes, sounds worth-while to me, let's try and make this a good one, eh?'

Darren and Sue nodded, and Wilson rose, indicating the meeting was at an end.

As Wilson left the office, Finding stopped Darren and Sue

just as they were following him out of the door.

'I'd like you guys to look into something for me while I'm following up on this.'

'Is it related to this 'Long Alley' thing?' Darren asked.

'I'm not sure,' Finding said, 'Perhaps, perhaps not. I want you to visit the Abingdon Town Archives, see what you can find out about this woman.'

He handed Darren a piece of paper, and Darren read the name written on it out loud.

"Mawyan Duhen?' who's she, I assume it is a she?'

Finding nodded, 'Yes. If you go to the Abingdon Museum, just down the road from 'Long Alley', you'll find a display about something called a 'Bastardry Order' that was made against her. See if you can find out any more information about her.'

Darren handed the note to Sue. 'Anything you say, Boss,' his smile was not returned by Finding, who seemed deep in thought once again.

SEVEN

Finding spent the rest of the day re-interviewing the witnesses in Abingdon. He didn't normally double-check on the work carried out by his researchers; the truth was that Darren and Sue were professionals and were more thorough and detailed in their approach than he would ever be.

But given the fact that he seemed to somehow have been targeted by the ghost Mary, a ghost that it would seem only he could see, he felt some personal connection that perhaps only he would be able to put together.

As it turned out, he discovered nothing that added anything further to what they knew already. Nothing, at least until at the very last minute a question had occurred to him, a question that perhaps had been sitting in the back of his mind since the briefing earlier, when Sue had mentioned the unusual nature of the sightings.

It had come to him just as he was leaving St Helen's Church, having had a pleasant but from the standpoint of the investigation, fruitless discussion with the Team Rector, a Reverend Thomas Baker, about the sightings.

Finding, being a staunch atheist, had absolutely no idea what a 'Team Rector' was, probably some trendy new title which was the product of that new breed of churchmen who tweeted the Lord's message from their iPhones. But the reverend seemed a very nice man, an American by birth who seemed not to struggle with, what seemed to Finding to be, the complete contradictions between faith and science.

As helpful as the churchman seemed to want to be, he was unable to throw any light on the sightings until Finding was set to leave.

Reverend Baker was showing Finding out of the church via the side door which led out onto the pathway that ran from the junction of West and East St Helen's Street, down past 'Twitty's

Almshouses' on the right before continuing on by the end of 'Long Alley'.

As they were shaking hands, it occurred to Finding that something must have triggered this spate of sightings.

It seemed to him that most of the many supposed 'supernatural occurrences' they had investigated over the years fell into three categories. Firstly, the type that basically emanated from the mind of the witness or victim effected. The Reading Poltergeist story was a classic; so-called demonic possession was another, but whether fraud, mental illness or illusion – typically they came from the mind of the victim. Secondly, there was the type that had some scientifically understandable physical cause, cold spots, drifting mist, blemishes on photographic paper and so on; and thirdly, what often could include elements of the other two, was location.

Put a witness in the kind of place where years of history, films, books and stories had created a classic backdrop for a supernatural story, and witnesses were almost predisposed to see something that is not there, particularly where the location had a history of such stories, sometimes going back centuries.

Finding could pretty much dismiss the first two: Multiple witnesses, unconnected to each other and apparently unaware of each other's sightings had given broadly similar descriptions that did not appear to have any element of collusion.

The physical or scientific answer did not seem to help either. Physical or atmospheric events tended not to suddenly crop up, an underground water table, draught, river mist tended to exist for quite a while which usually led to multiple incidents over a long period of time.

The third option, which Finding was feeling most comfortable with, was the location.

'Long Alley' certainly had the history, going back some 600 plus years and the presence of the graveyard and the church added to the likelihood.

But the puzzling thing was, why now? Why had all the sightings happened in the last few weeks, without any history, as far as he could tell, that dated back any longer than a month?

'One last question, Dr Baker,' Finding said, just as the Rector was turning back into the church, 'Can you think of anything, anything at all, that has happened in the last month that is out of the ordinary?'

'You mean like ghosts, spirits and demonic possession?' the rector smiled.

'No,' Finding said, returning the smile unconvincingly at the hint of sarcasm in the comment. 'No, anything unusual, something that started or is currently going on that is out of the ordinary.'

'Afraid not,' the rector replied, 'Apart from the complaints from our caretaker about the mud and dirt spread by our friends there.' The rector nodded in the direction of three men in yellow fluorescent jackets with red safety helmets, who seemed deep in conversation at the far end of the row of brick terraced cottages that made up the 'Twitty's' almshouses.

'How long have they been around?' Finding asked.

'They started a few weeks back. There's some problem with the wall at the far end of the 'Twitty's' block, a bit of subsidence I think. They turned up three weeks or so ago, a few complaints about their mini-digger tearing up the grass in that part of the cemetery and also, as I say some complaints about them spreading a bit of mud around the footpaths, but generally they have been no bother.'

'Thanks for your help,' Finding said, shaking the rector's hand.

Dr Baker smiled and turned back into the church as Fielding walked over to where the three workmen were standing.

'I want him sacked.' The workman speaking was wearing a fluorescent jacket over a suit and was clearly managerial, given that the other two men were wearing well-soiled work clothes, with the clear signs of dirt and dust on their hands and boots.

The man in the suit was furiously scribbling on a clip board as he continued, 'This job has over-run by a week already and now you tell me - having failed to turn up for work on two separate occasions, he has gone bloody missing again – sack him and get somebody more reliable on it! I want this job finished by the end of the week.'

'Sorry to interrupt.' Finding held out his hand to the man who had been talking, who took it automatically and shook it.

'I'm Steve Finding, I have a radio show and we are looking into some, shall we say, unusual sightings that some of the locals have reported. I wondered if your guys could throw any light on it.'

'Finding Ghosts,' the man responded, 'Yes, I listen to the show regularly. You investigate the paranormal. You looking for ghosts around here? – seems like you came to the right place,' he smiled, making a gesture around at the neat collection of burial grounds surrounding them.

'I'm George Williams by the way. I'm in charge of this renovation job, a minor bit of underpinning needed but we seem to be making a bit of a meal of it.' He looked at the two other workmen pointedly. 'How can we help?'

'I just wondered if you or any of your guys had seen anything unusual over the last few weeks since you've been here. Some of the residents have reported unusual sightings in that time.'

'No one has said anything to me,' Williams remarked as he turned to the other two workers, 'You heard or seen anything?'

The two workmen were taking the opportunity to roll cigarettes, but shook their heads in response to the question.

'When were the sightings?' Williams asked.

'Different days, but always early to mid evening, after dark.'

Williams shook his head. 'I have a job keeping these blokes here beyond four o'clock in the afternoon, let alone into the evening. Sorry, can't help you I'm afraid. The only other person you might ask is Colin Hobart, if I can ever get him to turn up; he is supposed to be working on this job. You might need to get in quickly though, I've had to warn him twice already over the last two weeks for going AWOL, and the lazy bastard hasn't turned up again today. Mind you, I wouldn't hold my breath anyway, I'd get more sense and work out of some of the residents in the graveyard here than out of that waste of space.'

'Okay, thanks.' Finding handed Williams his business card, 'Listen, I'd be grateful if you can have a word with Mr Hobart when you see him and if he has anything useful to say, or anything else occurs to you, perhaps you can give me a call.'

Williams looked at the card and held out his hand to Finding.

'I'll do that,' he said,' but frankly your ghosts might turn up a bit more regularly than Hobart does.'

EIGHT

Whether due to the fact that he now had something to occupy his mind, or because of the broken sleep he had endured over the last few days, Finding for once had a reasonably pleasant night's sleep.

He woke at 7.00 am. Tentatively opening his eyes, he looked nervously in the direction of what he had now started thinking of as 'Mary's Chair' and, reassured by her absence, he showered leisurely before going down to the kitchen and putting on coffee and toast.

He scanned the newspapers that had been delivered and, finding nothing of any interest to him, threw them onto a spare chair in the kitchen and sat at the table, sipping black coffee and crunching on buttered toast as he considered his next actions in the 'Long Alley' case.

He had a meeting arranged with Darren and Sue for the afternoon to find out how their investigations at the Abingdon Council Archives had gone, but until then he was not sure what his next move should be.

He still had no idea what Mary's role was in all this, and he contemplated opening up to Darren and Sue explaining what he was experiencing.

This, of course, would also necessitate him explaining his original sightings of Mary in the Jenning's Cottage case, and as he really wasn't sure himself whether he was just being delusional or not, he couldn't quite believe that a pair of trained scientists and researchers like Darren and Sue would come to any other conclusion than that Finding had finally gone off his head completely.

Thinking about it, he preferred to wait until perhaps he had a better idea of what was going on than he did at the moment, ideally with some kind of evidence that even Darren and Sue could not dismiss rationally.

If he only knew what the connection was between Mary and the 'Long Alley' affair, if any. But then there had to be didn't there? She had led him to the story, to the display case in the Museum. Surely also the coincidence of her appearing to him so close to the sightings at the almshouses was too great to ignore?

He decided that, before the meeting with his researchers, he would re-visit 'Long Alley'; perhaps he might have some inspiration or maybe Mary would turn up again. After all, she seemed to be there when he didn't want her to be. Perhaps now, when he needed some inspiration she might turn up again.

Finding spent a couple of hours wandering around the almshouses. He walked the length of the 'Long Alley' walkway several times without feeling so much as an unexpected draught of air.

He returned to the museum, re-reading the documents in the display case and then moving on to the other displays in the neat little museum, hoping that something would make some sense. Nothing did.

Eventually he gave up and left the historical exhibits, walking across to 'Local Roots' where he greeted Chris and ordered a coffee, taking his place on the bench by the window and looking across to where he had previously seen Mary.

Chris looked up as Finding muttered under his breath 'Just when you could do with some spiritual guidance...'

'Sorry?' Chris looked up from behind the counter.

'Nothing. Just talking to myself.' Finding said.

'First sign of madness,' Chris said, smiling.

'Exactly what I'm afraid of,' Finding answered as he continued staring out of the window.

At 2.00 pm, Finding met with Darren and Sue as arranged at the studio on the Banbury Road. Darren was carrying a brown folder within which was an impressively large pile of papers.

'So what have we got?' Finding asked as the three of them sat around the conference table.

'Interesting.' Darren started. 'Well, we met a very helpful lady, who is a part-time archivist for the Council. At the outset, it

180

seems that she really could only reinforce the details of the 'Bastardry Order' made on Mawyan Duhen, probably more accurately called an 'Illegitimacy Order' handed down in 1675 by William Cheney, the Mayor, and the Recorder Thomas Holt. The complaint they were ruling on was laid by the 'Church Wardens and Overseers of the Poor', great name, from St Helen's Church. That's the church next to 'Long Alley'.

Finding nodded. He already knew as much from his own reading of the display at the museum.

'Anyway, it seems Mawyan was ordered to be *Set on work and punished during the term of one whole year.*'

'They apparently also ordered someone called John North, described as a yeoman of Shippon, that's a village near Abingdon, to pay the sum of three shillings per week, back-dated to the 5th April 1675, when the child was born. The money was to go to the previously mentioned 'Church Wardens and Overseers of the Poor', for the length of time the child remained a charge on the Parish.'

'Okay,' Finding said, 'Do we know the name of the child or anything else about what happened to Mawyan or the boy afterwards?'

Sue continued the story, 'We have no direct evidence of the name of the child. It seems a bastard was pretty much a non-person in those days, most of the paperwork refers to him as *'it'* or *'the bastard child'*.

'So, not much more than was on display in the Museum?' Finding looked disappointed.

Darren smiled and Finding watched in anticipation, recognising the look that he often had when he was about, like some stage magician, to pull some metaphorical rabbit from a hat.

'Okay Darren,' Finding said, 'Out with it. What else have you found out?'

Darren placed one small bundle of papers, all put together with a paper clip to one side, whilst he picked up another larger pile of papers.

'It seems our 'Overseers of the Poor' had a little internal problem going on at about the same time Mawyan was under their

181

control, a problem by the name of Jeremiah Holdsworthy who was one of their own. Son of a rich landowner and a local employer. He also was involved, it would seem, in running the 'House of Corrections' where Mawyan was sent. By all accounts, he was giving the rest of the Overseers some serious headaches. Unfortunately, it seems he was too powerful for any of them to deal with directly or openly; they set up some kind of internal committee to investigate confidentially and to try and sort out a way to solve the problem whilst not ending up out on their ears themselves.'

'What kind of headaches?' Finding asked.

'Sexual ones,' Sue said, taking over from Darren who had stopped briefly, ostensibly to take a drink, but Finding suspected more for dramatic effect.

'You mean he was abusing the women in the workhouse? – I'm not sure that would surprise anyone unduly,' Finding said.

'It was a little more than that it seems.' Darren took over the story again from Sue. 'There were certainly a lot of allegations of him taking advantage of the women in his charge, I'm not sure that would necessarily have raised too many eyebrows. Nobody was representing these women, except the Overseers, and if it was one of their own doing the abusing; well, no one was going to take much notice of allegations made against the rich and powerful. Particularly, as many of these women had effectively already been declared immoral as a consequence of the actions that brought them to the attention of the Overseers in the first place. No, it seems our Jeremiah Holdsworthy did not restrict himself to adult victims; there are suggestions that he had paedophile tendencies, some of the alleged victims were babes in arms.'

Finding considered what Darren and Sue were telling him before speaking.

'Okay, so we have a 17th century paedophile here. Is there anything that connects him to Mawyan or her baby boy?'

'Not directly,' Darren said, 'But it seems this unofficial *'committee'* looking into the behaviour of Holdsworthy became very active around April 1676, in fact it seems they were running around like headless chickens, judging from the minutes of these private meetings which seem not to have been part of their usual activities.'

'So what makes you think there might be a connection with Mawyan?'

'Well, this shall we say, heightened activity, took place as I said, in April 1676. That would have been shortly before Mawyan was due to finish her *'punishment'* and her baby would have been a year old. Remember, his birthday was the 5th April 1675. It seems that a child was killed around that time, a boy, and whilst we have no information on a name for either the boy or the parents; whilst discussing the financial implications of the death of the child, it seems the Overseers had been receiving three shillings per week since the 5th April 1675 - which ties in perfectly with Mawyan Duhen's child.'

'Not conclusive,' Finding said, 'But I suppose, whilst there may have been quite a few unmarried mothers in the workhouse, the chances of there being more than one, of the right sex, born on the same day and also being supported at three shillings per week... Well, it seems too much of a coincidence to me.'

'Incidentally, without being pedantic,' Darren said, 'it seems Mawyan was in something called *'The House of Corrections',* not strictly the workhouse. I wasn't aware there was a distinction, but apparently they were two different places in Abingdon, and existed at different times.'

'Okay, let's assume it was Mawyan's child; where does that lead us?'

'Well it seems that, to coin a phrase, the shit really hit the fan,' Sue jumped in excitedly.

'The inference seems to be that our Jeremiah Holdsworthy was, in some way, responsible for the child's death, I really don't want to imagine how that might have been, but clearly he was 'in the frame', and whilst our committee of worthies were obviously metaphorically wringing their hands wondering what to do about it, providence took a hand. It seems the mother of the child; again she is not named; murdered Jeremiah. She must have been quite a woman. No knives, blunt instruments or anything like that; it seems she strangled him using a piece of rope. It must have been quite an effort for a no doubt, under-nourished young woman; but she managed to strangle him.'

Finding was beginning to get excited. He had lots of questions but didn't know where to start. Darren took over the story once more. 'Guess where he was killed?' he said to Finding.

'Don't tell me 'Long Alley?' Finding's mind was racing.

'Exactly,' Darren said.

'I need coffee,' Finding said as he broke off and walked out to the filter coffee jug in reception. He returned to the conference room, his mind racing. He sipped from the plastic cup before continuing. 'I'm a little puzzled. If Holdsworthy was murdered in 'Long Alley', I'm wondering why Mawyan, if it was Mawyan, is roaming the walkway and not him. Do we know what happened next?'

Darren turned over a few pages. It seemed he was way ahead of his notes and he obviously wanted to find the appropriate place to continue his story.

'I think I can explain that, assuming of course we do believe that *anyone* is haunting 'Long Alley', which I guess for the purposes of argument we should consider.'

He took another swallow of water before proceeding, 'Well. It appears that the committee again got a helpful break, and this might answer your question. The woman never came to trial. It appears she committed suicide. Before she could be brought to account for the murder, our friendly committee of Overseers appear to have got to her. Apparently, she was 'advised' that she should not make allegations against Holdsworthy in her defence case. Actually, to be precise it seems that the fear of God was put into her – literally. She was told that Holdsworthy was a pious and worthy man, beloved of God, and if she made allegations against this servant of The Lord she would be punished in this World and in the next.'

Finding interrupted Darren, 'Well, it seems to me that if Mawyan was not going to defend herself she would be found guilty,

184

and I assume in those days that meant execution. What more could they threaten her with? Unless they were promising to influence the Judge somehow and get him to commute her sentence.'

'It seems they didn't even need to offer her that,' Darren continued. 'They told her that any allegations she made against Holdsworthy would lead the Judge to consider she was unworthy of God's redemption. Not only would she be sentenced to hang, but the Judge would order her body to be cut down and handed over to surgeons for dissection. This apparently was a terrifying prospect to many people who honestly believed that your body needed to be intact to enter the Kingdom of Heaven. Seems she was so terrified that she hanged herself under the walkway in 'Long Alley'.'

'Why there? Wasn't she in custody? How did she manage to hang herself in 'Long Alley?' Finding asked.

'We're not sure really. Perhaps they put the idea into her head, suggested it might be her best option. I suspect her suicide would suit them all very nicely, no need to rely on her keeping quiet about Holdsworthy.'

Sue spoke, 'If that's true, they were of course being extremely duplicitous, given that suicide would have been considered a mortal sin anyway, but I guess as prominent members of the Church, they could interpret God's will anyway they wished. It would be hard for an ignorant and illiterate pauper to debate theology with church wardens.'

Finding considered for a few moments. 'I guess that makes some kind of sense. In any event she must have expected to hang anyway; at least she may have considered she had a little more control over her ending. The death of a child alone is enough to turn some people. I can't begin to imagine what sort of state of mind she must have been in, her son murdered, God knows in what horrendous circumstances; probably after months of abuse, the murder of Holdsworthy and then these evil Overseers putting the fear of God into her. People have certainly committed suicide for less.'

The three of them sat quietly for a few moments deep in

185

thought, until Sue broke the silence. 'I think she could possibly have been questioned in the halls attached to 'Long Alley', they were added in 1605 to house *'Christ's Hospital'* – I wouldn't mind betting the Governors and the Overseers could probably have served in both capacities. The dark walkway would serve as a convenient place to hang a rope. She might even have been left there to contemplate the wickedness of her crime. They seemed to like people to dwell on their sins in those days.'

'It certainly would seem to have been a convenient conclusion to a potentially embarrassing, if not explosive situation – she kills herself, thereby confirming her guilt, Holdsworthy was out of the way, no longer an embarrassment to them and with his reputation in tact. Works all the way around, except for Mawyan and her child of course.'

The three colleagues went over the information for another 30 minutes or so until Finding called the meeting to a conclusion.

'Well, whatever the truth or otherwise concerning the hauntings, I still think we have one hell of a story here, I need to run it by John, but there is certainly enough here to make up at least one episode of 'Finding Ghosts'. We still have a few missing pieces though. For example, if all this happened in 1676, why has it taken nearly 350 years for Mawyan to get around to haunting the place?'

Darren and Sue looked at each other and Darren shrugged, 'No idea,' he said finally.

'Well okay, let's call it a day and we can think about it overnight. I'm going to visit 'Long Alley' tomorrow night, spend the evening there, see if anything unusual happens. Who knows maybe we'll have some kind of mist cloud coming up from the river that only happens at that time of the evening, perhaps some shadow cast by a street light that comes on automatically around that time, anything that might account for the sightings.'

'We could do that, Steve,' Darren said, 'After all that's what you pay us for.'

Finding answered quickly, 'No, I want to do this myself, and alone. I don't want anything to be different. After all, whilst we have had multiple sightings, the witnesses have always been alone. Let's make sure we don't introduce any random elements.'

Actually, Finding had another motive far more pressing for him as to why he should do this alone. He still had not mentioned anything to Darren or Sue about the involvement of Mary. If she was a part of this, he was sure she would only come to him.

He needed to sort this out for his own peace of mind, if not to reassure himself of his own sanity.

NINE

Finding spent another fitful night as he seemed unable to switch off his mind. He tossed and turned, endlessly running over the facts as he understood them.

He finally fell asleep at about 4.00 am, with the help of two very large glasses of whisky and woke again, feeling totally exhausted at 8.45 am. Something had startled him. It took a few seconds for him to realise it was his mobile phone ringing on the bedside table.

He didn't recognise the number displayed, so rather than saying his name he simply answered 'Hello?'

'Steve Finding?' The voice at the other end of the phone asked.

'Who's this?' Finding responded, not wanting to identify himself until he was sure who the caller was.

'It's George Williams, we met in Abingdon, at 'Twitty's' the day before yesterday? You asked me to call you if I heard anything?'

'Oh yes George, thanks for calling. Have you? - heard something, that is'

'Not exactly,' Williams replied, 'But we've found Colin Hobart this morning, you know, the guy you asked me to speak to before I sacked him?'

'Yes, did he say whether he saw anything unusual?'

'No he didn't, I'm afraid. I've just got off the phone from the police. They want me down at 'Long Alley', apparently they've found Colin Hobart down there – he's dead.'

'Dead?' Finding responded, 'What the hell happened?'

'No idea,' Williams responded, 'I got the call from the Police first thing this morning. They asked me to meet them there. They want to know what he might have been doing on site as it seems he has been there all night. One of the old ladies discovered his body outside her door when she opened it this morning. He was

188

hidden from anyone passing by, by the wall along the walkway. The only thing I know is, apparently he was definitely not there at 7.00 pm last night, that's when she last opened the door before this morning. I thought you'd like to know, I was just on my way down there.'

'Do you mind if I come too? I'd like to try and find out what's going on down there,' Finding said.

'Be my guest,' Williams said, 'I guess it's up to the police whether you get anywhere close, but I've got no objections.'

'I'll be there in about 45 minutes.' Finding ended the call.

'What the hell is going on?' he said to himself as he climbed out of bed and hurried into the bathroom to shower.

Finding parked in a gravel lane alongside 'The Old Anchor' pub that led from the river to the footpath cutting through alongside 'Long Alley' towards the church and the town.

A number of police cars were also parked along the lane, some with their blue lights flashing rather redundantly, Finding thought.

As he approached from the back of 'Long Alley', he could see, on his left, the black iron railings separating the lane from a tree-shaded, small old burial area at the far end of which was the side wall of the end cottage in 'Twitty's'.

He noticed a mini digger parked close by, next to a pile of dark earth that had clearly been excavated from under the end wall of the cottage, presumably the site of the subsidence. A lonely looking shovel stuck, like a makeshift headstone at one end of the earth pile.

Standing on the footpath, close to the earth works was George Williams, who was talking to a rather dishevelled grey haired man in a dark suit that looked like it could do with a good pressing.

A considerable beer belly hung over the low slung suit trousers, and the shirt which had clearly originally been white, but now looked distinctly greyish was straining to hold in the man's substantial belly, the buttons looking in serious danger of popping at any moment.

Finding smiled as he recognised the bulky shape of Detective Chef Inspector Willie Baxter, an amiable Glaswegian who had been stationed in Oxford for as long as Finding could remember.

As Finding approached the pair, Baxter turned his head towards him and smiled, his eyebrows arching as he peered over the bifocal glasses perched on the end of his nose.

He smiled and held out his hand to Finding who shook it warmly, 'Steve Finding as I live and breathe,' Baxter said, 'Long time no see Steve. To what do we owe the pleasure of the company of Oxfordshire's foremost ghost hunter?' The obvious good-natured sarcasm was not lost on Finding.

'Good to see you Willie. Yes, long time. How are things? Hope I'm not in the way. I was talking to Mr Williams here the other day about some odd sightings some of the locals have experienced around here. What's going on, can you tell me? I'm not on the News Desk any more you know.'

Finding had known Willie Baxter for a lot of years off and on, as a young journalist on the Oxford Mail and later as a crime reporter both in newspapers and radio. He had formed quite a close relationship with him.

Willie, as far as Finding was concerned, was as straight as a die, a highly experienced detective and one of the good guys. He did his job and, unlike many others Finding had encountered, was interested in solving crime not advancing his career or playing politics, what used to be called a 'Thief Taker', he still saw his job as dealing with criminals not playing games.

Over the years a trust had built up between them. If Willie had asked Finding not to print or broadcast something he had told him in confidence, he had always honoured it. As a consequence, he was often the first person to get the inside track on an investigation, even if on occasion he had missed the opportunity to get a short term jump on the competition. Things tended to go in cycles, over time he knew he had won more than he'd lost as a consequence.

'Bit of an odd one,' Baxter said, 'We know our victim, bit

of a lad, well known to the Police as they say, but nothing serious, bloody nuisance rather than a career criminal to be honest. There are lots of local villains I could well imagine turning up dead in the street, but Hobart wasn't one of them.'

'Any idea what happened?' Finding asked, as he took in the ribbons of blue and white tape blowing gently in the breeze around the far end of the 'Long Alley' walkway. Uniformed police officers were talking to elderly residents, as forensic examiners dressed from head to foot in hooded anti-contamination suits busied themselves around where Hobart's body was lying.

Other officers were conducting fingertip searches in the pretty manicured churchyard in front of 'Long Alley'.

Baxter continued, 'Have to wait for the PM, but my bet would be a heart attack. He was a bit young, late 40's but a heavy drinker and smoker, and I doubt if he regularly got his 'five a day', but then who does?' he said, patting his substantial stomach.

'No sign of any injury or any kind of a struggle. Hobart could be a handful when he was into the drink. If someone attacked him, he'd have fought back. There are no signs of him hitting anyone, no swelling or grazes on his knuckles, no defensive marks or matter under his fingernails, which I'm sure there would have been if he had fought back, and no sign of a major trauma suggesting he was incapacitated quickly. Nope, looks to me like he just keeled over.'

'So, do we have any idea what he was doing here last night?' Finding asked.

'Nope. According to Mr Williams here there was no reason for him to be here in the evening. It was too dark for him to be working, they didn't have any floodlights set up, but we did find a torch which, I'm assuming Hobart brought with him and that spade.' He pointed at the pile of earth with the shovel sticking out of it.

'He must have brought that with him too. There are no tools left here overnight. Seems Hobart was doing a bit of excavating of his own, there was fresh dirt on his boots and hands. I'm pretty sure his conscience from missing a couple of days work wasn't pricking him and he had decided to do a bit of unpaid overtime, and we didn't find a map with a bloody great cross on it – so I'm ruling out buried treasure. God knows what he was up to.'

'So what's next?' Finding said.

'Well, I'll wait for the PM report obviously, establish the cause of death. We'll continue the house to house enquiries and I'll do some checking round his place and speak to some of his mates. But as of now, there is no sign that any crime has been committed unless the pathologist tells me differently. Actually, I could do with a nice 'heart attack' verdict, could do without another major incident if it turns out to be suspicious.'

'Will you keep me posted? I won't broadcast anything without your say so.'

Baxter shook Finding's hand. 'Yeah, no problem, and if you hear anything, well you'll let me know too, won't you – I've dealt with a few murders in my time, but never one committed by a ghost!' He chuckled to himself as he walked over to the forensic officers.

Finding talked a little more with George Williams, trying to get more background on Hobart, but apart from reinforcing Baxter's suggestion of his unreliability, he couldn't add much more, so he walked along the pathway, passed the church and up East St Helen's Street to 'Local Roots'. It was quite busy, which Finding was grateful for, because it meant he could sit, drink his coffee and think things through, without the necessity to make conversation with anybody.

He could overhear some of the customers remarking on the number of police cars and speculating on what was going on further down the road, but nobody seemed to have any real idea, despite Chris' attempts to tune his radio into the local station, seeking an explanation that, frustratingly, did not seem to be forthcoming.

The case was becoming more complicated as far as Finding was concerned. The Hobart death was peculiar. Was it connected or simply a coincidence? Finding had always said he didn't believe in coincidence, but it must happen sometimes. What was Hobart doing digging around in a graveyard after dark? Clearly he didn't seem the type to do manual work unnecessarily. He must have been looking for something; something he obviously thought was valuable. Then, why would he stop and go over to the walkway? Had he seem something? Gone to investigate? And, of course, the huge question, how did he die without a mark on his body?

It seems he was there in the evening, after dark. Perhaps he had seen the woman that the other witnesses had seen. Perhaps he went over to make sure she wasn't going to phone the police, warn her off or something. But then, how did he die?

He realised he was thinking himself around in circles. The logical thing for him to do was to wait until after the Post Mortem examination and find out from Baxter what the cause of death was. Perhaps Baxter's other enquiries might throw some light on what Hobart was up to. After he had finished up his coffee, he walked back down East St Helen's Street and along the footpath past the church and 'Long Alley'.

It seemed the forensic team had finished and the police and others were leaving, and he watched as a black unmarked van, which had been backed up to posts preventing vehicular access to the footpaths started up and pulled slowly away, disappearing around the bend to where Finding's car was parked.

Presumably this was Hobart's body en-route to the mortuary for the PM.

Finding returned to his car and sat for a few minutes watching the various police cars leaving the scene.

Hopefully, Baxter would have some news for him tomorrow. It depended, of course, how busy the pathologist was, how many sudden deaths were waiting for examination, but he was sure Baxter would be able to prioritise Hobart, particularly if there was any suggestion of foul play. With luck, he might find out something tomorrow.

In the meantime, he decided that he would follow through with his previous plan to visit 'Long Alley' after dark.

He started his car and drove out, past the 'Old Anchor' pub towards the town centre. There had been too much disruption today, so he decided to leave it until tomorrow night.

He would come back then to the mysterious walkway in 'Long Alley'.

TEN

Later that evening, Finding sat in an armchair in his living room, a large whisky in his hand, restlessly flicking from channel to channel on the TV with the remote.

The Hobart story had made the local news, but was obviously not important enough for the nationals. The feature was not terribly enlightening, apart from a few rather nice shots of 'Long Alley', a short interview with the Rector, Dr Baker, explaining how worrisome it had all been for the elderly residents of the almshouses, and a completely non-committal interview with Willie Baxter who clearly was keen to play down any potential premature over-excitement about murder enquiries. Backed up by an obvious police mug shot of the victim, Colin Hobart, the story was far from exciting.

He began to doze off from a combination of the whisky and tiredness his head dropping forward onto his chest as he fell into a fitful sleep. The muted television flickered, casting shadows around the room as darkness closed in, while Finding slept.

He awoke with a start. Had he heard a crash? Had he been dreaming? Reaching out in the darkness to a small table lamp next to him, he flicked it on and looked at his watch. 1.00 am.

As he stretched, he could see nothing to indicate that the noise that had awoken him had been anything other than a dream, and he walked into the small kitchen, took out a glass and filled it with cold water, swallowing it in one large gulp. The icy liquid slaked his whisky-parched throat. He refilled the glass and carried it back into the living room. It was then he noticed the light flickering in the bathroom.

Putting down the glass, he walked into the bathroom. A small fluorescent tube above the shaving mirror over the sink was flashing, like it sometimes did when it was initially switched on, or just before it failed. Finding tapped it on the side. Then, using the small pull rope dangling form one side of the fitting, he switched it off and then on again. Flickering once, it lit up and remained on with a steady white/yellow glow.

It was then he noticed a small bottle of after shave which had been on the shelf above the sink and below the light had fallen into the sink and smashed into thousands of small shards of glass, a strong perfumed smell rising from the sink as Finding put his hand down into it, only to withdraw it quickly when one of the shards dug painfully into his finger, a few drops of blood dripping into the sink and mixing with the remnants of water in the bottom which was permanently wet from a slightly dripping tap that Finding had meant to fix many times. He watched the drops of blood spread, diluted by the water as he automatically raised the finger to his mouth, sucking the blood from the small cut.

'Shit,' he whispered, shaking the finger, before returning it to his mouth as he left the bathroom to return with a small dustpan and brush with which he cleared up the glass, running the tap to wash the remaining tiny pieces and the blood down the waste pipe.

He then found a small plaster in the bathroom cabinet and covered the cut that was stubbornly refusing to stop bleeding.

He turned on the shower, went into the bedroom, stripped off and returned to the steam-filled room, stepping under the water and leaning with both hands on the tiled wall as he let the hot stream cascade over his head and down his body. He stood motionless in that position for a minute or two, before reaching for shower gel and washing himself and rinsing.

After he had finished, he climbed out onto a small bathroom mat and reached for a large white bath towel with which he began to dry himself vigorously, staring across the steam filled bathroom at the mirror above the sink.

As he dried he noticed a small, circular mark in the condensation on the mirror, near the top left hand corner, and while he was watching, it seemed to lengthen as it extended downwards for a few inches to create a vertical line in the opaqueness.

Then, his mouth dropped open as another line, starting at the top of the first stretched at an angle of about 45 degrees downwards before rising up again and down, until the letter 'M' was clearly visible on the glass.

Unable to move, Finding stood, clutching the towel to his naked body while the invisible finger continued its journey in the condensation until, clearly displayed on the glass was the sentence,

MAWYAN WANTS
TO BE
WITH JOSHUA

ELEVEN

Given the events of the evening before, Finding did not finally fall asleep until around 5.00 am, and when he awoke at a little after 10.00 am, he felt unable to force himself out of his bed.

He lay on his back staring at the ceiling, arms behind his head, for over an hour and a half until, just before mid-day, his mobile went and the caller display indicated it was Willie Baxter.

'You want to buy a poor, underpaid and overworked detective a pint?'

Finding sighed, rubbing his eyes hard, trying to drive the sleep from them. 'You got the PM result? What does it say?'

'Not so fast Laddie,' Baxter responded, 'this kind of information doesn't come cheap, it will cost you at least a pie and a pint. I'll see you in 'The Old Anchor' in Abingdon in an hour. I'll tell you then.'

Baxter hung up, leaving Finding holding his mobile to his ear and staring into space, before finally realising the line was dead and throwing the mobile down onto the bed.

He sat up for a couple of minutes before picking up his mobile again and calling Darren.

'I want you to go back to the Council archives and check any financial records they've got, dating back through 1645 and up to April 1646.'

'No need, I've already got copies.' Darren said, 'What am I looking for?'

'See if you can find a record for a Joshua.' Darren laughed briefly at the other end of the phone, 'Joshua? Joshua who?' he said

'Not sure, try Duhen or North. But if you find anyone called Joshua, get the details.'

'Are you suggesting Mawyan's child might be called Joshua? Where did that come from?'

'If I told you, you wouldn't bother looking,' Finding said

calmly as he cut off the call and threw the phone back on the bed.

Almost exactly one hour later, Finding pulled up and parked in the road outside 'The Old Anchor.' Inside the pub he found Baxter sat at the bar, an almost empty pint glass in front of him.

They shook hands briefly. Then Baxter lifted his pint and swallowed the remainder of the beer down and handed the glass to Finding.

'I'll have the same again,' he said jovially, 'and I've ordered fish and chips. Don't worry about paying now, you're running a tab,' he said, chuckling. 'You can pay at the end, I'll be over here,' he said walking to a 4-seater table, away from the bar near the window.

Finding ordered another pint for Baxter and a large scotch and a cheese sandwich for himself. He carried the drinks over to where Baxter was sitting and took a chair opposite, before staring out of the window across the road to the river on the other side, watching an assortment of water birds on the surface and a huge red kite with its forked tail prescribing apparently effortless circles on the thermals above the meadows on the opposite bank.

He took a swallow from his whisky as he watched Baxter sink the best part of half his pint in a single gulp.

'So, PM?' he said quizzically.

'Strange,' Baxter said, 'Cause of death was asphyxia apparently. Classic signs, according to the pathologist. Except, they would have been classic if there had been any external signs of trauma.'

'What do you mean?' Finding asked.

'Well, there are some fancy medical names for them, but Hobart had purple splotches on his eyes and in his lungs apparently, as well as a build up of foam in the airways that can happen when mucus from the lungs mixes with the air as the victim struggles to breath. This is particularly prevalent in drowning, but no evidence of water in the lungs, so no drowning here. His heart was enlarged, too and there were changes in his blood chemistry that also indicate asphyxia. Apparently, classic symptoms of manual strangulation, except...'

'Except, there were no finger marks or bruises on the throat,' Finding said.

'Exactly,' Baxter continued. 'No scratches, bruises from blows, signs of a ligature, no damage to the larynx. Nothing. It's as if he suffocated from the inside, not the outside. Which, the pathologist tells me, is pretty much impossible. He favours some kind of toxicological cause that somehow simulates asphyxia – but frankly he seemed to be struggling to identify one. He says he is going to speak to some colleagues, but frankly I think he's stumped.'

'So, no sign of heart disease?' Finding said, 'Or any life style causes?'

'Nope,' Baxter replied, 'Apart, as I said, the heart enlargement which the Doc thinks was caused by the asphyxia, no sign of anything that could have killed him that suddenly.'

The two men were interrupted by the barman who came over with a cheese sandwich for Finding and a huge plate of fish and chips which he placed before Baxter who immediately handed his now empty beer glass to the barman. 'I'll have another one of them,' he said.

Finding shuddered with a degree of horror at the huge amount of salt that Baxter shook all over the mound of fried fish and chips before proceeding to wash it all off again with copious amount of vinegar, finally topping it all off with a generous squeeze of tomato ketchup from a plastic bottle.

Loading a fork with chips, fish and mushy peas, Baxter shoved the large mouthful into his mouth, chewing vigorously as he continued talking.

'I think we know what Hobart was up to that evening, though,' he said between mouthfuls.

Finding paused, just as he was about to take a bite from his sandwich. 'Oh?' he commented.

'Yep, the sick little bugger was digging up bodies. Well, *a* body, to be precise. It seems, while he was uncovering the foundations at 'Twitty's', he brought up a skull in his bucket. A very small, very old skull. I'm not sure what he was thinking, maybe he thought it was valuable, or worth something, I'm not sure. The man was not the sharpest knife in the drawer – but the pathologist had a quick look at it, no full examination as yet, but he was able to say it was not recent, at least a couple of hundred years old, and it was the skull of a small child, so not likely to be triggering a murder investigation.'

'Why would anyone think a skull from a graveyard might be valuable?'

Baxter seemed to be thoroughly enjoying his food, and he stopped now and then to wash it down with a huge swallow of beer.

'I'm not sure he thought that much, if at all. We actually also found, with the skull, a small leather pouch. From the state of it, it was probably buried with the skull. It had a few coins in it that date from the 17th century apparently. Not particularly valuable, but I doubt Hobart would have known that. It would have been a hell of a clue though, if it had been a modern day murder enquiry. The pouch obviously didn't belong to the child who was about 12 months old according to the pathologist, so chances are it was dropped by whoever buried the body. Incidentally, although there is a graveyard there, the body wasn't strictly 'in the graveyard' – it looks like it was buried on the edge of it. 'Twitty's' wouldn't have been built at that time, so looks like the outer wall was actually on top of the grave. I reckon we are looking at an informal burial shall we call it, but I think I can safely suggest there is not much point in pursuing whoever was responsible after all these years.'

Finding had hardly touched his sandwich, so fascinating were Baxter's revelations.

'So you think someone killed a child and buried it on the edge of the graveyard, dropping the pouch while they were doing it?'

'Well,' Baxter replied, 'Without any conclusion from a pathologist of the cause of death, which might be tricky after all these years, we have no evidence that the child was unlawfully killed. But it does look like the burial was not a formal interment. No traces of a coffin or even any kind of burial cloth - looks like the body was just dumped in a hole and covered up.'

Finding finally took a swallow of his whisky while Baxter finished the last mouthful of his food, before wiping his mouth on a red paper napkin, emptying his glass and raising a finger to the barman and then pointing down at his empty glass, requesting a refill.

Finding watched as Baxter took a matchbox from his pocket, and taking out a single match, began shaping the end with his fingernails into an improvised toothpick and poked it into a gap between his teeth.

'No,' he continued, 'My guess is, Hobart found the pouch or purse, whatever you like to call it, found the coins, thought they might be worth something, then came back to dig around hoping to find some more. Perhaps he just thought the skull might help him prove they were worth something by showing how old they were.'

'I suppose that sounds reasonable,' Finding said. 'So how did he end up in the walkway a hundred yards away, do you reckon?'

Baxter shrugged, 'Who knows. Maybe he thought he saw somebody in the walkway, went over to check, maybe make sure they weren't about to call the police or something. Maybe he saw one of your ghosts!' Baxter laughed at Finding's obvious discomfort at the good-natured jibe. 'Whatever happened to him, happened to him and he collapsed and that was that. One dead tea-leaf.'

Baxter and Finding went over the facts that they were sure of and indulged in a little speculation, but what seemed clear was, they were never really going to know what had happened, unless a witness was going to come forward, which seemed unlikely.

'The pathologist will take a look at the skull and the rest of the remains of the baby we pulled out, but we checked thoroughly; there wasn't anything else to find, no gold doubloons or ruby necklaces. They'll check to get a more accurate date for the remains and probably see if there is any obvious cause of death, but frankly, it wont be a priority after all these years.'

Baxter knocked back the pint in a couple of swallows.

Finding, as usual amazed at the policeman's capacity for pints of beer as he watched him wipe his mouth with the back of his hand as he stood up.

'Better get back to work,' he said, offering his hand to Finding. 'Thanks for lunch, and if we get any more I'll let you know.'

Finding shook Baxter's hand and watched the policeman walk out of the pub before going up to the counter to settle the tab.

Had Hobart seen Mawyan in the walkway? It was probably the right time of day to fit in with the other sightings.

So diverted was he by the numerous thoughts that were running through his head, the barman had to call him back from the door as he was about to leave without recovering his credit card.

He decided that he would return early evening as planned and check out the walkway as the sun went down.

It seemed now his only real line of investigation.

TWELVE

Finding unlocked his car and stood in the doorway, briefly looking at his watch. It was fast approaching 4.00 pm, too late to go home just to turn around and come straight back.

The weak sun had disappeared behind the clouds and a strong wind had begun to spring up, sweeping along the river, causing the previously still water to become choppy as the wind blew against the natural flow of the river.

It had become colder and Finding shuddered. He slammed the driver's door closed and opened the back, pulling out a black raincoat and putting it on, raising the collar against the chill. After locking the car, he walked off in the direction of the town. It could be a long night and he was tired already from his disturbed night.

A couple of strong coffees in 'Local Roots' should wake him up, enough to keep him alert for his evening vigil in 'Long Alley'.

After two very strong coffees and sustained by a couple of sausage rolls, Finding left the shop and walked slowly along East St Helen's Street in the direction of the church and 'Long Alley'. The light was already beginning to fade, and it had become noticeably darker as a chill wind blew directly up the street into his face.

He shivered. Perhaps he should have taken Darren up on his offer to stand around in the dark in a graveyard he thought. He pulled his collar tight around his neck before shoving his hands deep into his coat pockets and hunching his shoulders against the cold.

Crossing the road, he passed the entrance to the church on his left, entering the open area behind it and looked across the fenced-off graveyard to the shadowy silhouette of the 'Long Alley' almshouses, its central clock tower and the roof, black against the last remnants of daylight in the sky beyond.

He stopped and leaned on the railings, staring at the already dark walkway from his position on the far side. He could just about make out the walls and doors on the furthest side of the walkway, except where supporting walls or dark corners blocked the light from street lamps which were already beginning to come on. He noticed with interest that each new light source effectively changed the shadows, almost as if something was moving in the walkway. He smiled to himself, knowing that these physical effects, changes in light, air temperature, air pressure even, could often trick the mind into creating movement where none existed, the human brain trying to make sense of external stimuli that seemed to run counter to normal experience.

This, he knew, was often the scientific rationale behind many so-called 'sightings'.

He stamped his feet briefly as the chill wind now blowing up from the river cut through his thin trousers and once again he began to shiver. He needed he thought, to get out of the wind, but still be able to observe the walkway.

The solution was obvious - he could stand in the walkway in a corner at one end, where he would be hidden from the pathways, and he would be able to overlook the full length of the covered alleyway and also be sheltered from the cold wind, so he moved around the pathway, opened the gate onto the gravel track that ran parallel and directly in front of the almshouses.

He walked to the central entrance and stepped onto the stone floor of the walkway, turning to the left and passing along to the far end, where he could turn to view the entire length of the covered area. He squatted down and leaned back against the wall, once again shoving his hands deep into his pockets, still cold, but sheltered from the biting wind.

He squinted at the luminous hands on his watch, struggling to see the time in the dim light. 6.25 pm.

He leaned back and waited.

Finding was not sure how long he had been squatting there. An hour? Two? But however long it had been, it seemed the lack of sleep from the night before had finally caught up with him and, despite the black coffee, it appeared he had dozed off as he leaned,

205

supported in the dark corner.

He pushed himself painfully to his feet, rubbing life back into his cramped legs and breathing in deeply. He tried again to check the time, but was distracted by what he thought was the slightest of movements deep in the shadows at the far end of the walkway.

He rubbed his eyes and stared, trying to acclimatise them to the almost full darkness that had now fallen. For a moment he could see nothing. Then just the slightest hint of a sideways movement appeared and then disappeared again. It was impossible to make out exactly what it was. Then it returned, disappeared and returned again, a fleeting movement, moving laterally across the walkway. What was it?

Finding held his breath, and he was embarrassed to notice that his heart was pumping faster. He inched forward towards the movement, as silently and slowly as he could.

He had moved perhaps two metres along the alley when he realised that the movement seemed to be a garment of some kind, wafting slowly in the wind, side to side.

A long, dirty looking beige shift gently swayed before him, accompanied by a faint creaking, and as Finding took a few more steps forward he suddenly realised, this was not a piece of laundry.

Two small feet, in worn black and tiny slippers, hung below the hem of the shift around two feet above the ground, toes pointing downwards. Thin arms hung lifeless to the side of what was clearly a young woman's body hanging from a beam in the roof.

Finding's eyes travelled up the lifeless form, towards the head but it was not visible, obscured as it was by the deep shadows beneath the eaves.

He stopped, open-mouthed, as he took in the full horror of the body of a young woman, swaying backwards and forwards from the roof, accompanied by the eerie creaking of rope on wood.

He stood frozen to the spot, mind racing, as he wondered what to do next. Record it! No one would believe this. He needed a picture, why had he not brought a camera, or a torch? He was totally unprepared; he was absolutely sure neither Darren nor Sue would have been so slapdash.

Frantically he hunted through his pockets, looking for his phone, eventually pulling it out and activating the light which briefly illuminated the area with a cold, ice-blue glow, his cold fingers scrabbling to activate the camera feature.

Finally, he managed to orientate the phone so as to take in the full length of the hanging body and he clicked the shutter, firing off a bright flash as the hanging body froze in the display window.

Finding stepped in closer and then orientated the camera upwards, towards where the head of the body was hidden in the darkness. He had managed to activate the light on the screen and he used it as an improvised torch to light up the head.

A small pale face was angled down to the side, eyes closed, and a swollen tongue hung obscenely from an open mouth. Untidy long blonde and greasy hair obscured the noose so that only the segment above the head, which travelled upwards and was knotted around a beam, was clearly visible as it swayed and creaked, the ancient wood protesting under the dead weight of the corpse.

Finding swallowed hard, desperately resisting the urge to gag at the horrific sight and he struggled to stop his hands from shaking as he tried to frame the girl's face in the centre of the screen for a picture.

It was at that moment that the girl's eyes opened, exposing black, dilated pupils surrounded by what normally would have been white, but were instead, blood-red.

The whole head slowly turned in the noose until the girl was staring directly into his eyes, as the mouth opened, exposing broken and yellow-black teeth. The look of pure evil on her face caused Finding to drop the camera that clattered noisily on the stone tiles of the walkway.

He staggered backwards, not taking his eyes off the face of the creature staring menacingly into his eyes, as the previously limp arms rose from her side, and her entire body angled around to face him, arms outstretched in his direction.

A small cry of terror escaped his lips. He stumbled backwards, trying to put the maximum distance between himself and the apparition which suddenly seemed to float towards him at tremendous speed.

Finding tried to turn and run, but he lost his footing and he fell heavily, cracking his forehead painfully against the low outer wall of the walkway.

Rolling over on to his back, he felt bony fingers dig deep into his throat. The spectre hung horizontally over him, the evil grimace inches from his face as he felt the breath being squeezed out of his burning lungs and he struggled frantically, unable to breathe. He began to lose consciousness.

Then, without warning, he felt the pressure on his throat slacken. He opened his eyes to see that the girl had turned away from him and was looking over her shoulder, back down the walkway from the direction she had originally come. Letting go of Finding, she turned in mid air and hung above him as Finding pushed himself painfully up onto one elbow and also looked down the corridor.

There, standing facing them, was Mary. In her arms, wrapped in a blanket, lay a small child.

THIRTEEN

Finding sat dazed for a few minutes while he watched the two young women facing each other, the babe in arms between them; as they both looked down, the hanged woman pulled the blanket down to uncover the face of the child which was still hidden from Finding.

Mary handed the child slowly to the girl, smiling gently as she did so.

Without looking at either Mary or Finding, the girl pulled the child to her breast and turned towards the wall, her back to Finding. He watched in disbelief when she floated through the wall at the end of the walkway and disappeared from sight.

He tentatively dabbed his fingers at his hairline and felt a large swelling which had suddenly appeared on his head and he withdrew his hand. His fingers were covered with blood.

Searching in his pocket he found a handkerchief, and despite its obviously dubious state of cleanliness, bunched it up and pressed it to his head, holding it there to staunch the blood.

Looking up, he jumped when he saw Mary standing directly over him and she reached out with one hand, palm upwards, clearly indicating he should take it. Nervously, he stretched out his hand and placed it in the offered palm. He was not sure what he had expected, whether his hand would pass through, but as she closed her fingers around his, her hand felt soft, not cold and not warm. She pulled gently and he struggled to his feet, bracing himself against the small wall, before standing up straight and breathing in deeply.

He felt a slight tug when Mary pulled him in the direction of the exit from the walkway and he followed meekly as she led him, holding his hand and slightly ahead of him while they walked slowly away from 'Long Alley' and down the path, towards the church.

Perhaps he expected her to lead him into the sanctuary of St

Helen's, but instead she led him, pulling gently, passed the church and across the road, back along East St Helen's Street.

Finding felt he was in some kind of a dream as he watched people passing, looking at him suspiciously. He realised he was staggering slightly and clearly he must have looked a peculiar sight, clutching a handkerchief, soaked with blood to his head, his other arm held out slightly ahead of him.

It was clear that no one but he could see Mary, and he was sure the people passing must have assumed he was drunk; he noticed how they looked away nervously when he made eye contact with them, some tutting silently as they scurried by. Some, ahead of him, deliberately crossing the street to avoid passing too closely by him.

They passed by 'Local Roots', long since closed, and crossed the busy junction and under the archway, towards the Abbey, turning right down towards the Old Abbey buildings.

Eventually, Mary led him through the gate and into the gardens, round the side and stopped in a small grassed area alongside the river.

Exhausted, Finding sat down clumsily on the damp grass, breathing heavily while Mary remained standing, looking out on the river, and finally letting go of his hand.

She turned towards him and, crouching down once more, took hold of his hand and pressed it with surprising strength into the soft mud on the edge of the bank beside him and, closing her fingers over his, scraping at the soft earth and drawing it through the mud, claw like, a small mound of grassy, black slime forming in his palm. Lifting it, she returned it again to the starting point and once again, drew it back, pulling clinging mud. She repeated this cycle two or three times, Finding wasn't sure. Then he fell backwards onto one elbow and, turning his head to his and Mary's hands, he could see that the scrapings had left a small, shallow dip in the mud, which was slowly filling with water.

He began to feel dizzy and slowly laid back until he was lying full length on the grass and mud, looking up at the stars in the dark sky above, wisps of clouds scudding across, in front of a watery moon.

He felt Mary continuing to pull his hand through the damp earth as he passed into unconsciousness.

FOURTEEN

Finding opened his eyes briefly, before closing them again quickly as his pupils were assaulted by a stark white light, so bright that a sharp pain shot across behind his eyes like a knife stabbing into his already throbbing head, and an involuntary groan escaped his parched throat.

Tentatively, he opened his eyes again, squinting against the harshness of the light as he saw a shadowy face, features blurred, looking down into his.

'Mary,' he whispered through dry and cracked lips.

'Who's Mary, Laddie?' The strong Glaswegian voice probed into his head as the image of the face above him cleared and became the soft features of an attractive young nurse, jet black hair pulled fiercely back into a tight ponytail and she shone a small pen-like torch into his eyes.

'This is Jessica,' the Glaswegian voice continued, 'Not polite to get a young lady's name confused, even if you have got a nasty bump on the head.'

'Where am I? Where's Mary?' Finding mumbled and groaned again. He rolled his head to one side as he took in the room around him.

Slowly, he lifted a hand to his throbbing head, finding it encased in soft bandages that came down on one side to his eyebrow. He noticed the clamp of a blood pressure monitor on the end of one finger; a short plastic tube emerged from a cross of white sticky tape on the back of his hand and further up his naked arm, another piece of white tape concealed an IV needle attached to a transparent tube which curled its way upwards to a plastic bag full of some unidentified clear liquid which was obviously pumping into his veins.

Turning his head to one side, he noticed the starched white pillow and tightly bound sheets which held him snugly in what was clearly a hospital bed, his eyes settling eventually on the source of

212

the voice, the dishevelled and bulky shape of Willie Baxter, as he lounged in a low armchair by the side of the bed.

'Where am I?' Finding said eventually.

'You're in The Radcliffe Hospital Laddie,' Baxter responded, 'You were picked up in the grounds of the Abbey in Abingdon, some local couple found you. Had sneaked around the back, looking for a quiet place for a bit of old fashioned courting; found you lying on the grass, one leg in the river, covered in mud and your face soaked in blood. They thought you were dead. Would have been if you'd been there a bit longer. Luckily, a paramedic got to you quickly, saved your life, I reckon. The doctors say your skull is fractured and you have a serious concussion, but looks like you're out of the woods now, in fact they're talking about kicking you out tomorrow - can't have the like of you blocking off beds for days on end.'

'Days?' Finding said, 'How long have I been here?'

'You were brought in in the early hours of the morning four nights ago; you were completely out of it for two days and raving for the next 24 hours, almost completely incoherent. Nasty bang on the head, apparently. You are lucky to still be with us it seems.'

'Four days?' Finding said, 'I've been here four days?' He was clearly struggling to make sense of what had happened to him.

'That's right Laddie,' Baxter said. 'They called me in. It looked like you'd been mugged, left to die, frankly looked like it might be a murder enquiry. Odd thing is your wallet is still there, cash, cards in tact, your watch untouched. I've been waiting to get some sense out of you. I haven't got much out of you so far.'

Finding turned his head away from Baxter and stared up at the ceiling. What did he remember? He remembered the horrific encounter with the girl in the walkway at 'Long Alley'; he remembered the fall and cracking his head, the moment he thought he was breathing his last as the breath was squeezed out of him. And he remembered Mary.

He knew, she had saved his life and he remembered her leading him to the river close to the Abbey. He raised his hand, now washed spotlessly clean; it was as if he could still feel the clinging mud between his fingers and under his nails as she clawed with him in the soft mud. He remembered the stars. And then he remembered... nothing.

He turned his head again towards Baxter. 'I don't know.' he said quietly.

'Well,' Baxter eased his huge bulk in the chair. 'We took a look the morning after you were found, no blood - so it doesn't look like you were attacked there, no footprints, apart from yours and the couple's who found you. My best guess is that you were clobbered somewhere else and staggered round there yourself. The severity of the blow to your head would suggest you would have probably not have known much about what you were doing. I'd say you collapsed. Can't think of anything else that fits the bill, frankly, there is no way anyone could have been there with you without leaving a trace, there would have been footprints, something, unless he could fly!'

'I think you should let Mr Finding rest now, he is looking tired and I need to get him something for the pain he is obviously still in. Sleep is the best thing for him right now.' The nurse checked the various tubes and monitors once more, before straightening the sheets around Finding, tucking him in like a mother did with a small, helpless child.

Baxter heaved himself with difficulty out of the low armchair, grunting with the effort.

'Okay Laddie. I'll leave you alone to get some rest. But we will need to talk some more. I need to know how you knew about the body.'

Finding turned his head back towards Baxter, a look of confusion on his face. 'What body?' he said.

'The body buried in the garden where you were found, in fact right underneath the exact spot you were found.'

'I don't understand...' Finding was struggling to concentrate.

'Look,' Baxter turned back to face Finding. 'We've known each other for a lot of years, and I don't want to be forcing you into explaining things whilst you are still confused. Fact is, anything you say now would probably not be allowed in court, anyway, given your condition. But I need to know how you knew a girl was buried at precisely that spot, and I need to know who this Mary you keep talking about is. I hope to God she doesn't turn out to be the girl in the grave, because, as the way things look right now, the only person who knew about it was you.'

'But I didn't know, I didn't know anything about any body buried there,' Finding was beginning to become agitated.

'You should leave Inspector,' the nurse said firmly.

'*Chief* Inspector,' Baxter said equally firmly to the nurse, before turning again to Finding.

'Think about it Laddie,' he said calmly. 'During the 24 hours when you were raving, after your couple of days in a coma, I came to see you; I sat with you for hours. You kept mentioning a Mary, and you were rabbiting constantly about someone being buried there. There were signs that you had been digging. Not very effectively, but it seems you were trying to dig into the ground with your bare hands. I got the forensic guys to take a look. I used Hobart's recent excavations as an excuse. Said an informant had suggested Hobart might have been digging around here too, said it was a statement from an unnamed informant, which isn't strictly true, but hey, you can't go digging around in historic buildings, based on the incoherent ramblings of someone in hospital with a head injury, can you?'

Baxter took his coat from where he had thrown it - over an aluminium walking frame by the door and pulled it on.

'Anyway, on the strength of my 'informant' we dug up the garden and found the remains of a young woman. We'll have a PM, of course, but she has clearly been there quite some time, some blonde hair left, and she was wearing some kind of beige shift, with buttons down the front.'

He opened the door and started to leave, stopping briefly to turn again to Finding.

'I wondered if her name might be Mary.' he said, before he closed the door behind him.

FIFTEEN

The following day, Finding sat silently on the edge of the hospital bed, dressed and waiting for Darren to pick him up, having completed the formal processes of his discharge.

He stared at the boxes of medication in their little paper bag, along with the large plastic carrier by his side containing the muddy clothes he had been wearing when he was brought into the hospital.

Now dressed in clean clothes, he vaguely remembered Darren bringing them to him the previous day and he sat, feeling as he imagined a child awaiting evacuation must have felt.

The constant pain in his head, whether suppressed by medication, or as part of the healing process, had subdued to a kind of dull ache and he had the strange feeling that his skull was packed with cotton wool.

Suddenly, he felt the need for fresh air as he began to feel slightly claustrophobic. The air he was currently breathing seemed to lack the clean sharpness that his aching body craved. He needed to be out of here.

Standing up, he felt dizzy and needed to lean on the bed with one hand to stop himself from falling until the imbalance sorted itself and he stood, for the first time in several days, unaided.

After having picked up his dirty clothes and his medication, he walked gingerly towards the door, opened it and stepped out of the room. He leaned briefly against the door frame, before setting off slowly down the corridor, following the signs to the lifts, down three floors and along the corridor to the exit.

He sat on a wooden bench outside the hospital, breathing in the cold air gratefully, intending to wait for Darren who was due to collect him. Then, on impulse he hailed a taxi driver who was dropping off a patient at the front entrance.

'Can you take me home?' he asked the cabby.

'Where too?' the driver asked, as he opened the rear door of

216

the cab.

Finding climbed painfully into the rear of the taxi, leaning back and closing his eyes as he gave his home address.

Four hours later, opening his eyes he stared at the ceiling and realised he was lying in his own bedroom, a ringing sound in his head which he initially put down to his injury until he realised his front doorbell was sounding persistently as if somebody was leaning on it.

Finding dragged himself to the front door, opened it slowly to find Darren and Sue standing on the step.

'Where the hell have you been?' Darren said, 'You were supposed to be waiting for me at the hospital and you're not answering your phone. We thought something had happened to you.'

For some reason this struck Finding as amusing, and he chuckled as he held the door open wide, turning his back on the couple he walked slowly back into the living room, Darren and Sue following, concerned looks on their faces.

Finding slumped into an armchair, leaned his head back and closed his eyes.

'Are you okay?' Sue asked as she and Darren took a seat on the settee opposite.

'Am I okay?' Finding repeated, 'Now that's a difficult question.'

He breathed in deeply and opened his eyes again, looking at the concerned faces of his two colleagues.

'Yes,' he said eventually, 'I'm okay. You know what? What I really need is a cup of tea.' He leaned heavily on the arms of the chair as he tried to push himself up.'

'No, you stay there, I'll make it,' Darren said, crossing to the small kitchen.

'Can you tell us what happened to you?' Sue said against the backdrop of the domestic noises emerging from the kitchen.

Finding ignored the question. 'Did you find Joshua?' he shouted to Darren in the kitchen.

'What?' Darren said, poking his head out from the kitchen.

Finding repeated the question, 'Did you find anyone in the archive records called Joshua?'

'Yes, I did,' Darren said. 'I found a Joshua North, under the care of the Parish, died in April 1646 it seems, when the three shillings per week being paid to the 'Overseers' ceased.'

'Mawyan's boy,' Finding said quietly.

'Almost definitely, I'd have said,' Darren responded, 'given that his alleged father's name was North. The facts fit. But how did you know to look for someone called Joshua?'

Finding ignored the question. He closed his eyes again. The effort to talk seemed to be extreme.

'I need you to do something for me. I need you to arrange a meeting tomorrow at the studio, I'd like you two to be there along with John of course, but I also want you to contact Detective Chief Inspector Willie Baxter in Oxford, ask him to join us at the meeting. I'm not strong enough to keep this to myself any more. I'm not sure what the consequences will be. Probably I'll be out of work or even committed, but frankly, I can't handle this alone, whatever the consequences.'

Darren and Sue shared a worried look.

'What is it you can't handle?' Darren said.

'Tomorrow,' Finding replied, once more leaning his head back in the armchair and closing his eyes.

SIXTEEN

Finding arrived at the studios in Banbury Road at 10.30 am and stopped as usual in reception to help himself to a coffee from the filter machine.

The receptionist offered a considerable stack of letters and notices to him that were clogging his in-box which he obviously hadn't cleared for over a week.

Acknowledging the receptionist's welcome with a brief smile and nod, he then shook his head at the proffered mail. 'I'll deal with that later,' he said. The receptionist pressed the hidden button that buzzed open the internal door and he passed through into the corridor beyond.

Entering the conference room, he found Darren, Sue and John Wilson already sat at the table, chatting amiably with Willie Baxter, coffee in one hand, a Danish pastry in the other, a good proportion of which had crumbled down his front and was scattered on his belly. They all stood up as Finding came in, moving forward to enquire about how he was feeling.

'I'm fine, fine,' he said unconvincingly, 'Please, no fuss, just sit down. Let's get on with this.'

Finding edged his way slowly along the table to take up his usual place at the far end by the window. He turned to look out onto the passing pedestrians and vehicles outside as the others took their places.

After a few seconds he swivelled back towards them, looking from one to the other as they watched him expectantly.

'Where to start,' he said eventually. 'I've been up most of the night, deciding how I was going to explain all this. Now I'm here, all that seems meaningless. So, I'm just going to tell you everything I know. You can then decide where we go from there.'

He coughed, the act obviously causing him some pain as his palm went immediately to his head and he scrabbled in his jacket pocket, removing a small tablet container, struggling to open

219

it with trembling hands, before finally giving up and handing it to Darren who opened it for him and handed it back.

Finding shook out two tablets, threw them into his mouth and with a swallow from his coffee, screwed his eyes up as he gulped them down.

'Some of this, Darren and Sue already know, but for the benefit of John and particularly Willie here, I will repeat some things they already know.'

'The last little bit of this investigation was provided by Darren yesterday,' he said.

'In their usual inimitable way, Darren and Sue dug out from the archives information that I would never have managed to find. Usually, I just get the glory of coming in at the end and putting it all together.'

'I'm conscious of the fact that Willie is here, and his standard of proof is likely to be far higher than anything we have, but then, apart from a fleeting moment when Willie here seemed to be suggesting I had some explaining to do, there is no one in this case who will ever be prosecuted for anything.' He paused. 'Reason? - They're all dead. The first criminals, at least in my view, were the pious and frankly vile hypocrites, who called themselves 'Church Wardens and Overseers of the Poor' and who took a young lady called Mawyan Duhen and threw her into some God-forsaken place called the 'House of Corrections' for the 'sin' of having an illegitimate child.'

'If that was not abuse enough, it seems that she, and even more horrifyingly her infant child, was then further abused by someone called Jeremiah Holdsworthy, one of the previously mentioned Overseers of the Poor. We are not sure how it came to pass, but it seems Holdsworthy killed Mawyan's child.'

'I'm pretty sure, given Darren's latest snippet, that the child was called Joshua North, and Holdsworthy, from his position of authority, was able to bury the child in an unmarked grave, upon which the 'Twitty's Almshouses' were subsequently built.'

He paused to swallow coffee before continuing.

'Unfortunately it seems, despite her lowly and clearly

220

fragile state, Mawyan was not prepared to let the matter go, and after being brow-beaten into believing that any attempt at justice against Holdsworthy would be useless. We can only guess at what the mental state of this poor woman was, but in any event, it appears she decided to take matters into her own hands and killed Holdsworthy by strangling him with a piece of rope. She then committed suicide, by hanging herself beneath the beams in the walkway of 'Long Alley'. Basically, that is it. Interesting; but as it all took place in the 17th century, of purely academic interest.'

Finding looked across at Baxter, expecting that he might be losing interest in this history lesson, but he seemed happy enough as he munched his way through a second Danish pastry.

'It seems Mawyan was buried in unconsecrated ground, near the site of the 'House of Corrections' which we understand was close to the Old Abbey buildings, and that, as they say was that. Holdsworthy, the child and Mawyan were all dead and the 'Overseers of the Poor' were able to quietly hush-up the whole embarrassing situation created by their peer, Holdsworthy, and their life went on, no doubt pretty much as normal.'

'That is, until a few weeks ago when Colin Hobart and his colleagues started digging at the end of 'Twitty's' and Hobart discovered Joshua's body along with a purse containing some coins, that I have no doubt belonged to Holdsworthy, which had presumably been dropped by him while disposing of Joshua's body. Hobart took the skull, along with the purse and coins, leaving the rest of the skeleton behind. He then came back in his own time to do some more digging, no doubt hoping to find more, what he thought might be treasure trove.'

Finding paused. Obviously still in a certain amount of discomfort, he took a few calming breaths before continuing his story.

'This is where I might start to lose, well, all of you really, but certainly you Willie. I believe Hobart disturbed Joshua's body, and that triggered off the sightings. I think Mawyan came back to try and protect her son's grave.'

Willie Baxter coughed loudly, spraying bits of Danish

pastry across the desk as he shot upright in his seat. 'You believe what?' he spluttered, 'Have you lost your mind?'

'Maybe. Maybe, Willie – I said this would be difficult for you to believe. This is what has been giving me so much cause for concern. Do I say what I believe and risk ridicule and possibly my job, or just keep quiet. Up to now, I had thought the latter was best.'

'Not sure about ridicule, Steve,' Baxter continued, 'I think you are stark raving mad!'

Darren and Sue looked at each other and then at Wilson, who in turn was looking quizzically at Finding.

Darren spoke first. 'Hang on a second Steve; we've worked together for years, investigating these incidents. Some much more convincing than the sightings of four old people in a church yard, and you're saying that for the first time, in all those cases, you have suddenly decided, with no real scientific support or investigation, that this is a genuine case of haunting?'

'Second time,' Finding said.

'Second time? What do you mean 'Second time'?' Darren said, looking for support from Sue who also seemed totally confused by Finding's comment.

'You're right Darren; we have always managed to find logical and scientific answers to all our investigations, usually conducted by you guys. All, that is, except one – the first was the *Jenning's Cottage case*, and now this case has become the second one.'

'I'm sorry, I don't understand what you're saying, Steve. The Jenning's Cottage case was explained. We found solid scientific evidence for all the so-called manifestations in that place. Unfortunately, because of the tragedies associated with it, we decided not to broadcast it. But we did explain everything, the temperature differences, the collapsing ceiling, the...'

Baxter interrupted, 'Would someone like to explain to me what the bloody hell the 'Jenning's Cottage Case' is? I have no idea what you are talking about!'

'Look,' Finding said, 'Let's come back to that, shall we? I'd like to focus on the Mawyan Duhen affair for the time being. I

222

promise I'll come back to 'Jennings Cottage' later.'

Baxter frowned. 'Okay, but I hope some of this starts making sense soon, because at the moment, much as I'm enjoying your ghost stories, I'm not convinced all this is a particularly productive use of my time.'

'I realise this is difficult to take in, but I think we are all sure Hobart was digging around, looking for something valuable that he might be able to sell and we also know, for some reason he walked across to the 'Long Alley' walkway where he collapsed and died. We have assumed he must have seen something and gone over to investigate. We also know it coincided with the time frames for the other sightings.'

Baxter responded, 'The timing is coincidence, given that Hobart was 'grave robbing'; it was highly unlikely he'd be doing it in broad daylight when he could easily have bumped into his boss, or one of the residents, *of course* it was after dark.'

'True,' responded Finding, 'But, remember the Post Mortem results. We know, Mawyan strangled Holdsworthy, and Hobart had all the internal evidence of a strangling, but with none of the external signs, How do you account for that?'

'It's not my job to explain causes of death,' Baxter replied, 'Yes; the pathologist seemed troubled by it. If *he* couldn't explain it, it would be silly for me to try. In any event, he said he was going to refer it to other experts, toxicologists and so on. I don't recall any suggestion that it might be strangulation by ghost!' Baxter's tone was one of exasperation.

'And did they find any other explanation, these other experts, toxicologists or any one else for that matter? Tell me, did they find an explanation?'

'Well, no,' Baxter said, 'But just because they couldn't come up with a cause of death does not mean we can jump immediately to the conclusion he was throttled by a 300 year old ghost, for Christ's sake!'

Finding started to say something and then paused, looking down at the table before him.

'He's right, Steve,' Sue broke the silence. She seemed to

want to calm the situation and used her most level and conciliatory tone. Voices were getting raised and Baxter's face had gone bright red, there was a need to cool the situation.

'Absence of a clear cause of death may be interesting but it really doesn't mean we can assume that he was strangled by Mawyan. There is no supporting evidence, other than the most tenuous of circumstantial coincidences,' she continued.

'I know she strangled him.' Finding said quietly, still staring down at the table in front of him.

'But how do you know?' Sue spoke as gently as she could.

Suddenly, Finding raised his head and stared at the others, defiantly, his voice raised in frustration as he answered.

'Because she bloody well tried to do the same to me!' he shouted.

The silence that followed Finding's outburst was palpable as Darren, Sue, Baxter and Wilson stared at Finding, clearly trying to make sense of the incomprehensible.

Baxter was first to break the silence. 'Look, I know you've had an almighty bang on your head, but thinking you have been attacked by a ghost, for God's sake...'

Finding cut Baxter off in mid sentence. 'Please don't patronise me Willie, I know what I saw and I know what I felt. I went to 'Long Alley' specifically at that time to see if anything would happen. I wasn't expecting anything to, and I was fully anticipating that if it did, there would be a logical explanation, after all, there always had before.'

'So, what are you saying, happened?' Wilson spoke for the first time.

'I positioned myself at one end of the walkway, crouched down and fell asleep for a while, when I woke up I saw Mawyan, hanging at the far end from a beam.'

'You were dreaming. Dreaming you were awake, while you were still asleep,' Baxter said, 'Happens all the time.'

'I was not dreaming. Dreams have no beginning and no end. Believe me; we have investigated this kind of thing many times. Darren, Sue, you know the difference.'

Darren answered, 'Typically, dreams follow a pattern. Whichever strange situation you find yourself in, in dreams you just, sort of, 'find' yourself there. There is no lead up to it, certainly not any logical lead up anyway, and no end. You experience it and then it ends. Typically, when you wake up. They are also usually very short.'

'Exactly,' Finding responded, 'I remember everything leading up to the sighting and most of what happened afterwards, until I passed out in the Abbey Gardens.'

'And you didn't think to take a camera,' Darren said, frustrated, 'I offered to go for you as per usual; we would have had the right kit.'

'I'm not sure she would have come if it had been anyone other than me. I did actually take a couple of pictures, with my phone.'

'Photos? Now, photos I can work with,' Baxter perked up quickly, 'Where's your phone?'

'I dropped it when Mawyan attacked me. It fell on the floor inside the walkway, from then on I was fighting for my life, and frankly, with a fractured skull I was more concerned with staying alive than proving what I was seeing.'

Baxter sat back in his chair and folded his arms across his chest. 'Very convenient,' he smirked.

Finding climbed painfully to his feet, leaning on the table with both hands. 'Convenient!' he said angrily 'What is convenient about it – you think I enjoy being treated like an idiot!'

He stood panting with the effort and Darren left his chair, took his arms and gently returned him to a sitting position. Finding closed his eyes, breathing heavily.

They sat in silence for a few minutes, until it was suddenly broken by the sound of a mobile phone ringing. John Wilson pulled his mobile from the breast pocket of his shirt and held it to his ear, listening briefly.

'Tell him I'll be right out,' he said, replacing his phone in his pocket, before addressing the others. 'I think we need to calm down a bit here, and this shouting is not helping Steve. He has

225

suffered a fractured skull, for goodness sake. His well-being comes first. I have to speak to someone. I suggest we all calm down, take a break for twenty minutes and continue then. Agreed?' He looked to each of them in turn, waiting until he received a nod of confirmation from everyone in the group.

'I'll be back.' he said, standing up and leaving the room.

SEVENTEEN

It was actually 40 minutes later when Wilson returned to the room, closely followed by the receptionist who brought in a coffee jug and proper cups and saucers.

She poured for everybody, before stepping outside into the corridor and returning again with plates, napkins and a large platter full of assorted sandwiches which she placed on the table before leaving, closing the door behind her.

'Right, where were we?' Wilson said, 'And can we try to keep the tempers under control this time.'

Baxter had grabbed himself a plate and was busily piling sandwiches onto it. 'He was telling us about being strangled by a ghost,' he said, pointing in Finding's direction with a cheese sandwich.

Finding sighed. 'Look, I'm telling you the truth, I was not dreaming, I tried to photograph the girl hanging there, I *did* photograph her, then she came at me, I stumbled back, trying to get away from her and dropped my phone. As I tried to get away, I stumbled, I suppose, knocked myself senseless on the wall, then she was on me. I can see the look on her face now, she was strangling me. If she hadn't stopped I'd have been as dead as Hobart.' Finding gave an involuntary shudder as he remembered the sheer hatred in the dark eyes of the girl as she throttled him.

'Knocked senseless is about right,' Baxter mumbled almost to himself.

Wilson turned to Baxter, 'Can we just save the personal comments and stick to the facts.'

Baxter laughed; 'When I hear one or two I'll be happy to!' he said sarcastically, 'So how come you're still alive and not 'brown bread' like Hobart? Why didn't she kill you, too?'

'She would have done,' Finding said, 'But Mary stopped her. She was suddenly there in the Walkway behind Mawyan. She was carrying a baby, I'm assuming Mawyan's baby. She left me to go to her child and then she left.'

Baxter sighed, made to say something and then held back, clearly frustrated as Sue intervened.

'So, who is Mary?' she asked.

Finding answered with a sigh, 'You remember Mary, Mary was the ghost, the dead maid from Jenning's Cottage, you remember?'

'I thought the maid was called Rose?' Sue looked puzzled.

'No,' Darren said, 'Remember, we *thought* her name was Rose, that was what her employer called her, but she was christened Rosemary, although we suspected she might have been commonly known as Mary.'

'Yes, I remember now,' Sue said 'are you telling us you saw the ghosts of Julie and Mary at Jennings Cottage?'

Finding looked at Darren and Sue. 'I'm sorry; I just couldn't say anything at the time. I saw her, you see, I saw her in the house along with Julie Palmer, the dead wife. I saw them both, but I could not bring myself to tell you about it. I was the only one who saw them, you see. I just couldn't face the thought that everyone would think I was mad.'

Baxter was raising his voice again, 'Is someone going to tell me what the hell this is all about, this Mary, Jenning's Cottage, are you all stark staring mad?'

Wilson waved his hand at Baxter. 'Leave it,' he said firmly. 'We'll give you all the details later. I want to hear what happened after the attack.' He looked expectantly at Finding.

'Mary handed the baby to Mawyan and she went away. Then Mary led me to where they found me. She was telling me that Mawyan was buried there. She wanted me to know. I believe she wanted me to know that Mawyan wanted to be at rest with her child, Joshua.' Finding thought briefly about mentioning the writing in the mirror. Then obviously thought twice about it and returned his eyes to the table in front of him.

'I've heard some claptrap in my life,' Baxter began, 'But I haven't got the time to waste, listening to the lunatic ravings of a madman.'

Wilson looked at Baxter. 'Shut up,' he said loudly, 'Just bloody shut up for one minute, will you!'

Darren and Sue looked shocked, they had never heard this usually conciliatory man even raise his voice, let alone tell someone to shut up, especially a Detective Chief Inspector. Even Finding looked at him in surprise.

'I believe him,' Wilson said eventually.

Baxter seemed about to protest when Wilson held up his hand to stop him.

'I believe him,' he repeated. 'That call I took a while back, just before we broke up. It was from reception. Someone had called in, wanting to see me urgently. One of your colleagues, as a matter of fact, Chief Inspector, a uniformed police officer.'

'He'd driven over from Abingdon, apparently. They'd had a call from an old lady from 'Long Alley'. Obviously, when she went out this morning she found a mobile phone in the walkway outside her house. It had blood on it, and there also was a substantial amount of blood on the wall nearby, she thought somebody had been badly injured.'

'It seems, because of the blood the police didn't just record it as lost property, they sent someone here to make sure the owner was okay. I explained that Steve was fine and they left the phone with me to give back to you, Steve.'

Wilson reached into his trouser pocket, pulled out a phone and held it up to Finding. 'This yours, Steve?' he said, and without waiting for an answer began pressing buttons, before sliding it across the polished desk to Willie Baxter. 'Take a look at this.'

Baxter picked up the phone and looked at the screen, his mouth fell open as there, staring out at him, was the most terrifying picture he had ever seen.

Dark and bloodshot eyes, filled with hate, stared out from the pale face of a young woman, with wild blonde hair, mouth open and a swollen tongue lolling out of bloodless lips.

EPILOGUE

It was 3 months after the events of 'Long Alley', as Steve Finding stood inside the small and pretty cemetery outside the almshouses and behind St Helen's Church, where the Rector, Thomas Baker, had performed a simple but moving ceremony to re-inter the remains of Mawyan Duhen and her son Joshua in a joint grave.

The episode of 'Finding Ghosts', concerning what had become known as *'The Long Alley Haunting',* had met with a good response from listeners and had also attracted the attention of the National media, despite the fact that Wilson had deliberately toned down the more spectacular elements.

An experienced producer, Wilson's decision had created a far more adult response than the hysteria that might otherwise have followed any tabloid-type sensationalist story.

Finding had been interviewed several times by credible reporters, and talks were advanced on the possibility of a book on this and a number of others of their investigations.

But right now he was enjoying the warmth of the sun on his face as he stood alongside Willie Baxter at the graveside.

'How you feeling?' Baxter asked as the two of them thanked the Rector after he had finished up and left the two of them alone, 'to pay their respects' as he had put it.

'Fine. I'm fine,' Finding said. 'Still get the occasional headache, but otherwise...' he let the sentence trail off.

'Well, seems that there have been no more sightings of our local ghost in the last three months. Whatever else is certain, it looks like our restless spirits are not restless any more.'

The two men stepped back to one side, to allow the grave attendants who had been waiting patiently to come forward, fill the grave and replace the turf that had been carefully rolled back in order to minimise the impact on the otherwise perfect lawn.

'How about you?' Baxter said as they watched the men

begin to work, 'Any more sightings?'

Finding turned towards the centre entrance to the 'Long Alley' walkway.

He looked at Mary and Mawyan as they sat on the steps, playing with little Joshua, passing him back and forth, lifting him high in the air, the child chuckling with delight at the two laughing women.

While he watched, Mary looked across at him with a look of affection on her face as she made eye contact with him.

Finding turned back to Baxter and smiled at the policeman. 'No.' he said, 'No more sightings.'

'Pint?' Baxter said as he slapped Finding on the back good naturedly.

'Why not?' Finding said as the two men set off down the path from 'Long Alley' in the direction of 'The Old Anchor.'

-END-

About the Author

David P Elliot was born in Reading in the UK and, apart from 8 years in the Police Service in the 1970s, he spent almost 30 years in the IT industry before leaving to concentrate on his first love, writing.

His debut novel 'CLAN', a historical, supernatural thriller, was published in December 2008 and so far has sold in 16 countries.

It has also been released as an e-book and as an audio book, read by the author. Unabridged, it has a run time of 540 minutes and is available on CD (8 CD package) and as a download in both MP3 and AAC (iPod) format. It has also been translated into German.

The supernatural is a recurring theme in much of his writing.

He has 3 grown up children and 3 grandchildren one of which inspired the novel 'Clan'.

He now lives in Faringdon, UK, with his partner, a native of Munich.

You can find out more at www.davidpelliot.com

About 'Clan' by David P Elliot

The story of 'CLAN' is told through the eyes of David Elliot, who at 57 years of age is alone, frustrated and with three failed marriages behind him. When in 2007 he finds himself out of work he goes to the Borders of Scotland to seek some validation of his life through his bloodline, the notorious "Border Reiver" Elliot Clan.

Accompanied by his daughter, son-in-law and beloved grandson Thomas, far from resolving issues, he finds that he has led his family into terrifying danger as 700 years of Scottish Border history and the myth and reality of "The Bloodiest Valley in Britain" combine to threaten all he holds dear in his life.

The corruption of the rich and powerful meets legend as Good and Evil clash for the ancient throne of Scotland and power in the modern world.

William Wallace ("Braveheart"), Robert the Bruce, Border Reivers, creatures of supernatural horror and past heroes of the Elliot Clan are all involved as the Master of Hermitage Castle, the evil Lord, William de Soulis, actions his plan to assume power over an unsuspecting World.

All that stands against him is an ordinary family fighting desperately to protect a child.

"It's a great read. In his youth my father and some friends tried to stay the night in Hermitage, but they were driven out by 10 pm."
Madam Margaret Eliott of Redheugh, Clan Chief of the Elliots.